The Music Box Killer

A DEREK REED THRILLER

Victoria M. Patton

Dark Force Press – www.darkforcepress.com

Dark Force Press
City of Publication: Piedmont, OK
www.darkforcepress.com

Book Layout © 2016 BookDesignTemplates.com

The Music Box Killer/ Victoria M. Patton. -- 1st ed.
ISBN 13: 978-1-946934-29-1
ISBN 10: 1-946934-29-1

Library of Congress Control Number
2022901140

To my husband:
I am the luckiest woman on earth.
Thank you for choosing me to spend your
life with.

Thank you to my fabulous editor Judith Boling, and my beta readers
Without you guys my books would suck.

CONTENTS

CHAPTER ONE

Charlene danced a jig as she stared at the package. It had arrived earlier that morning, but events of the day kept her from opening it until now. She checked the return address. "Hmm. Who could this be from?"

This added to her excitement and curiosity. Her fiancé liked to send her things, and she figured this was another gift from him. She ripped open the box and flung out the tissue paper. There were two presents inside.

"Ooh," she said, pulling the first one from the box. A beautiful pink sheer nighty. She removed her clothes and tried it on. The heart-shaped neckline accentuated her full breasts. As she spun around, the baby doll shape of the gown floated in the air. The matching panties made it look more classy than trashy. It hung to her knees, but the sheerness of the material kept it from looking like something a grandma would wear.

She admired herself in the full-length mirror. "This is so pretty." She stopped spinning. "I can't wait to see his face when I tell him he can't see me in it until our honeymoon." She giggled at her devious plan to torture him for the next three weeks.

Charlene stopped twirling. Her gaze landed on the gift. She pranced to the bed and took out the plain white box. Her eyebrows drew together. She opened it and lifted out the contents.

Made from antique metal, the oval shape made it hard for her to recognize it. The ornate design on the outside had birds and butterflies etched into the surface. In between the metal work, colored glass made the butterflies and birds pop.

She lifted the lid, and a butterfly spun slowly to a classical song. When it stopped, she flipped the music box over and turned the heart-shaped key. The butterfly spun again. Captivated by the beautiful lullaby it played, she didn't hear the doorbell chime.

When the music stopped, she heard someone at the door. She threw clothes all around until she found her heavy robe. "I'm coming!" she yelled as she put on the robe and hurried towards the door.

The bell chimed again.

"I said hang on," she yanked the door open. "Can I help you?"

A delivery person smiled at her. "Did you receive a package earlier?"

She squinted at the woman. "Yes." She looked at the badge hanging on the front of the uniform.

"I'm so sorry, but my colleague was supposed to get a signature. If I don't get one, I can be in a lot of trouble. See, I'm training him, and I don't want to lose my job."

"I understand. Please come in. I don't want to let all my cool air out." Charlene stepped back, holding the door open for her.

"Thank you so much," the woman said.

As Charlene closed the door, a hand clasped over her mouth and nose. Another arm reached around her waist. She struggled against her attacker, but couldn't get a firm grip on her arm.

A sweet odor filled her nostrils, then the same sweet taste coated the back of her throat. She clenched her fists. Her eyes widened, burning as the tears stung. Adrenaline rushed through her system. She jerked violently before she passed out.

The intruder dragged Charlene into the living room and removed her robe. "How nice. You are wearing my gift. Saves me a lot of work." The woman searched the rooms looking for the music box. Retrieving it from the bedroom, the woman returned to the entryway.

Kneeling next to Charlene, the woman pulled a ribbon from the front pocket of her pants. She caressed Charlene's hair. "I know you don't understand why I'm doing this, but I promise, it's for your own good. Your fiancé will do nothing but hurt you and crush your soul."

The woman placed Charlene in the position she wanted. Before proceeding, she ensured the ribbon was in the correct spot around her neck. "I'm going to set you free, Charlene. You won't suffer any longer. The lies he will tell, and the embarrassment you will suffer at his hands would be too much for you."

The woman lifted the gown. It had to stay perfect. She glanced one more time at the young woman. "I'm here to save you. Think of me as your angel of mercy."

CHAPTER TWO

Tuesday early morning.

A light snore woke Derek. He reached his arm out to pull Lizzy close to him. Instead, he got a handful of fur. Cracking one eye open as Lola, Lizzy's boxer, greeted him with a big wet kiss.

"Really? Why are you here?" Derek lifted his head. "Lizzy?" he called out looking at the other side of the bed. "Where is your mama? Huh?" he asked, scratching the dog.

Lola groaned, rolling over and exposing her belly.

Derek rose, pulling on the pair of underwear lying on the floor. "Lizzy?" he called out as he walked down the hallway. "Lizzy?"

Lola ran past, hoping to get an early breakfast.

"Lola, it's not time to eat yet." Derek peeked into the kitchen as he walked by. Empty. He walked through the archway and around the corner into the living room.

Lola stopped. Her hackles bristled. A low rumble emanated from her chest.

The hair on his arms lifted. His stomach felt rock hard. The room looked empty. Yet his body and Lola said otherwise. "Lizzy?" Derek walked over to the sliding glass door and touched a button on the wall.

The opaque coloring cleared, allowing the dim lights of the early morning to shine into the room. The dew on the grass looked undisturbed. He turned to see Lola staring at him.

She made a move towards the spare room, then turned and looked at him. Lola barked and took a step, glancing back at him.

"Okay. What's up, girl?" He followed her.

Lola stopped outside the second bedroom's door, growling.

When Derek reached for the doorknob, a static charge arced. "What the hell?" he said, yanking his hand back. Reaching for the knob again, he hesitated, then grabbed it. Twisting with force, he pushed on the door. It didn't budge. He took a deep breath and repeated the same steps. This time, he used his body weight and forced the door open.

Swinging open with ease, Derek caught himself before he fell to the floor. "Crap," he said. "Lizzy?" Derek called into the room. No answer.

The room's creepy darkness engulfed him. As he reached for the light switch, he felt a hand on his. He jerked his hand back touching his skin.

Lola's low growl turned into a high-pitch bark.

Derek quickly scanned the room. The dim light from the hallway cast a shadow around him. "Lola. Stop barking."

Lola's bark intensified as a rush of cool air swirled around them.

Derek heard a woman's voice.

"Help me."

"Lizzy?" Derek flipped the light switch. It didn't turn on. "Shit." As he pushed open the door to let more light in, it slammed shut.

Lola growled. She placed herself between Derek and the perceived threat of harm.

"Help me! Derek."

"Lizzy, where are you?" It was almost pitch-black, but there was enough light coming through from under the door to keep him from bumping into furniture. As he moved around a shelf next to the wall, a full-length mirror came into view. He jumped back and grabbed his chest when he saw his reflection. "Fuck." His pulse raced.

Lola stopped. She glanced up at him.

"Sorry," he said reaching down and scratching her head. When he looked up, a young woman's reflection glowed in the mirror.

Lola saw her. She shifted her stance, putting herself at the ready to protect Derek. Her growl intensified.

Derek froze. The young woman wore a nightgown, and her long brown hair cascaded over her shoulders. She held out a music box. When he took a step closer, he saw blood oozing from a wound beneath a large white ribbon around her neck.

"Help me. Please."

Lola barked at the mirror.

Reaching his hand out, he placed his fingers inches from the glass. Just as he was about to touch it, the bedroom door flew open.

"What the hell are you two doing? Didn't you hear me calling you?" Lizzy asked, standing in her running gear.

Derek jumped.

Lola ran to her, wiggling her tail and yapping with excitement.

Derek turned back to the mirror. Nothing but glass. He looked at Lizzy. "Um. We heard a noise. Me and Lola came to investigate. I thought it was you."

"Why would I be in here?" she turned and walked towards the kitchen.

Hot on her heels, Lola ran to the cupboard holding her food, and sat waiting for her breakfast.

Lizzy filled her bowl, then turned towards Derek. "You don't look so hot. Do you feel okay?"

"Yeah. I guess I got startled when you weren't in the bed." He filled a cup with coffee. "Did you brew this before your run?"

She nodded as she added milk and sugar. "Yes." She sighed, as she took the first sip. "I couldn't sleep. I needed to clear my head."

Derek glanced over his shoulder at the spare room.

"Derek?"

"Huh?" he said as he turned and faced her.

"What is going on with you?" Lizzy stared at his green eyes. Emerald in color with pops of gold flecks. His mix of boyish features and strong jawline coupled with those eyes, made it hard not to be attracted to him.

Running his hand through his wavy hair, he tugged on the ends. "I don't know. I guess I'm worried about you."

She went to him. "You have nothing to worry about." She tussled his hair. "You know how much you mean to me. No one can ever take your place."

Derek took her in his arms. "And what about Congressman Jackson?" he regretted it the minute he said it. He stepped back looking down. "I'm sorry. I shouldn't have said that."

She lifted his chin. "You and I have a unique relationship. I care for you, and I care for him. But it isn't the same. I just need some time to figure out the best way to deal with things." She raised up on her toes and kissed his lips.

He pulled her close to him and soaked it in. His hands roamed across her body. The kiss deepened. He was about to lift her up and carry her to the bedroom when his phone rang. "Shit."

"I'm too sweaty, anyway." She waited as he answered.

Lola had wedged herself between their legs, making sure not to be left out.

Lizzy bent down and kissed her nose. "You silly dog."

Derek moved towards the kitchen counter. "Okay. Yeah. You don't want me to bring my crew? I don't understand." He sipped his coffee.

"Okay. Just me. I'll be there."

Lizzy eased herself up and sat on the edge of the counter. "What's going on?"

"That was Dr. Callahan. He's with my director and Dr. Chelsea. I need to go to a crime scene."

"Sounds a little cryptic."

Derek finished his cup of coffee. "I'm supposed to show up alone."

"Do you have time to eat?"

"No. I need to get dressed and go." He took her by the hand. Kissing her fingertips, he reached out and caressed her cheek. "I love you, Lizzy. I don't want you to think I am trying to keep you from living your life. You don't owe me anything. And I will take whatever kind of relation-ship you want to give me," he said as he kissed her lips.

She laid her head against his bare chest. "I know that. I just need some time. But you have must know I love you. That will never change." She leaned back, looking up at him.

"I know that, too," Derek said, heading towards the bedroom.

Lizzy followed him.

Along with Lola.

She sat on the bed as he got dressed. "Do you know when you might be done?"

He popped his head out of the closet. "No. But I will text you."

"I need to take care of some business today." She laid back. "I know I need to see Congressman Jackson. I keep putting it off. I'm just not in the mood to go to the gala. I'm not sure he will understand."

Derek put on a pair of new tennis shoes and tucked his short-sleeved oxford shirt into his jeans. He stepped over to her, clipping his gun and badge to his belt. "If you don't want to go, don't. Jackson will under-stand." He bent over, holding himself above her face. "If he gives you a hard time, tell me. And I will shoot him."

She laughed as she sat up. "I totally believe you would." She scratched Lola's ears. "I may leave Lola here and go home before I run some errands. Plus, she loves the yard."

"Lola can stay forever." He moved towards the doorway. "So can you. I'll call you later."

She listened as he headed out to the garage. She grabbed Lola by the cheeks. "That wouldn't be so bad, huh, Lola? To stay here forever?"

CHAPTER THREE

Derek looked at his phone, checking the address. Not sure where he was going or why he had to be there at the butt crack of dawn, he longed to be back in his comfy bed with Lizzy. His shirt already sticking to him, he cranked his AC. Even in the middle of October, it was still too damn hot in Phoenix.

He considered some possibilities that would bring his director to a crime scene. And none of them were good. A knot formed in his stomach and a sour taste inched up his throat. Breathing slowly, he kept himself from throwing up his morning coffee.

Derek pushed the girl from the mirror out of his mind. He didn't have time to think about who she was or what she wanted. Yet the vision was too real to say it was his imagination. Lola had seen her, too. His anxiety level rose with every mile he drove.

His phone pinged to make a right-hand turn. Pulling into a modest neighborhood, he saw the house at the same time the app said he'd arrived. Two police cars blocked off the street on either end.

A police officer approached his vehicle.

Derek rolled down his window.

"This area is restricted. Do you live here?"

"I'm Agent Derek Reed with the FBI," he said, showing his ID to the officer.

"Go on in, Agent. They are expecting you."

Derek drove to the home and parked in front of the house. As he exited his car, his heart beat at a sluggish rate. He twisted his head, making a popping sound. Looking at the entrance, all he could think about was how much he wanted to hide. Escape. Run as far away as he could.

The sour taste lingered at the back of his throat. He reached back into his car and grabbed a pack of gum from the middle console. Chewing on one piece, he then added another.

A Phoenix police officer checked his credentials at the door. "Go in, Agent."

Derek nodded as he glanced back over his shoulder. The sun and police presence brought out the neighbors. He had a sneaking suspicion news crews would soon be on the scene. "Fuck. This will not end well."

Entering the foyer, an iron taste filled his mouth. "Oh hell," he said. He knew that taste all too well and not even the gum he chewed could hide it.

The cries of a woman filtered from a room down a short hallway off to his left.

"Derek? Is that you?" Dr. Callahan called out.

"Yeah, it's me," he said following the voice to the small living room. Derek saw his AD and Dr. Chelsea. Dr. Ronald Chelsea looked physically ill. The AD stepped to the side. The blood-soaked carpet came into view.

Derek took a few steps into the room. "Holy shit." Air rushed out of his lungs. A young woman in a knee-high nighty lay on the floor. Her body was slit open from her groin to her sternum and her entrails were spread out in some sort of pattern. Derek tilted his head. If he didn't know better, the girl's guts looked like butterfly wings.

He glanced over his shoulder. Shaking off the feeling that someone stood right behind him, he focused on the dead girl. Her nightgown's sheer material gave her an ethereal look. A white ribbon tied in a bow had been wrapped around her neck.

Blood from the ear-to-ear gaping wound had dried, causing the edges of the skin to curl up and poke out from underneath the ribbon. He stepped closer. His skin broke out in a clammy sweat. She didn't look like the girl from the mirror, she looked like the girl he saw when he had a CT scan a few weeks ago.

He avoided looking Dr. Ronald Chelsea in the eye. That didn't stop him from feeling the weight of the man's stare as he looked over the crime scene. In the moments following the CT scan, Derek described the dream he had about a girl who had appeared to be murdered. This girl. Focusing on his Assistant Director, he did what he did best. Played stupid. "Why am I here?"

"You and your team will take over this case." His AD fiddled with a cigarette in his fingers.

"You smoking again?" Derek asked.

"No."

"Why couldn't I bring my team?"

"I needed you to hear about this first." Assistant Director Fretz nodded towards Dr. Chelsea. "Tell him about the case."

Dr. Chelsea waited before he responded, taking a moment to gather his thoughts. "Ten years ago, four women were murdered. The one connection we could establish was each of the victims were either days or weeks away from getting married." The doctor cleared his throat. "Dr. Callahan and myself worked on this case with Special Agent McDougal. Four months and we couldn't come up with a suspect."

"The guy was never caught?" Derek's gaze fell around the room. Landing on each man.

"That's correct," Fretz said.

"Maybe this is a copycat killing." Derek adjusted his stance.

Dr. Callahan shook his head. "No way. There were three things we never released to the news. One, the women were all dressed in a nighty. similar to what our victim is wearing. Two, each woman had her throat slit and a white ribbon tied around the wound, and three, we never mentioned that." The doctor pointed to the young woman. "We never let out that each victim had a music box in her hand."

Derek kneeled next to the girl and studied the design on the box. "Did the other murders have the entrails in this same design?" he asked, stepping back.

The AD handed him a folder. "That is the only difference. The earlier women were not gutted like this. All the photos from those cases are in here. I need you and your team to find this killer. Last time, he killed four women. Then stopped for ten years. I don't know if he plans to kill four or double that. But he needs to be stopped."

Derek took the folder but didn't look through it. "Who else will work this case? Anyone else from the FBI?" he asked his AD.

"Just you and your team. I need you to go over the original case and find the link between all these women. That is how you will stop this killer." Assistant Director Fretz pursed his lips. "I called the captain of the PD department. The men who are here know if they breathe a word of this, I will deal with them."

He paced. "This can't get out at all. No mention of this case or the first four murders. I need this to be a generic murder for as long as possible. Let's keep it to—at this time we believed the victim knew her attacker. Do not, under any circumstances, say anything to the press. I will handle all releases."

"I will need to do this my way." Derek raised an eyebrow at his director.

"No problem," he said. "I will get you the complete case file later.

That folder just has the photos."

Derek squinted at the ME and Dr. Chelsea. "I need to interview both of you. I would prefer you to come to my office so my entire team can be in on the interview. This way, they hear the information directly from you. Any problem with that?"

"Not at all." Dr. Callahan looked at his watch. "I can be at your office this morning."

"I can be there whenever," Dr. Chelsea said.

Derek glanced around the room. The clock on the wall said 6 a.m. "How about 9:30?"

"I can be there." Dr. Callahan bagged the music box.

"I need pictures of that. From all sides. I also want photos of the crime scene. From every angle." Derek stood still for a few moments.

His AD headed for the door. "I want updates as you have them. Do not give updates to anyone but me." AD Fretz waved as he left the house.

Derek frowned. "Who found her?"

"Her sister. She was supposed to meet her at their parent's house at 5 a.m. When she didn't show up, she came here." Dr. Callahan pointed to the other side of the house. "She's that way in the kitchen. Waiting for someone to come get her. She can't drive in her present state."

Derek nodded at them. "I need to ask her a few questions, then I'll head to my office. See you both later this morning."

Dr. Chelsea chased after him. Before he spoke, he peered over his shoulder, making sure Dr. Callahan wasn't paying attention to them. "I need to know how you knew about this."

"I didn't know about this."

"The day of the CT scan. You had a dream about this. This girl. You described her. Is this the girl you saw? How did you know?" Dr. Chelsea grabbed his arm. "Tell me."

"I don't have an answer for you. Maybe I heard about it. Maybe it was one case Emma pulled for our crew to work on. I must have seen it somewhere. That's all I can tell you."

Dr. Chelsea gripped his arm tighter. "That's a lie. They buried this case. It wouldn't have been available to you and your team. I need to know how you knew. Derek, please. Is this the same girl from your vision?"

Derek took a moment before answering. He laid his hand over Dr.

Chelsea's. "I can't talk about this now. I promise I will talk with you later when it's just you and me. Please."

"I have to stop this killer. He got away once. I can't let him get away again. Help me stop him."

"I will. I promise." Derek left his friend in the middle of the foyer. Deciding to ask the sister questions later, he left. He had no clue how he knew about this case. But after Josiah Craig beat the shit out of him a year ago on one of the worst cases he ever had, his life hadn't been the same. He didn't think it would ever go back to normal. Derek had a feeling this was his new normal. And he didn't like it.

CHAPTER FOUR

Tuesday 6:45 a.m.

Derek drove into the Legacy Unit's parking lot. The old Catholic church fit the desert of Arizona. During the afternoons, the warmth of the day brought the incense smells out from the wood within the building. For him, it was the best part of the day, despite the heat.

He parked next to Agent Marcum's car. Derek had texted him when he had left the crime scene and asked him to come in before the rest of the crew. He had a fondness for Kyle. With his blond hair and surfer looks, he didn't look like the typical agent. However, the kid proved himself a genius when it came to hunting down information on the web. Once a hacker, Derek was glad the young man used his skills to bring the bad guys to justice.

Derek scanned his thumb and entered the code to get into the building. As he stepped in, his phone pinged. Removing it from his pocket, he read the text. Assistant Director Fretz gave him Agent McDougal's phone number. The agent died a few years ago, but his widow agreed to speak with him if he needed to.

"Great. Just what I wanted to hear." Dealing with the widow of a dead agent didn't brighten his day. "Kyle?" Derek called out as he headed towards the kitchen.

The FBI had remodeled the interior to suit their needs, but the bones of the building remained the same. They had removed the pews to make way for desks and computers. Two small bedrooms were on the other side of the main area. Along with a small laundry room.

Off the kitchen, stairs led to the basement and several other small rooms. Most of which were probably used as storage. The largest one had become Kyle's headquarters.

In the kitchen, Derek heard music from downstairs. "That explains why I didn't get an answer." The aroma of fresh coffee filled his nose. Pouring himself a cup, he called a local donut shop and placed an order.

He figured it was going to be a long day, and he expected the interviews with his two favorite doctors to last quite some time. Derek knew he had to keep his crew focused.

Leaning against the counter, he closed his eyes and listened to the music. The office seemed weird and too quiet without Lola. She always came with him to work. Having to leave so early, he couldn't bring her with him, but he would go get her after the interviews.

"Damn," he said pinching the bridge of his nose. "That was so stupid." He could kick his own ass for bringing up the congressman. Something seemed off, though. Lizzy seemed a little distant.

"Why don't you ask her to stop seeing him?"

"Seriously?" He squeezed his eyes shut. "Please. Not today."

"You knew this was coming. I tried to tell you. Wait, your subconscious tried to tell you."

Derek opened one eye in the girl's direction. "It's been a while, Chrissy." Josiah Craig murdered Chrissy in front of him. He carried the weight of that guilt ever since and talking to her seemed to help. Maybe in his mind making her real allowed him to ease the pain of that day in the carnival tent.

"It hasn't been that long."

"New dress?"

She twirled around. "Let the guilt go. Man, that shit is going to eat you alive. As soon as you release it, you will see things much more clearly. And maybe I will be able to go."

"Go where?"

She stopped twirling and shrugged. "Wherever dead people go when they're dead. I don't know. I just know I'm not supposed to stay here forever. At least I don't think I am. I'm not sure yet. I seemed to be tied to you." She sat on the counter. "I can't explain it, however," she wiggled her finger at him, "there are others who need your help more than me."

"What others?" Derek sipped his coffee.

She played with the hem of her dress. "Some are alive and some are dead. The dead ones won't be as well-kept as me." Chrissy patted down her dress. "You need to be prepared for what you will see."

Derek looked at the ribbon around her neck. "You're bleeding again."

"Every time you summon me, it bleeds. It may be your way of reminding yourself of something.

"Maybe it's just the way I remember you. Perhaps it is nothing more than that."

"Right. Is that what you are going with?" She hopped down from the counter. "You ready for this case?"

"No, not really." He refilled his coffee mug.

"You already have a head start."

Tilting his head to the side, he raised an eyebrow at her. "No, I don't."

"You do. You saw the dead girl in the CT scanner. You know Dr. Chelsea knows. How are you going to explain it to him?"

"I don't know." Derek sipped his coffee.

"It's going to get worse. You need to let the others talk to you. If you would just give in, Derek. Your life would be so much easier. One has already reached out to you."

"What do you mean, one has already reached out to me?"

"Hey, um, who are you talking to?" Kyle asked, looking around the kitchen.

"What? Huh?"

"You were talking to someone. Who?" Kyle lifted the coffeepot and filled his cup. He grabbed the creamer from the fridge and added two sugars.

"Just myself. Hey, I'm going to need everything you have on those victims I sent you. I need to brief everyone. Could you add Charlene Marshall to the list? She is our latest victim."

Kyle raised an eyebrow at his boss. "I thought we were dealing with a cold case."

"I had to go to the crime scene this morning. I will explain it all later. How much time do you need to hunt down information on Charlene?"

Kyle pondered his response as he sipped his coffee. "Maybe thirty minutes."

"You have an hour."

"Great. I've started on the four you gave me earlier. The runs on those are almost complete. Remember, though, these are simple runs. Not in depth. I need more time to run a more complete scan." Kyle sipped his coffee. "I've never heard about this case. The FBI must have kept it under wraps."

"If you can't stop a killer, the last thing you want to do is broadcast the case. It never ceases to amaze me how the FBI can bury things and keep the news from ever finding out."

Kyle cocked his head at him. "That should show you how much power they have. How about when they leak what they want covered to spin the story?" As he headed towards the stairs, he smiled at his boss.

"I'm glad I work for them. That's all I can say."

A pang of worry hit Derek. He knew the FBI could cover up things. The Pink Diamond case showed the reach the FBI held. Or at least the reach one man in the FBI held. That case had the power to blow the entire agency apart.

Besides himself and AD Fretz, only Kyle knew the details of the Pink Diamond case. He worked on it when he could, and right now, he had to push that case aside. "One case at a time," he said as he sat at his desk.

He glanced at the floor and realized he hadn't brought his laptop from home. His shoulders drooped. "How the hell did I forget that?" The alarm at the front door buzzed. He focused on the large overhead screens.

Agents Rogers and Warden entered.

"I can't believe how hot it is already." Felicia Rogers said, stepping into the cool office. She wore a light pink shirt. Lifting it off her chest, she blew some air down the front. "Man, I may never get used to the Arizona heat. And I'm tired of my clothes sticking to me."

"I like it. I'm so tired of the winter months. It's nice to know winter won't last that long." Kelly Warden smiled at Derek. "Hey boss." She removed her blazer and hung it on the back of her chair. The crisp white button-up shirt had no wrinkles.

"Good morning." Derek lifted his coffee mug. "There's a fresh pot."

"Oh yum. I need it," Felicia said heading towards the kitchen.

Derek checked his watch. The donuts should arrive in about twenty minutes. His stomach growled.

The door alarm pinged again.

This time, Emma and her trusty sidekick, Marc Anthony, entered.

Derek picked up his phone to call Lizzy and have her drop off Lola. His thumb hovered over the call button. Deciding against it, he laid his phone down.

Marc Anthony made a beeline to everyone in the room. His wagging tail whipped around in a frenzy as he howled to get attention.

"Hey, Emma," Derek said, scratching the giant Great Dane's ears. "Hey buddy."

Marc Anthony stopped wiggling and ran around the room, looking for his best friend. When he couldn't find Lola, he ran back to Derek. He sat and pouted.

"I know buddy," Derek said. "She's not here today. She will be here this week. I promise."

Marc Anthony sulked over to Felicia and sought comfort by placing his head on her lap.

"You are so pathetic," she said. Felicia looked at her boss. "Where is Lola?"

"She's with Lizzy," Derek said as the front door buzzed again.

Agent George Peterson entered, followed by Agent Michael Finch.

George wore a pair of Chino pants with a pair of shoes which looked like a cross between a tennis shoe and a hiking shoe.

Derek glanced down at his choice of attire. As he looked at the youngest agent, Michael Finch who also wore jeans, he thought of how unofficial they all looked.

"Good morning," George said as he removed his gun from his waist and placed it in his desk drawer.

Marc Anthony had followed him from the door and sat patiently waiting for smooches.

"Oh, my. You are so spoiled, aren't you?" George said scratching his ears.

"Yes, he is," Emma said as she walked back in from the kitchen. "Of course, it's my fault." She sat at her desk.

"Dogs are so much better than kids." Agent Kelly Warden straightened her desk. Moving her to-do basket a micrometer to the right. She leaned back, making sure it lined up with the cup that held her pens.

Felicia watched her coworker clean an already immaculate workspace.

Kelly lifted her chin. "You should clean your desk."

Felicia frowned. "My desk is fine. Mind your own beeswax."

"Okay. Can I have the file for the Freestone case?" Kelly held out her hand.

Searching her desk, Felicia's brow wrinkled. She lifted folders and pads of paper. "Oh," she said, snapping her fingers. She opened her desk drawer and pulled out a file. Several empty candy wrappers came out with it. "Here."

Kelly shook her head. "I don't need it. Just wanted to prove a point."

Felicia put the folder back on her desk. "The only point you proved is you have a mental problem." She held out her empty coffee cup when Kelly headed to the kitchen.

"You're in serious need of help." Kelly smirked as she took Felicia's cup with her to fill her own mug.

Agent Michael Finch sat at his desk and turned on his computer. Glancing at the big screen when the doorbell chimed, he slapped his leg. "Hot damn. I was just thinking about how hungry I am."

Derek headed towards the door. Emma stood, but he waved her off. "I got this," he said as he unlocked the door and took several boxes of donuts from the delivery guy. He tipped the driver and then locked the door behind him.

He nodded to Michael. "Make sure there is a fresh pot of coffee brewing for me, will you?"

"No problem." He headed towards the kitchen.

"I could make a pot," Felicia said.

"No," everyone said at the same time.

Kelly handed a mug to Felicia. "You are no longer allowed to touch the coffee pot."

"One time. I burned the coffee, one time." Felicia sipped her coffee.

"No. Not one time. Every time you touch the coffee maker, you screw it up." George stood to get his own cup. "We love you, girl, but you suck at making coffee."

"Just leave it to the professionals," Michael said as he entered the room. "I put the remaining coffee from the first pot in the thermos on the counter." He directed his comment towards George as he passed him.

"Thanks," George said.

Derek placed the donuts on a long table situated against the far back wall. "When the new pot is done, fill the thermos and bring it in here, with two extra coffee mugs," he said, looking at Michael.

"I'll go get that done now." Michael jogged into the kitchen.

Derek buzzed Kyle using his desk phone. "Come up as soon as you can. Bring what information you have so far."

"On my way," he responded.

George moved to inspect the boxes of donuts. He crossed his arms and stared at Derek. "What gives?"

"I'm sure I don't know what you're referring to?" He smiled at his agent as he sat in his desk chair.

"Sure." George turned around as Michael returned from the kitchen carrying the large thermos and several paper plates. "Let me help you," he said taking the plates and setting them on the table with the donuts.

Kyle entered the area as Michael set down the coffee. "Oooh, are those donuts?" he asked as he made a beeline towards the table.

"Okay. Everyone grab some donuts, fill your coffee mugs, and take a seat. I need to fill you in on a few things." Derek stood and waited for everyone to go ahead of him. After selecting his donuts, he topped off his coffee, set them down on the corner of his desk and pulled the white board around from the back of the office area.

George moaned as he swallowed his first bite of pastry. "These are great."

"Best Donut Shop in Phoenix," Derek said.

"Okay, but what is the name?" asked George.

"Best Donut Shop," Derek repeated.

"Who's on first?" Kelly said, laughing.

George smiled as it dawned on him. "I got it. The shop is called Best Donuts Shop."

"Now that we have that straightened out." Derek turned towards Kyle. "Did you find the information I needed?"

He handed Derek a file. "I found as much as I could. I'm looking at social media from back then. It has been ten years. I have a few web searches running. I wish people understood, nothing is ever deleted from social media."

"When will that run be done?" Derek glanced through the file. Setting it down, he grabbed the file his director gave him at the crime scene. Scanning the photos from the previous cases, his fingers clenched the edges of the folder.

The woman from this morning in the mirror stared back at him. Margaret Sanchez, the third victim. His chest hardened as he held his breath.

"As long as it takes. I should have some results by tomorrow." Kyle waited for his boss to look up. "Hello?"

Derek glanced up. "Hmm?"

"Um, did you hear what I said?" Kyle asked.

"Oh, yeah. Good." Derek took a gulp of his coffee, then pulled the whiteboard into the center of the room.

Kyle made the crazy sign as he sat next to Felicia's desk.

Derek shook off the vision from earlier that morning as he turned and faced his crew. "Alright. This morning I was called to a murder scene. Told to come by myself, so don't get your panties in a wad."

He placed the photos from the previous victims and the original music box on the whiteboard. "What I'm about to tell you does not leave this room." He glanced at each person, including Emma. "Under no circumstances should any of you answer questions from the press or any other person. If someone asks you something, direct them to me."

Kelly gave George a sideways glance.

He shrugged, shaking his head.

Felicia held her coffee mug inches from her mouth. "I don't think I like the sound of this case."

Kyle looked over at her and winked.

Her eyes smiled at him over the rim of her mug.

"Ten years ago, four women were murdered. April Fontaine, Betty Shore, Margarite Sanchez, and Lana Berkshire." Derek pointed at each photo as he spoke. "Both Dr. Callahan and Dr. Chelsea were involved in the case, although in a limited capacity. Special Agent McDougal, who is now deceased, worked the case before he retired."

George raised his hand. "I'm guessing they didn't get anywhere?"

"No. They didn't. When the killings stopped, they buried the cases from the news and the public." Derek leaned against his desk.

"How do we know this isn't a random murder made to look like those other ones?" Felicia asked.

"There were three things that weren't released to the public. The women were dressed in nightgowns, each woman was weeks or days from getting married, and each victim held a music box in her hand." Derek lifted his cup of coffee.

Agent Kelly Warden raised her hand to speak when the door chimed.

George looked at the monitor and then back at his boss. "This is bigger than just a ten-year-old case and a new murder. That's why they are here, isn't it?"

Derek didn't answer. He pushed the button and let his guests in.

CHAPTER FIVE

Derek walked towards the two men. "Come on in guys."

Dr. Callahan and Dr. Chelsea peered around the remodeled sanctuary.

Marc Anthony bounded towards them.

"Oh, my." Dr. Chelsea stepped backward.

"He really is harmless," Emma said.

"He's huge." Dr. Rory Callahan scratched the dog's ears and patted his side.

Marc Anthony tilted his head, leaning into the attention.

"Marc Anthony, go lay down," Emma said, pointing at his bed.

The dog sulked over and spun several times, finding the right spot.

"Hey," Derek waved them to follow him. "For those of you who don't know, this is Dr. Callahan. He is our ME. And this is Dr. Chelsea. He is a forensic psychiatrist and therapist. He works with the FBI and if you ever have to do a psych eval, he will be the one to do it."

Agent Michael Finch smiled at the man. "Hi, Dr. Chelsea."

"Hello, Michael. How have you been?" Dr. Chelsea reached out to take his hand.

"I've been doing well. Thank you." Michael remembered the many sessions he had with Dr. Chelsea. During the last case, he had shot and killed the suspect. In order to be cleared for duty, he had to spend some time with the doctor. As therapists go, there wasn't anyone Michael would ever want to go to but Dr. Chelsea.

Derek pulled over two extra chairs and motioned for the men to come sit down. "Before you get comfortable, you two want some donuts and coffee?"

Dr. Chelsea moaned. "Coffee sounds great."

Derek pointed at the table. "Please, help yourself."

Dr. Chelsea and Dr. Callahan grabbed a cup of coffee and a plate with a couple of donuts each.

Dr. Callahan handed Derek a manilla folder. "This has the latest crime scene photos. And a few stills of the music box. I will have more in a few hours. Better ones of the music box."

"Thank you." Derek thumbed through the folder. Seeing the dead girl from the CT scanner again gave him a jolt. He felt a tightness in his chest. When he fell asleep during the scan, he thought he had a dream. Not that he saw an event which hadn't happened yet.

"Derek? Derek?" Dr. Chelsea stood next to him.

"Huh?" he responded.

"Are you okay?" Dr. Chelsea asked.

"Yeah. Sorry." Derek looked up at his crew. "I've asked these two to come in for an interview. Since they were both involved in the first case, I wanted to ask them questions as a unit. Plus, they are vital to this current investigation."

He took a photo of the latest victim and placed it on the whiteboard separate from the previous victims. He also placed the best picture of the latest music box up next to her.

"Wow," Kelly said. "There is a definite difference between the earlier murders and this one."

Kyle licked his fingers. "Are we going to come at this from a cold case perspective first?"

Derek nodded. "Yes. I think we need to revisit the first four cases." Before he sat in his chair, he grabbed a pad and pen from his desk. "Let's start with what you guys discovered during your investigation." Derek pointed to the first girl on the whiteboard. "When you interviewed all the parties, what stuck out about April?"

Dr. Chelsea smiled at the crew. "I'm going to let Dr. Callahan discuss the forensics first." He took a bite of his donut.

"You just want to stuff your face," Dr. Callahan said.

Dr. Chelsea wiggled his eyebrows at him as he took another bite.

Both Derek and Dr. Callahan rolled their eyes.

"Okay," Dr. Callahan started, "April Fontaine, along with the other victims, had their throats slashed. A white ribbon tied around their necks over the wound. They all held a music box in the palm of one hand. The killer left these at every crime scene."

He pointed to the photos on the board as he stood and walked towards it. "You can see the first four victims were laid out the same as the latest victim. However, the entrails were not removed as they are in the latest killing."

Derek pointed to one of the music boxes. "This is the music box from the original murders. It isn't the same as the one left today. It's vastly different. What can you tell me about the music boxes?"

"All the previous ones were identical," Dr. Callahan said. "The original music box had a woman posed like she was dancing. You can just see it in that photo. The music box played *A Dream Is A Wish Your Heart Makes.*"

Felicia frowned. "What song is that?"

"Cinderella," George said.

"Huh?" Felicia responded.

"Ilene Woods sang it in Disney's animated version of Cinderella in the 1950s. Since then, lots of artists and composers have covered it."

Derek crossed his arms. "Do you know what the song is in the new music box?"

Dr. Callahan sipped his coffee. "Yes, it's Tchaikovsky's *Waltz of the Flowers.* There is a little butterfly that spins around."

Felicia leaned forward. "Why do you think the music box is different now if it is the same killer?"

"Ronald, you could probably best answer that," Dr. Callahan said.

Dr. Chelsea reached to his side, placing his coffee cup on the edge of Derek's desk. "This is the reason I thought a woman might be the killer." He pointed to the picture of the first music box. "This clearly looks like something a woman or girl would have. With the dancing woman and the choice of song."

He paused for a moment, looking at Felicia. "The song is about the animals telling Cinderella to never stop dreaming. I'm not sure what the message is for the murdered women, but I think it's more for the killer. Never stop dreaming. Your wish will come true." He glanced over at Derek. "Just my opinion."

Pointing to one of the music boxes, he spoke. "This one is so different. It's metal. More ornate with butterflies and birds cut out in the metal. It's not as dainty or girly as the original box. The song itself is from the Nutcracker. Maybe the killer can no longer get the older music box. But I think the two different boxes represent two different times in this killer's life." Dr. Chelsea took a deep breath.

"Kyle, I want you to find this new music box. I will have more photos for you later today." Derek looked at Kyle. "As soon as I get them, I want you to make a 3d rendering of this box and the original one."

Kyle slapped his leg. "Hot damn."

"Somehow, I knew you'd like that." Derek took a sip of his coffee.

"Back to the original cases."

Dr. Callahan sighed. "The killings were spread over four months."

"Four consecutive months?" Michael asked.

"Yes. Besides the three things we didn't release to the public, there was one more item." Dr. Callahan nodded at Dr. Chelsea. "Ronald."

Ronald Chelsea leaned his head back. "I don't like talking about someone when they aren't here to defend themselves, but there was one other item. However, Special Agent McDougal didn't really think it had any significance at all to the case."

Derek's brow wrinkled. "Um, okay."

"The women were all killed on the same day of the month. The sixteenth." Dr. Chelsea took a sip of his coffee.

George sat up in his seat. "You've got to be kidding me?"

Dr. Chelsea shook his head. "I wish I was."

"We battled the agent in charge on this point," Dr. Callahan said.

Derek made a note of the date on the board above the other victims. As he wrote, he paused. He quickly pulled up the calendar on his phone. "Shit."

"What?" Dr. Chelsea asked.

"Today is the twenty-first," Derek said.

"Charlene, our latest victim, was murdered yesterday, last night, or early evening. Damn it." Dr. Callahan grunted.

"The killer isn't following the same pattern." Derek put the date above Charlene's name.

"What about the victims, Dr. Chelsea? What can you tell us about their victimology?" Kelly asked.

"As you can see from the pictures, they all had different looks. Different ethnicities. There isn't a physical characteristic that binds them together." Dr. Chelsea stood and moved next to the board. He studied the pictures of the dead women, almost as if he searched for something he might have missed. After a long pause, he turned towards the group. "I couldn't find anything that connected these women. Other than they were all about to be married."

Kelly scribbled a few notes. "The sixteenth had some kind of significance during the first set of murders. Were the women to be married on the sixteenth?"

Both Callahan and Chelsea shook their heads. "No. The women had different dates for their wedding."

"How about the grooms? Any information regarding them?" Michael sipped his coffee. "Could they be the missing link to the killer?"

Dr. Chelsea filled his coffee mug. Then took his seat. "I couldn't find anything that linked the men. Either to each other or the killer. They didn't work near each other. None of the couples knew of the other. They didn't have any common friends or acquaintances."

"Then at the time of the murders, the date had to be important to the killer." Felicia finished her second donut. She threw her plate in the small trash can next to her desk.

Derek sat in his chair. "That is one of the most important pieces of our puzzle. If we know the why, we can find the who."

"Is the date not important now?" Michael asked.

"Not necessarily." Derek nodded towards Dr. Chelsea. "Do you agree since this latest murder didn't occur on the sixteenth?"

Dr. Chelsea rubbed his neck. "I would just be speculating. I think this killer does things for a reason, so I'd be willing to say the date ten years ago was important. Now, I'm not sure of its importance."

"What else can you tell us about the victims?" Kelly asked.

"Two were middle class, one was very wealthy, and one was doing okay, but on a tight budget, you could say," Dr. Chelsea said.

"What about their venues for the weddings?" George asked.

Dr. Callahan and Dr. Chelsea glanced at each other.

"We didn't do that part of the investigation. I do not know what Agent McDougal looked for," Dr. Callahan said. "The agent in charge shared little with us. We stayed in our lanes. I covered the forensics, and Ronald covered the psychological aspects of each victim."

"Again, not trying to speak ill of the dead, but Agent McDougal was a short timer. He didn't want to be on this case from the get go. He kept us out of it as much as he could. We gave him what we had, and that was the end." Dr. Chelsea wiped his brow with his handkerchief.

Derek glanced at his agents. "McDougal died a few years ago. I'll get the notes on the case from the AD." He turned towards Dr. Callahan. "Did you do any toxicology tests on the victims?"

He nodded. "Each victim was subdued using chloroform. I ran the tests on samples of blood and tissue after the second case. The lack of any signs of a struggle led to the assumption the killer used something to incapacitate the women."

Kelly scribbled a few notes. "This bolsters your opinion, Doctor, that it could be a woman killer."

"Good point." Derek pointed at the pictures. "Although the MO doesn't lend towards a woman being the killer, it isn't out of the question."

Dr. Chelsea cleared his throat. "I remember one conversation with Agent McDougal. I had made the comment that we may have a woman as the killer. He blew me off completely. He didn't want to even consider that line of thinking."

"I agree with Dr. Chelsea that the killer could be a woman," Dr. Callahan said. "Not just because of the chloroform, but the way the bodies were posed." Rising, he walked to the board. "All the victims wore a nightgown. Sheer, but not slutty, in any way. Almost like one might wear on the first night of the honeymoon."

Dr. Callahan pointed to the ribbons around the neck. "Each ribbon came from the same spool. The cut end on April's ribbon matched up to the cut end on the second victim, Betty Shore. The same pattern repeated for the remaining victims. It seemed to me the killer took great care concerning the ribbon and the outfit on the victims."

"What about the current victim, Charlene?" asked Michael.

Dr. Callahan lifted his hand, almost in surrender. "I don't have the results in yet. However, at first glance, it seems this is a new roll of ribbon. The width is slightly larger than the others. Not by much, and there is no discoloration on the ribbon. Like one might find on a ten-year-old spool of ribbon. Also, each victim seems to match the nightgowns. Like the killer knew what style they liked."

Felicia rose and walked to the table, filling her coffee cup. "Did you guys ever look into the victims' wedding registries? That could explain how the killer knew what the victims liked."

Dr. Callahan and Dr. Chelsea exchanged glances, both shrugging.

"Maybe Agent McDougal did," Dr. Chelsea said.

Derek looked at Kyle. "Do you think you could find that information?"

Kyle moaned. "I'm not sure. I would need a store to start with. And then it may be a long shot."

Derek took the file Kyle had given him and looked through it. "Kyle did some research for me this morning. I asked him to hunt down everything he could on our victims. I want each of you to take one."

He handed each agent a victim. The papers contained the victim's history and information. "This is preliminary information. Kyle will get us more as he uncovers it. Call the families. Tell them we are looking into their loved one's case and see if they will answer a few questions for you. I've included information about the husbands-to-be. Call them as well. Ask the families about the registry thing. Maybe they remember."

Dr. Callahan shifted in his chair. "We didn't find any packages or any evidence of an intruder. I had my guys search each of the homes. There wasn't anything out of the ordinary or left behind."

Derek opened his mouth to speak.

"Wait," Dr. Callahan said, holding up a finger. "In the latest case. One of my techs searched each room. In the master bedroom, he found a box under the bed. There was no return address or postage, but it was addressed to our victim. Inside the box were tissue paper and a smaller box. I am assuming it held the nighty and the music box."

"Did you find anything on it? Anything of significance?" Derek asked.

"Not yet. The techs are still working on it. We are testing for fingerprints and DNA," Dr. Callahan said.

"They found nothing like this at the other crime scenes?" George asked.

Dr. Callahan shook his head.

"Well, this is good. This means the killer made a mistake," Michael said.

Derek rubbed his chin, nodding. He turned towards Rory Callahan. "How do you think the killer got into the homes during the first murders?"

He looked over at Dr. Chelsea.

Dr. Chelsea responded. "We never got any word about what the FBI thought. We assumed the killer presented themselves in a non-threatening way to gain entrance."

"When I showed up this morning, it didn't look like anything was disturbed. I didn't see any forced entry. The victim must have let the killer inside. If that is true, the killer must be someone the other victims trusted or possibly knew. Which again could point to a woman as the killer." Derek made a note on the board.

"The one person I open my doors to that I'm not scared of is a delivery person," Felicia said.

All eyes turned towards her.

"What?" she asked.

Dr. Chelsea's shoulders slumped. "Why didn't some of this come out ten years ago?"

"Listen, Doc. It's clear that Agent McDougal kept you out of the loop. Both you and Dr. Callahan were very close to the investigation. Sometimes it just takes some fresh eyes to see things." Derek smiled at the men.

"I don't like this." Dr. Chelsea hung his head. "For ten years, I have revisited this case. When the murders stopped, no one, and I mean no one, mentioned it. The FBI all but shut down any inquiry I had."

"Tell us about that. Was there anything different about the last case, Lana Berkshire?" Derek asked.

Dr. Rory Callahan frowned. "Nothing. The killer murdered Lana on the evening of the sixteenth of September, 2012. Her murder was exactly like the others."

Derek searched the file and placed the dates of each murder above the corresponding picture of the victim. "The murders started in June. Ending abruptly in September." He turned towards his team. "We have our work cut out." He spun around towards the visitors. "Is there anything else we should know moving forward?"

Both men looked at each other.

"Dr. Chelsea," said Kelly, "What do you think is driving this woman to kill? Assuming it is a woman."

His mouth puckered before the corners turned down. "Not sure I can give you an answer."

"I believe you can," George said.

Dr. Chelsea lifted his cup of coffee, taking a sip. "The earlier murders," he stood and moved towards the crime scene pictures. "The previous murders are so neat. The killer slit their throats, then took great care when posing them. Making them look—pretty."

Pointing to the latest victim's picture, he waited, gathering his thoughts before he spoke. "This murder is so much more. Look at the way the body is posed. The entrails aren't just strung about. They look like a work of art."

Dr. Chelsea stared at the photo of April. The first victim. The one he held an attachment to. He faced the agents. "I'm not sure if she was angry at the first four women or if they represented a bigger group. Maybe she killed them because they were about to get married, and she wanted what they had for whatever reason. Maybe the jealousy became too much.

"But the new murder, this doesn't feel like the others. Whatever spurred her to kill ten years ago, she has moved on from those emotions. She's motivated now by something completely different. Yet she is still killing the same type of victim."

He made eye contact with each person in the room. Then focused on Derek. "I think she sees herself in a different role. She needs to kill the same type of victim, but her purpose is entirely different."

Derek held eye contact with his mentor. His friend. He stepped away from Dr. Chelsea, averting his gaze. "Is there anything else we should know?"

"Everything I know is in the folder, and my preliminary notes are in there as well," Dr. Callahan said.

Dr. Chelsea nodded in agreement. "I can send over my notes from the case. But everything should already be in the folder that Rory gave you."

"I want everything, Dr. Chelsea. What you may not think is important might be the biggest help to us. Send me everything. And make sure I get everything from the crime scene techs," Derek said.

"I'll bring what I have by your house this evening." Dr. Chelsea smiled.

Derek withered under the heat of his stare. "That would be great."

Felicia walked to the board as everyone stood and spoke with the doctors. She studied the previous victims and then stood in front of the latest victim.

"What do you see, Felicia?" Derek asked.

She spun around. "Nothing. Nothing, really."

George tapped his foot. "I don't believe you. Spill."

She looked over her shoulder at the board. "Okay, we are going on the assumption it is a woman. That could change, I realize that. But using that line of thought, the first set of murders could represent her losing a marriage."

Derek raised an eyebrow at her. "Go on."

"I've been spurned before. The song from the music box." She snapped her fingers. "Dream a wish...."

"*A Dream Is A Wish Your Heart Makes*," George said.

"Thank you. What if she killed the first women because of jealousy, like the doc thinks? She was jealous of the other women. They were still getting married, but she no longer was."

Dr. Chelsea crossed his arms over his chest. "That makes sense."

"Why is she killing now?" Michael asked.

George stepped next to her. "The second song, *Waltz of the Flowers*, basically represents finding true love."

"I'm not seeing the importance of the second song." Michael leaned against a desk.

Emma, who had been sitting at her desk listening but staying in the fray, spoke up. "If I could interject."

All heads turned towards her.

"Absolutely, Emma. You're part of this team," Derek said.

"If the killer murdered the first women because she lost a chance at marriage. Maybe the killings now represent her wanting to keep the women from experiencing another kind of loss," Emma said.

Dr. Chelsea moved to stand next to Felicia. He studied the board, looked at Derek, then faced Emma's direction. "I think you might be on to something."

Derek smiled at his secretary. "I knew you were going to be a great fit here." He clapped his hands. "Okay. We have our starting point. Get started on the previous victims. I will take the latest. If any of you find out that the bride-to-be was registered somewhere, please let Kyle know. If you need to go speak with someone, take another agent with you."

His mouth puckered, then he frowned. "I feel as if I am forgetting something. Kyle, don't forget the photos of both music boxes. See what you can find. Dr. Callahan, get me any photos you can as quickly as you can, please."

"I will get you those by this afternoon," Dr. Callahan said as he rose.

"I think it is time for us to go. Derek, I will see you later this evening. Say 6:30?" Dr. Chelsea said.

"That will work. Thank you for coming here this morning. I appreciate you two taking the time to answer questions." Derek followed them towards the entrance. He watched them on the screen as they both headed to their cars. When he turned around, his team stared at him. "What? Is my hair on fire?"

Felicia's eyes turned into slits. "Why did the FBI hide this case?"

Everyone waited for an answer.

"I don't have those answers. A lot of things were at play. I think the agent in charge at the time didn't want to be on the case. And I think when they couldn't find any leads to help narrow in on a killer, and the killings stopped, they shoved the case into a box somewhere and forgot about it." Derek moved his chair back behind his desk.

A quiet fell over his agents.

Derek sat and rested his elbows on his desk. "Emma, your thoughts on this give us a few avenues to look at. Thank you."

She sat in her seat. "I'm not an investigator. My feelings won't be hurt if you think I'm a nutter."

"Emma, I think you're fabulous," Derek said. "However, we still have a problem."

Everyone looked at him.

George was standing at the table getting another plate of donuts. "Besides a serial killer back from the past, what could be a worse problem?"

"If the killer is no longer sticking to killing their victims on the sixteenth of every month, and the date has no significance anymore, then the killer could strike again, at any time."

CHAPTER SIX

Anastasia lay in Dimitri's bed. She missed him so much. Her life would never be the same. She rolled on her side and clutched his pillow. She inhaled deeply and held it. His smell filled her nostrils. Tears moistened the pillowcase.

The last few months had been the worse. She did all she could to make him comfortable. But in the end, there was nothing she could do. His little body couldn't take it anymore.

She squeezed her eyes shut, concentrating on the years before when her life was wonderful. She and Dimitri spent every summer traveling until last year. The doctors advised against it, and she regretted to this day that she didn't follow her heart and take him on one last trip.

There were things she had to do, but they would have to wait. She grabbed Dimitri's teddy bear from the other side of the bed. She tucked him under her arm and curled up under his favorite blanket. As she drifted off, she could hear her son's laughter. She heard him calling for her.

"I can fly now, Mama. I have wings. Come fly with me."

She smiled as her hand lifted off the bed, reaching out. She whispered as sleep overcame her, "I'll be there soon, baby. Just a little longer."

CHAPTER SEVEN

Derek walked down the stairs to Kyle's work area, better known as the cave. He heard music and his agent's horrible singing filtering down the concrete hall. He stood in the short walkway, enjoying the coolness of the basement. No matter what the heat was outside, this area of the old church always remained cool.

As he entered the small office, he paused at the doorway. Kyle sat facing three screens on the wall. There were two more on his desk. Derek smiled as he watched Kyle sing his music, scrolling through endless data on the screens. Derek moved towards the desk and tapped his agent's shoulder.

Kyle jumped and flew back in his chair, rolling up against another desk behind him. "Jesus, man," he said, grabbing his chest. "Stop sneaking up on me."

"Quit making it so you can't hear when someone is coming." Derek took a piece of candy sitting on the desk. "Why don't you set up some kind of alarm, silent alarm, that tells you someone is coming down the hallway or entering the office?"

Kyle's eyes lit up. "Will the FBI pay for it?"

Derek rolled his eyes. "You're like a kid at Christmas. Give me some idea of cost and I'll let you know." He glanced over his shoulder towards the door. "Have you found any movement in that file from the Pink Diamond case?"

Kyle leaned in to him. "Nothing. No one has accessed it yet."

"Okay. That's not why I came down. I want to see if you could do something for me. In the first four cases, there was no packaging found at the residences. In this latest case, the killer delivered a package at some point. How, I'm not sure. Can you pull up an aerial view of the neighborhood from this morning's murder? Shoot it to me by email when you have it. Keep the view at about three-square miles."

"Yeah, I can get you that."

"Next, go through the addresses of the prior victims and do the same. Then overlay it with this latest murder. I don't need a rush on that, but as quick as you can, would be great." He smiled at his young agent.

Kyle smirked. "You don't want much, do you?" He chuckled. "No problem, Derek. I can get both pretty quick."

Derek patted his shoulder and headed back upstairs. His phone pinged as he reached the top. Lizzy.

I need to head to Tucson. I forgot I promised Jackson I would accompany him. I'm going to leave Lola at your house. I'll be back in two, maybe three, days.

Derek's stomach knotted. He hated that man. He wanted to scream at the top of his lungs and tell her to stop. But it was her life. She owed him nothing.

Okay. You can bring her to the office. If you have time.

I do. I'm at my place now. I will be there in about thirty minutes.

Okay.

Derek pocketed his phone and leaned against the wall. He needed a breath of fresh air and went out the back door to a small garden area. A concrete bench sat near the back under a small gazebo like structure. Plenty of shade covered the area, provided by the many trees planted years ago.

He sat on the bench, taking in the view. When the FBI took over the building, they cleaned up the garden and made sure the plants and flowers would attract birds and bees. Several patches of poppies, chuparosas, and marigolds filled the small area.

They had installed an eco-watering system strategically placed to water periodically and set up a rain collection system to use the city's resources as little as possible.

The stifling air wrapped around him like a wool blanket. Yet the shade made it somewhat bearable. He leaned back, trying to let the tension ease from his mind and body. No longer taking any medication for his anxiety, he tried to implement tools he had learned from Dr. Chelsea.

They didn't really work. But the meds were making his visions, delusions, or whatever they were more vivid, and he couldn't deal with them. With his eyes closed, he tried to clear his mind. He couldn't. Instead, flashes of previous cases swirled around his brain.

He concentrated on the dream he had in the CT scan weeks ago. He had been heavily medicating himself to deal with the reminisces of the Josiah Craig case. Josiah Craig forced him to watch as he raped and murdered Chrissy. He still shuddered at the memory. He pushed Josiah aside. "Go away," he whispered.

The day of the CT scan came into view. He had fallen asleep in the scanner. In a dream, he had awoken and thought they had left him behind. The straps that had held him on the bed had been removed.

In the dream, he got up and was dressing when he heard someone calling from inside the room where the techs sat during the scan. As he moved through the memory, he entered the small room to investigate. The smell of blood hit him the moment he stepped through the doorway. As the memory continued, the smell turned putrid.

He opened one eye, making sure he was still in the garden. His breathing slowed as he shifted on the bench. Relaxing, he was back in the CT room. Inside the tech area, the lights were off. He flipped the switch, but it wouldn't work. A cry for help echoed behind him.

While he sat on the bench with his eyes closed, he began touching his thumb to each fingertip as the memory of that day intensified. As he searched the small room, he moved around the desk that held the monitors for the CT scanner. There, on the floor of the small office, he saw the dead girl. The same girl from the early morning crime scene.

He fought desperately not to open his eyes. He wanted to see all the details. Maybe something he saw that day could help him now. He heard a girl's voice. A soft whisper. In the memory, he had reached for the doorknob. It was at this moment he expected to see the CT room, but he didn't. When he pulled the door open, he was in another house.

His head thumped as his pulse beat against his skull. He glanced around. He was in a child's room. Airplanes hung on fishing wire from the ceiling. Model cars lined shelves around the room.

Posters of race car drivers were tacked to the walls. Clearly, he was in a boy's room. *Why am I here? What happened to the CT scanner?*

He spun around looking for a way out when he saw something in the corner. It rested on a shelf. With his eyes still closed, he gave into the vision. He moved towards the wall and shelf, reaching his hand out. His fingers trembled as he grazed the metal surface.

Before he could pick up the music box, something behind it caught his attention. A picture of a pinned butterfly in a display case. As he reached for the butterfly, he heard Tchaikovsky's song playing. Except it wasn't coming from the music box in the room, it was coming from behind him as he sat on the bench.

His eyes shot open. He was in the church garden and heard the tin prongs as they tapped against the metal spool playing out *Waltz of the Flowers*. The hair on his arms stood on end. A line of sweat beaded down his back.

The whimpers of a girl tickled his right ear. "Why didn't you save me?"

He jumped off the bench, and spun around. The girl from the crime scene stood behind him. Blood soaked through the white ribbon around her neck. The skin around the ribbon had peeled back further, revealing the soft pink tissue underneath. Her entrails dragged behind her like a train on a dress. Clumps of soil stuck to the sticky leathery intestines.

She reached out, holding the music box. "I don't like this. Please, make it quit playing." The music box was open, revealing a small butterfly. As it spun, it looked as if the wings fluttered in time to the music.

Derek froze. His lungs burned. The air stuck, searing his chest from the inside. He stared at the same music box from the boy's room. The same one from the crime scene. He took a step backward and tumbled to the ground.

The woman inched closer. She stopped when her entrails snagged on a bush.

He watched in horror as she tugged and pulled. When it broke free, the smell of fecal matter and blood rushed over him like a wave at the beach. He gagged, turning on his stomach. Trying to pull himself, he clawed at the ground, but couldn't get his legs to move. When he glanced over his shoulder, Josiah Craig stood where the woman had been. He held one of Derek's legs in a tight grip.

Pieces of flesh hung from Josiah's head. Maggots and roaches crawled through his rotting teeth. "You ain't going nowhere, boy. I got you. And I ain't ever going to let you go."

Derek struggled and yelled out a screech like sound.

"Derek?" Kelly called from the back doorway of the church.

His head ripped around towards the door. He turned back to see Josiah Craig was gone.

Kelly walked towards the gazebo. "Derek?" she saw him on the ground near the bench. "Are you okay?" she asked, walking towards him.

"Yeah. Yeah, I'm fine. I tripped getting up when I heard you call my name. I just came out here a few minutes ago. Needed some air." He stood, brushing himself off.

"A few minutes ago? Kyle has been looking for you for about thirty minutes." Kelly had turned back towards the doorway. "Come on, Elizabeth is also up front."

At that moment, Lola bounded out the door, running towards him, with Marc Anthony close on her heels.

"Oh boy. I bet you're glad to see him," Kelly laughed. "The minute that dog came into the building, she has been searching for you."

Derek followed the dogs and his agent. Before he shut the door, he glanced over his shoulder—nothing there but an empty bench.

CHAPTER EIGHT

Dr. Ronald Chelsea pulled the old, ratty folder from his locked desk drawer. He laid it on his desk but didn't open it. Several coffee stains made an abstract design on the dingy old manilla color.

He held the tab with his fingertips. His hand trembled. Stalling, he shook out his shoulders, opening and closing his hands, making a few tight fists to expel the anxiety. Several times over the last few weeks since the CT incident, he pulled the folder out but couldn't open it. He would stare at it, then put it back in the bottom drawer.

This time, he was going to force himself to look. He took a deep breath and twisted his head from side to side, like what a boxer would do just before the fight. He shifted in his chair and glanced up at the clock on the wall.

The office was closed for lunch, and he didn't have any patients scheduled for the rest of the afternoon. He blew out a breath and opened the folder. Even though he had seen these photos at Derek's office, the first photo brought up all the emotions he tamped down while at the Legacy Unit. Sitting in the quiet of his office, he was transported back to the day April Fontaine's body was found.

April was younger than the latest victim and much prettier. She had been a nursing student, about to graduate and marry her high school boyfriend.

He sat for hours one day with the family. Listening to them talk about her. What she was like. The kinds of jokes she laughed at. They described how she treated her patients, and Dr. Chelsea saw where she inherited her kindness from.

After listening to them, Dr. Chelsea had no doubt she would've made a wonderful nurse. He moved his thumb across her picture. His sadness turned to anger. "Someone cut your life short. Too short."

Ronald had attended the funeral. At the time, he didn't understand why. He chalked it up to getting a little too close to the family. He had spent countless hours with them. By the time they released the body, going to the funeral seemed like the natural thing to do.

His nostrils flared at the thought of Agent McDougal. "You were such a son of a bitch." The words spewed out. The rage he felt during those four months returned. His lips flattened as he recalled countless conversations with the irritating man.

"I should have pushed harder. I should have gone over his head," he said as he went to the next picture in the folder. Betty Shore's dull blank eyes stared at him. In her thirties, she was much older than April. Set to marry a longtime friend after both had become widows. Dr. Chelsea thought back to the videos he had seen of Betty. Her robust laughter filled any room and drew people to her.

Flipping to the next victim, Dr. Chelsea sucked in a sharp breath. Margarite Sanchez. Staring at her deep blue eyes, he could see the oceans of the Caribbean. He will never forget the heartbreak her parents suffered when they found her two days before the wedding. When Dr. Chelsea arrived at the crime scene, the mother lay on the floor in a crumpled heap, wailing, and clutching rosary beads.

Ronald felt the sting as tears filled his eyes. He stared for a long moment at her photo. The music box sat perfectly placed in her hand. He wiped his eyes and looked more closely at the crime scene photo. His skin prickled. He tapped his foot against the hardwood floor.

Lifting the photo of Lana Berkshire, the last victim, he stared at the young woman. She was about to graduate from college and go to medical school. Looking beyond the dead girl, he focused on the music box.

Ronald pulled the first two pictures and focused on the music box in each one. He rifled through his center desk drawer and pulled out a small magnifying glass. He had to shift it back and forth until he found the right spot. "Oh my," he said as he did the same in each photo. "How did I miss this?"

CHAPTER NINE

Derek walked into the office area. Lizzy stood next to Marc Anthony, giving him kisses. He smiled at her when she glanced up. "Hey. Sorry. I didn't mean to keep you waiting."

Marc Anthony nudged her for more attention.

"I can't pet you all day." Lizzy turned towards Emma. "He is such a sweetie. Now I see why Lola loves him so much."

"Lola and him have become fast friends." Emma watched as Lizzy moved towards Derek. It didn't take a rocket scientist to see how much these two cared for each other. She tilted her head down while eavesdropping on their conversation.

"Are you heading right out?" Derek asked.

"Yeah." She motioned towards the front of the building. "Congressman Jackson is waiting outside."

Derek kept himself from going rigid. He looked at his feet.

"Hey," Lizzy said, reaching for his hand. "It's nothing like that. He has a three-day event in Tucson. I forgot I promised I would go."

"You don't owe me an explanation. You know that."

"I know."

Derek pulled her by the hand towards the front door. He glanced over his shoulder at his crew. "I will never tell you what to do. And I will always be here for you."

Lola came up and sat next to Derek's leg. She moaned at her owner.

"Oh, don't you start. I know you love being with Derek." She patted her head. "I need to go. I'll call you later today, or at least tomorrow."

Derek leaned in and kissed her cheek. He put his lips next to her ear. "I love you. Always."

Lizzy hugged him. "I love you, too."

He watched her on the big screen above him. He clenched his fists as he watched Congressman Jackson step out of the limo and hold the door for her.

Lola whined at his side, staring at the door.

"It's all right girl. You and I will have a good time." He scratched the head of the boxer.

Marc Anthony ran up to her, distracting her from her sadness.

Derek watched them run to the kitchen, no doubt looking for treats. His phone pinged on his desk. Sitting down, he read the text. Dr. Chelsea said to look at the photo of the original music box.

Derek stood, walking over to the whiteboard. He got as close as he could to the one photo of the music box. He couldn't see anything that stood out. "Does anyone have a magnifying glass?" he asked as he continued to stare at the photo.

"Yeah," said George. He rummaged through his desk drawer. "At least I thought I did." He hunched over, reaching towards the back. "Here it is." He walked over to Derek. "What are you looking for?"

"I'm not sure. Dr. Chelsea texted and said he had missed something in the photo." Derek held the magnifying glass and inspected small sections.

"Do you see anything?" George asked.

"No. But then I don't know what I am looking for." He looked over the entire photo. He handed the glass to George. "See if you see anything. I'm going to text him."

Derek typed a message. When it pinged back, he moved to the board. "Here." He pointed to the music box and the girl who spun around. "Do you see anything?"

George moved the magnifier over the area. "No, I—wait. Look at this." He pointed to an area for Derek to look at.

Derek stared through the magnifier. "Holy shit." He glanced at George. "What do you see?"

George chuckled. "It looks like a piece is broken off."

Derek squinted at the photo. He turned back to George. "Like maybe another figurine is missing?"

"Yeah. I think at one time there were two people who spun around dancing." George took the magnifier again, studying the photograph.

"Like a man and woman?" Derek asked.

"I think so. I mean, I guess it could be two women, but I'm thinking this is a traditional type of music box. Based on our victims and the killer, I'm thinking it was a man." George said.

Derek moved to stand behind his desk. "If our theory is correct and we go back to what Dr. Chelsea said about the killer being in a different time of her life, this could be the clue we need."

"I'm not following," George said.

The other investigators came over to look at the photo under the magnifying glass.

Felicia looked first, then handed it to Kelly. "Something prompted this killer to break off the dude."

Derek pointed at her. "Yes."

"Okay. Then that means our killer, at the time of these murders," George pointed to the early killings, "our killer had been spurned in some way."

Kelly handed the glass to Michael. "Something bad enough to make her break the music box. Which could be a symbol for her actual husband-to-be."

Michael frowned as he laid the magnifier on Derek's desk. "What could be so bad that it would make this lady buy perfectly good music boxes, break off the guy, then kill four women?"

"I can tell you what caused her to break off the guy from the music box." Felicia leaned into Michael. "He dumped her."

Kelly sat on the corner of her desk. "Not only dumped her. But more than likely dumped her right before the wedding."

Felicia snapped her finger. "And not only dumped her before the wedding, but dumped her for someone else. Trifecta."

Derek sat in his chair. "Okay. This gives us a starting point. It makes sense." He picked up his phone and texted Kyle to come up when he could. He also texted Dr. Chelsea back.

Thanks for the tip. We have a little more to go on.

I can't believe I didn't see that years ago.

It's easy to miss. You have to really be looking at the music box to see that there had been a second figurine on it.

It seems things were so messed up years ago. They didn't catch this in forensics. At least, the agent in charge never told us. Four girls died.

Not your fault, Ronald. Come to the house tonight. I'll get us some pizza.

All you eat is pizza.

Okay. I'll get a salad too.

I'll be there after 6.

Derek knew this was eating at Dr. Chelsea. He held himself responsible for something he couldn't control. He was also well aware of how those feeling could eat someone alive. Guilt. It came in all shapes and sizes. Derek carried a lot with him. He often thought it was the sole driving force behind his life. He leaned back as he dialed his director's number.

"Derek, what's up?"

"Listen, I need the complete file on the previous cases. I couldn't find it on the system."

The AD huffed into the phone. "It's not on the system. I told you I would get it to you."

Derek heard papers shuffling. "Where is it?"

"I will have the file pulled. The FBI didn't want any leaks. It was never entered into the system. I can get you the paper file by the end of today."

"That's odd. Don't you think? The case not being put into the system?"

"The powers that be thought putting it in the system might cause more problems. When I hang up, I will have my assistant pull it. It's downstairs in records."

"Do you want me to come get it?"

"I'll have someone run it over to you. Give me a few hours."

"No worries. Emma is always here."

"How is she working out?"

"She's great. This place runs a lot better with her here."

"That's for sure," Felicia yelled from across the room.

"Sorry AD. That was one of my agents."

Laughter filled the phone. "I think you assembled a good team."

"Thanks for getting the file."

"No problem," AD Fretz said.

"One more thing before I let you go."

"Sure, Derek. What is it?"

"Do you know who did the forensics on the case? I know Dr. Callahan collected items for testing, but the music box, did the FBI crime lab handle that?"

"Did you find something?"

"Can't say for sure. Just a question."

"I can say that the FBI took over everything after the second murder. I would assume that meant all physical evidence as well."

"Okay. When I get the file, I will get a better handle on some information. I would like to wait until then to fill you in."

"No problem, Derek. I trust you."

"Please make sure all the reports are in the file. Including all forensics."

"I will do that."

The phone went silent. He laid it on his desk. He heard Kyle whistling in the kitchen. Looking at the clock, Derek decided he needed a snack.

Kyle placed the two-liter bottle of soda back in the fridge. "Hey. I was just coming to see you."

Derek grabbed a glass from the cabinet and filled it with cold water from the refrigerator. He searched the snack cabinet for something to munch on. A protein bar was the one item that looked appetizing. Something he was sure Kelly brought in. "What do you have?"

Kyle sat in one of the two chairs at the small round table. He held out the file he had tucked under his arm. "These are aerial shots of all the neighborhoods where each victim was found. Including the latest victim."

Derek took the folder but didn't open it. "Thanks. Have you found anything out on the music boxes yet?"

"Yes, and no." Kyle sipped his soda.

"Maybe this will help. We found what looks like another figurine in the original music box."

"You mean like a couple dancing in circles?"

"Yeah."

"Well then, that explains my results. I couldn't find any that looked like the one in the photo. I found one that was identical, but it had a man and woman dancing around."

"That's great."

"Not really. The manufacturer went out of business years ago."

"After the murders?" Derek asked, taking a bite of his bar.

"Yep. About two years after, the murders stopped. The company went belly up."

"Can you get anything from the previous owners? Maybe track down some old order slips or anything?"

Kyle guzzled the last of his soda. "I found the owner. I tried to call. Got a voicemail. The owner lives in Dallas."

Derek's eyes narrowed. "How do you know where the owner lives?"

Kyle laughed. "Nothing too illegal. I pulled the financials on the company."

Derek shook his head. "Don't tell me. Just don't break any laws."

"I skim the laws... skim."

Derek pinched the bridge of his nose. "You scare me."

Kyle stood. "If the guy calls me back, I'll let you know what I find out."

"If he doesn't, let me know. I could have one of the Dallas agents go to his residence and interview him. I'm hesitant to do that though. I don't want to bring any other agents in on this case." Derek threw the protein bar wrapper away, placed his glass in the sink, and grabbed a soda for his desk.

CHAPTER TEN

At his desk, he studied the aerial photos from the file. Kyle had blown them up and circled the homes of the victims. He moved to the whiteboard and flipped it to the blank side.

He placed each photo on it with the names of the victims above each. "Okay, guys," he said as he turned towards his team. "These are the aerial shots of each victims' home. And this one is an overlay of the first murders and today's murder.

"Use this when you are talking to the family. Ask them if anything back during the time of the murders, stood out to them about the area. Ask them if the victims ever mentioned getting unusual packages in the mail or delivered by another service. Ask about any unusual phone calls or if suspicious cars were ever reported in their neighborhoods."

Felicia glanced up to look at the photos. "I can't see the connection. They aren't in any kind of pattern. Nor do they seem related. Something made this killer pick these victims but it doesn't look like where they lived had anything to do with it."

"We may never see the connection," George said. "Killers pick their victims for very random reasons. It could be the color of hair or eyes. It could be where each victim lives. Hell, it doesn't even have to be a real connection. It could be something the killer perceives to be real. There is often no understanding as to why a killer chooses who they do."

"Well, I don't like it." Felicia laughed. "I need these damn killers to make it easier for me."

"Don't we all," Kelly said.

Emma was cleaning the table that held the donuts and coffee.

"Thank you, Emma. That isn't your job. But I appreciate it." Derek took the coffee thermos off the table and helped her carry things into the kitchen.

"I don't mind at all." She set the empty boxes in the trash and smiled at Derek. She started to say something but stopped herself.

"What? What do you want to know?"

Her brow wrinkled. "How do you do that?"

"Do what?"

She sat at the little table. "You seem to always know when I want to say something."

He leaned in to her. "I'm psychic."

She waved him off as he took the seat across from her. "It's none of my business, really."

"Ask anyway."

"It's clear you have powerful feelings for Lizzy. I don't understand why you don't ask her to stop spending time with the congressman."

Derek looked at his hands.

"I'm sorry. It's really none of my business. But I saw how hurt you were when she left." Emma reached across the table and took his hand. "I don't have any kids. My husband and I couldn't have any. I have become quite attached to everyone here. I'm sorry if I overstepped."

"You didn't overstep, and you are not the first person to ask me that." Derek took a deep breath, blowing it out slowly. "I met her during one of my early cases. It's a long story, but she and I became close. I don't have the right to ask her to stop. We have a very weird relationship and I'm happy just being a part of her life."

"You do. You have the right. You just aren't that kind of guy. Lizzy doesn't know how lucky she is." Emma stood. "Thank you for letting me be nosy."

Derek rose. "You can always be nosy." He watched her walk back to her desk. Lola ran in and sat at his feet. "What? What do you want?"

She barked and ran to the doggy treat drawer.

As soon as he opened it, Marc Anthony ran in and howled.

"Okay, okay." He pulled out two big milk bones and gave them to the dogs, who promptly ran off to their dog beds. As he sat down, his head throbbed. The pain was piercing. As if someone stuck an ice pick through his eyeball. He closed his eyes, controlling his breathing. The pain passed as quickly as it had started.

He shook it off and opened the file that held everything from Dr. Callahan so far on the current murder. He studied the crime scene photo that held the music box. "George, can I borrow your magnifying glass?"

"Sure." George stepped over to him, laying it down on Derek's desk. "As he sat back down, his phone rang. "Agent Peterson." He grabbed a pad from his desk. "Hey, thanks for calling me back. Yes, I'm working on your sister's case. I understand this is hard. But we specialize in cold cases and we could really use your help." He nodded and scribbled on his pad. "I can be there in about thirty minutes. Thank you."

"What do you have going on?" Derek asked.

"That was Betty Shore's sister. Our second victim. She has agreed to meet with me at her home." George took his gun from his drawer and clipped it on his belt.

"Take someone with you," Derek said.

George looked at Kelly. "You want to go with me?"

Kelly stretched. "Absolutely. I could use some fresh air."

Derek watched as the two agents left. He needed some fresh air and didn't want to go anywhere near the backyard. "Emma, I'm going to go see Dr. Callahan. I will be back before you leave. I'm letting Lola stay here."

"Oh, that's no problem at all. I will take good care of her," Emma said.

Derek gathered his keys and made sure he had a pack of gum in the front pocket of his jeans. Before he exited the building, he spoke to his crew. "If any of you need me for anything, call me."

Felicia was on the phone and waved at him.

Michael nodded as he went back to searching the computer for information.

Derek stepped out into the bright October sun. The temperature was not as bad as during the heat of the summer, but for early fall, it was still hot. He started his car and sighed as the cool air blasted from the vents.

Leaving the parking lot, he changed his mind and drove to the home of the latest victim. Lizzy popped into his thoughts. He had never been a jealous man, but he couldn't give her what Congressman Jackson could. He didn't have private planes, galas to attend, or an enormous estate. His grip tightened on the steering wheel. "Damn, I hate that man."

Midday traffic moved fast. A truck pulled up next to him. The music blared, causing the sound to be distorted as it reverberated against the metal of the doors. He glanced over, shaking his head. "Seriously, rap music?" As the truck sped off, it pulled in front of him as soon as he cleared the intersection.

Derek noted the license plate. "Too bad I can't write you a ticket." He watched the driver look up in his review mirror. Derek kept his eyes trained on the vehicle. He rubbed the back of his neck.

A sticky sheen of sweat beaded at the base of his hairline. His eyes darted to his review-mirror. *Empty.* His heart thudded against his chest. "Relax." He said the words, but anxiety crept through his bones.

The truck stayed several car links ahead of him. As Derek continued to watch the vehicle, he noticed a person in the back seat. He squinted at the back window of the truck.

"What the hell?" Derek increased his speed. As he came closer to the truck, a young boy waved at him through the back window. A cloudy haze seemed to float around him. Derek changed lanes in order to get closer to the truck and get a better view.

As he maneuvered next to the left rear fender, he could see the boy looked very pale, sickly pale. The truck slowed, giving Derek a chance to pull alongside. As he monitored the traffic in front of him, he eased closer to the driver's side.

He glanced to his right, getting a side view of the driver. When the driver turned towards him, he had an evil toothless grin on his face. A swarm of flies buzzed around the driver's head. Derek stared at Josiah Craig. Beetles wove themselves through openings in his rotten flesh. "This isn't real."

Derek tapped the steering wheel, shaking his head. "You aren't real. You aren't real." He turned to look at the driver one more time when the truck flew through the red light. Derek pushed on his gas before looking straight ahead. Looking up in the nick of time, he slammed on his brakes. Another vehicle traveled at a fast rate of speed, coming through the intersection. The second vehicle had no time to stop and t-boned the truck.

Derek threw his car into park. Before he exited, he flipped a switch under his dashboard, turning on the red and blue flashing lights he had installed in his vehicle. Both his blinkers and parking lights flashed the different colors alternating between red and blue, while his headlamps and taillights blinked bright white.

He grabbed his phone from his pocket and dialed 911. "This is FBI Agent Derek Reed. I need immediate help at the intersection of 59th and Bell Road. There's been a major car accident. There are injured. Possible fatalities."

Derek ran to the second vehicle first. A small Toyota hatchback of some sort. The impact obliterated the front of the vehicle. The entire front cabin had been pushed into the back seat, compacting it. Derek didn't have to take vitals on the driver. A large piece of the metal frame from the windshield nearly decapitated her.

Several people came to help. Some recoiled at the sight of the dead driver.

Derek pointed to a man who looked like he was in his thirties. "I'm an FBI agent. Do me a favor and keep people back from this car wreck. Don't let anyone take pictures if you can help it."

The man nodded. "Yes, sir." He began pushing people back.

Sirens blasted in the distance.

Derek ran towards the truck. He had to yank on the door handle several times before he got the driver's door to open. The young teenage boy sat unconscious in the driver's seat. He touched his neck. Relief washed over him when he found a pulse.

The force of the impact had broken all the side windows and shattered the front as well. One large piece of glass shard stuck out from the young man's throat.

He inspected the wound and the piece of glass. Not knowing if the shard blocked the flow of the artery and kept the driver from bleeding out, Derek did not remove it. He quickly glanced in the backseat. There were no other passengers.

Another man ran up to the truck. He was about to yank the young driver out when Derek stopped him. "Don't move him. Let's wait for the paramedics."

The sound of sirens blared loudly as several cop cars, two firetrucks, and two ambulances entered the intersection. Derek waved one of the ambulance crews over to him. He stepped to the side before walking towards one officer. "I'm FBI Agent Derek Reed."

The cop's eyebrows wrinkled.

"I was next to the truck when it ran the red light."

"Oh. For a minute, I thought there was a major incident." The cop sheepishly glanced at his feet. "I meant like a terrorist or something." The officer motioned toward the truck. "Why do you think the boy ran the light after stopping?"

"Listen, the young boy had his music loud. I can only assume he wasn't paying attention and thought the light turned green. Or maybe he was tired of waiting. All I know is he blew through the red light and the second car," Derek pointed to the Toyota, "the driver didn't have time to do anything. From what I could tell, the deceased driver was moving fast."

The officer took notes on a little pad. "Could I see your badge? I need to make a note of who witnessed the accident."

"No problem." He fished out his FBI badge from his jean pocket. When the officer finished with it, Derek clipped it to his belt loop. He watched as the crew of the second ambulance removed the dead driver.

They removed the dead woman, paying close attention to her head, held on by a few strands of tendons and muscles. They secured it before lifting her onto the gurney. The last thing anyone needed—a head rolling into the intersection.

The young boy remained unconscious as the paramedic packed gauze around the glass shard, keeping it secure until they reached the hospital.

A few other witnesses gathered around Derek and the police officer. As he asked them all questions about what had happened, Derek glanced over at the boy's truck. He half expected Josiah Craig to pop out.

"Sir?"

Derek spun around. The cop stood before him, waiting for an answer. "I'm sorry, I didn't hear you."

"Do you have anything else to add?"

"No. I've told you everything."

The police officer handed out several cards. "If anyone has anything else to add, you can reach me at this number."

As Derek walked back to his car, the last remnants of the accident were being cleared and traffic began moving. As he sat and waited for a police officer to direct his lane of cars, a movement to his left caught his eye.

He twisted his head and saw the same young boy from the truck standing in a crowd of people. Derek watched as the crowd seemed oblivious to the young boy. The boy turned around and stared at Derek. He waved and then vanished.

Derek scanned the area. No boy. No Josiah Craig. He questioned his sanity. Who was the kid and why was he seeing him. Chrissy popped into his head. Their earlier conversation made him uneasy. "I don't want this gift. Whatever it is. I don't want it."

CHAPTER ELEVEN

3 p.m. Tuesday

Derek pulled into the driveway of the latest victim's home, next to an empty police officer's vehicle. Another car was parked on the street in front of the house.

Making his way to the front door, he glanced up and down the street. He thought about the aerial view he had seen back at the office. The victim's home was on a main thoroughfare. The killer had an easy in and out. He walked to the edge of the yard to get a better look at the street.

A woman walked out of the home directly across from him. He raised his hand. "Excuse me," Derek said, jogging across the street.

The lady shut her mailbox, looking over her shoulder. She took a step back.

"It's okay." He pulled his badge off his belt. "I'm FBI Agent Derek Reed. Can I ask you a few questions?"

She nodded, smiling at him. "Yes. That would be fine."

"What's your name?"

"Darla Stevens."

"Darla, can you tell me if you noticed anything yesterday evening? Or maybe even a few days before the murder?"

The woman crossed her arms over her chest. "I saw someone deliver something."

"Deliver something. Like a delivery truck, the mailman?

"No. No delivery truck. But the person was wearing what looked like a delivery uniform."

Derek scribbled on his notepad. "When did you first see this person drop something off?"

The woman's face wrinkled. "I had just finished watching my show. I usually check the mail between 2 and 3 p.m.

"Did you notice what car the person drove?"

"With all the delivery people using their own vehicles these days, I didn't think much of it. But I think it was a SUV of some type. A small one, though, not big."

"Color?" Derek asked.

"Dark. Maybe blue or green. Could've been black."

"How about the delivery person? Was it a man or a woman?"

"Oh, I didn't get a good look. They wore a hat, dark pants, and a dark shirt. I guess that's why I thought it was a man."

"I'm sorry. What made you think it was a man?"

"Their hair. It was short. I could tell. Even though they had on a hat. Their hair was cut very short. At least in the back."

Derek smiled at the lady. "Is there anything else you can think of?"

She snapped her fingers. "The same delivery person came back that evening." She shrugged. "I had forgotten about that. I thought it was odd, but I just figured they forgot to leave a package."

"What time did this person come back?" Derek asked.

"Let me think. My husband and I had just finished dinner. He went out to the back to sit by the pool. I went into the sitting room." She pointed to the big window facing the street. "From there, I saw the same delivery person. I think around 7 p.m."

"Did they carry anything up to the door with them this time? You said you thought they were delivering another package."

She frowned. "I don't think I saw another package. But the person was carrying something." She paused for a moment, closing her eyes. "It looked like one of those things you sign when you get a package. You know, like when UPS delivers something you need to sign for, like that."

"You have been a tremendous help." He pulled a business card from his badge holder. "If you think of anything else, or you see the same vehicle and person again. Please call me."

She took the card. "I will." She turned to leave, then turned back. "Do we have anything to worry about? We can't get any answers."

"You have nothing to worry about. This was an isolated incident. We don't have any reason to believe it is anything more than that." Derek took a step back. "Thank you again for your time."

He headed back across the street. Not much else to go on, but she gave one piece of information. The person did not drive a delivery truck. He rang the doorbell, then tried the door. Unlocked. He walked inside. "Hello?"

He craned his neck, listening for a response. "Hello?" Derek walked further into the home. "Anyone here?"

An officer and a woman carrying a box came to the top of the stairs.

"Who are you?" the officer snapped.

Derek held up his badge. "FBI Agent Derek Reed."

"Okay. I was just escorting Claudia, the victim's sister, so she could get a few items."

"No worries." He reached out to grab the box from the woman's hands. "I didn't have the chance to speak with you, Claudia. May I ask a few questions?"

"Yes." Her eyes darted down the short hallway. "Can we go outside? I don't enjoy being in here."

Derek leaned his head towards the doorway. "Lead the way."

The officer followed both out, locking the door behind them.

"Are you staying?" Derek asked the cop.

"Yeah," the cop said as he followed Derek, stopping at his vehicle. "The chief wants this place to be watched until further notice." He glanced at his watch. I'm here for three more hours, until my relief shows up."

Derek continued to Claudia's car. "I can't imagine how hard this must be for you and your family."

Claudia opened the back driver's side door.

Derek placed the box on the back seat and closed the door.

She leaned against car, wiping a tear from her cheek. "I can't believe what has happened. Her wedding is—was just days away. We don't know what to do."

Derek pulled his notepad from the back pocket of his jeans. "Can you give me her fiancé's name and how I can reach him?"

She nodded slightly as she unlocked her car. She retrieved her cell phone from her purse and held it out.

Derek copied the name and number. "Thank you. Do you know if your sister had received any threatening emails, text messages, or phone calls? Anything?"

Claudia shook her head. "No. Nothing like that."

"Did she mention anything about possibly someone new in her life? Maybe they asked a lot of questions about her wedding, anything at all?"

"No. She mentioned nothing. Except for a phone call she received regarding the wedding. Someone from a local store she had registered for wedding gifts."

Derek raised an eyebrow at her. "What store was that?"

"It was either Target, Walmart, or Amazon. I'm really not sure which. I remember she said a few days ago, someone called and wanted to verify the registration and make sure their date was listed correctly."

"Is that something that happens? I mean, people verifying that kind of information?" Derek asked.

Claudia crossed her arms over her chest. "I got married years ago, and we chose Walmart. No one called me during that time."

Derek scribbled some notes. "Did she say anything about the call? Like whether they asked inappropriate questions. Maybe they were too nosy?"

Claudia straightened, stepping closer to Derek. "Do you think the caller had something to do with her murder?"

Derek held up his hand. "No. I am simply trying to get a clear idea of her movements in the days before her death. I know it's hard not knowing. I am trying to get answers for you and your family as quickly as I can." He dropped his shoulders, letting his arms sag at his side. "Listen, can you think of anything which seemed out of the ordinary the days before her death?"

Claudia fell against the car. The tears crested over. "I don't think so. Other than what I have already told you. I'm sorry I don't have more information."

"It's okay. One last thing, did her fiancé have an ex that was jealous or anyone else that objected to the wedding?"

"No. Douglas had nothing but supporters. All of his family loved Charlene." She looked at her watch and quickly opened her driver's side door. "I need to be somewhere. I can call you if I think of anything else."

Derek handed her one of his cards. "That would be great. Any time." He stepped back and watched her drive away. He walked towards the officer's vehicle. "Hey, I need to get inside and look around. I didn't want to do it with Claudia here. Can I get the keys, or do you need to let me in?"

The officer handed him the key. "Be my guest. That place creeps me out."

Derek smirked. "Really? Why?"

The officer scratched his head. "I can't explain it. I've been around murder investigations, but something about that house just doesn't feel right."

Derek held the key up. "I won't be but a few."

"Take your time." The officer went back to reading his book.

CHAPTER TWELVE

Beth's mother watched her daughter search the newspaper. "What are you looking for?" She saw her daughter's pale blue eyes widen as she covered her mouth with her hand. "Tell me."

Beth Cahill giggled with delight as she held out the newspaper. "Look."

Her mother took the paper. "Well now, that is a fabulous picture." She laughed as she handed it back to her. "Does Ralph know you sent that in?"

"Yes. Maybe. Okay, no. He didn't want me to make a big deal about it. But I have always wanted to have my wedding announcement in the paper."

Her mother laughed as the waiter set down their drinks. "I remember when you were little. You would read the newspaper for all the weddings and funerals announcements ."

"Funerals? I never did that."

"Yes, you did. You would read someone's obituary and then say you were going to pray for their family."

Beth smiled. "I was such a weird kid." She took a drink of her water. "Why would I read the obits? I don't remember that."

"You did. But you were more concerned about the weddings," she snapped her fingers, "and the baby announcements."

"Oh, I can't wait to have a baby. I'm so ready, Mom."

"Don't be in a rush, sweetie. Enjoy your time with Ralph. Once you have kids, your marriage will never be the same. You two will be at the beck and call of that baby. Who will grow up to be a teen." Cindy reached over and took her daughter's hand. "I know you will be a wonderful mother."

Beth covered her mother's hand with hers. "If I can be half the mom you are, I will be a damn wonderful mom."

The waiter set a tray at their table and placed their food in front of them.

"Don't you think Ralph will be upset about the announcement?"

"He might be. That's because he would rather live as a recluse sometimes. Besides, I'm hoping a few people see this."

Cindy pointed at Beth with her fork. "You shouldn't poke the bear. You know his ex-girlfriend has never gotten over their breakup. She just might try to ruin your big day."

"First, the weasel is engaged. Second, the TRO is still in effect. If she comes anywhere near our wedding, we will have her arrested." Beth took a bite of food. "You know, now that you mention it, that may not be such a bad thing to happen." Beth winked at her mother.

CHAPTER THIRTEEN

Derek unlocked the door. Stepping in, he closed it behind him, but didn't lock it. He stuck the keys in his front jean pocket and walked into the living room, where he first saw the victim.

A large blood stain filled the carpet. Looking at the stain from all sides, he pictured the victim laying on the floor. He closed his eyes, recalling the position of the body.

He stood where the victim's head would've laid. Glancing up, he could see the front door. Closing his eyes again, he pictured the scene. Charlene heard the doorbell. She either came from upstairs or was already down on the first floor.

His eyes popped open. "She was in the nightgown," he said out loud as glanced up the staircase. "If she was in the gown, I'm betting she was upstairs when the killer came to the door." That made sense too, because they found a robe on the sofa near the body. "I can't imagine the killer went upstairs, grabbed the robe and brought it down to the living room."

He moved towards the bottom of the stairway. He studied the tile floor at its base and right in front of the door. Stepping back, he inspected the floor. There were no drag marks. The victim had been barefoot when found.

"Even if she was barefoot, the killer still had to subdue her and drag her to the other room." Derek pretended to be let in by the victim. He bobbed from side to side as if he talked to someone.

He closed his eyes. Whatever the killer said to get the victim off her guard made it easy for the killer to attack. He opened his eyes and imagined the victim turning her back on the killer. It would've been at this point that the killer could use a rag with chloroform to cover her mouth.

Derek reached around an imaginary victim and place a rag over the nose and mouth area. *The victim had to struggle.* Using his dominant hand to hold the rag, he to use his other to wrap around the waist of his victim.

Again, closing his eyes, he imagined the woman would go limp after a brief struggle. Pretending to drag the victim to the other room, Derek walked backwards.

He heard a noise coming from the second floor. He stood still, tilting his head towards the noise. Straining to hear, he held his breath. Silence. He returned to his task when he heard the same noise again. A soft cry. As if someone wept.

He walked back to the foyer and looked up at the top of the stairs. A tingle spread down his back. He turned his head from side to side, trying to release the tension. His neck bones popped, echoing throughout the empty home. Derek started up the staircase. Stopping halfway, he glanced up.

He listened intently, forcing his limbs to relax. Continuing up the stairs, he clenched and unclenched his hands. Spreading out his fingers to dissipate the anxiety. At the top of the landing, he stepped into the first bedroom, which had been made into some kind of craft room. He used the jack and jill bathroom to get to the second bedroom.

A full-size bed, dresser, and small chair filled the room. It looked unused. Back in the hallway, he continued towards the last room, the master.

Checking doors as he walked down towards the master; he slowed his pace as he neared the bedroom. He stood several feet outside the doorway. Tilting his head, he listened. Silence.

He blew out a long breath as he walked the last few steps and entered the room. Not very large, as masters go. A rush of cold air surrounded him. Shrugging it off, he scanned the room.

The bed was on his right. Two identical nightstands, with matching lamps, sat on either side. Derek frowned at the lampshades. Fringe lined the edges of each one. The deep red color made him think of burlesque.

"I hate fringe," he said as he looked around the rest of the room. A tall dresser sat on the opposite wall, with a long shorter one against another wall. To his left, a girly vanity with an ornate chair were in one corner with a standup mirror in the other corner.

Diverting his eyes away from the mirror, he moved towards the bed. Bending over, he looked under it. "Nothing." As he moved towards the vanity, he heard a faint cry. His heart thudded against his chest. Inhaling through his nose, he blew the breaths out slowly and steadily through his mouth.

Turning slowly, towards the bed, he wiped his clammy hands on his jeans. The vein in his neck throbbed. The room appeared to be empty. "I know I heard a cry. I am not losing my shit."

He pushed it out of his mind and walked towards the vanity. The chair was pulled out. Makeup littered the entire surface area. He pulled the pen from his little notebook and moved things around. Using it, he opened the little drawer. More makeup. He used the top to push it back in.

His mouth was dry, and he tried to swallow. His tongue stuck to the roof. He sucked in his cheeks, trying to get saliva to build up. When his mouth watered enough, he swallowed. He patted his jeans, looking for gum. He pulled the package out and placed it in his mouth. He chewed and swallowed several times coating his throat.

"Get a grip. It's just a house." Still avoiding the mirror, he turned to leave the room. He heard the cry again. Coming from the bed area. Derek stared at the cover. No indentations. Nothing or no one sat on the bed.

He blew out a breath and started for the door. The cry happened again, this time it was louder. Derek moved towards the foot of the bed. He felt rooted in place. Frozen. Closing his eyes, he could hear a light sobbing.

His muscles tightened; his body told him to run. Instead, he stepped next to the foot of the bed, crouched down, lowering himself onto his knees. His racing heart caused sharp pains in his chest. But the overwhelming pull to look under the bed made him push through it.

He gulped down his breath to stay as quiet as he could. Lowering his head, he closed his eyes just before he reached out to lift the overhanging bedspread. As he lifted it, he opened his eyes and peered underneath.

He saw nothing at first. The darkness under the bed was black as night. As his eyes adjusted, he heard a noise behind him. He glanced over his shoulder. Nothing. He turned back to look, one more time.

Jerking back, he fell onto his ass. He scurried back, using his hands and feet to propel him away from the bed. A young girl stared at him. She had pale blue eyes. Her mouth opened up as she let out a primal scream.

She grabbed his ankle, pulling on him and tugging him towards the bed. Derek screamed, digging his hands into the carpet. He kicked at her with his free foot. "Let go of me!" he screamed at the ghostly figure.

"Help me. Please. Don't leave me here. I'm scared."

He yanked on his leg, clawing at the carpet. He freed his foot at the same time the police officer came into the room.

"Are you okay?" he asked as he moved to help Derek up.

"Yeah," Derek's voice quivered slightly. "I thought I saw a giant spider. Man, that thing was huge." He laughed, smiling at the officer. "I hate spiders."

The officer stepped back. "I hear you on that. My wife screams when she sees one."

"I'm sorry. I must have taken longer than I thought." Derek handed the keys to the officer.

"Oh, no worries. I was just doing a quick round before my relief shows up." He took the keys.

Derek checked his watch. Almost forty-five minutes had passed. "I didn't pay attention to the time." He followed the officer out of the house. "Thank you for your help." He walked to his vehicle. Waving as he pulled away from the home.

He looked in his rearview mirror at the house as he drove off. His hands shook as he held onto the steering wheel. The girl didn't look familiar. She wasn't a victim from the past. He had no idea who she was or what was going to happen to her. And that scared him.

CHAPTER FOURTEEN

4:30 Tuesday

Derek pulled into the Legacy parking lot. As he exited, his phone pinged. Lizzy.

Hey, we are going to be gone a few extra days. Do you mind keeping Lola longer?

No. Not at all. Be safe, Lizzy.

I will. Thank you. ILU.

Me too.

A sour taste filled his mouth. He wanted her in his life, but he wasn't sure how much longer he could do this. Entering the unit, Lola ran to him. She howled at him as she wiggled, bumping into his leg.

Marc Anthony ran full speed from the kitchen area, sliding as he tried to stop.

"My goodness!" Emma called out. "Marc Anthony!"

The big dog slid into Derek's leg, almost knocking him over. "Whoa there." He reached down and petted him. "You will scare the shit out of someone if you do that to anyone else."

Marc Anthony howled at him.

"Yeah, I know how you feel, buddy," Derek said.

"I'm so sorry. He has been acting so weird today." Emma pointed to his bed. "Go lay down."

He obeyed but sulked as he followed his master's command.

"What do you mean, acting weird?" Derek asked as he headed towards his desk.

"He and Lola have been barking at nothing. All day. Scared the crap out of me a few times." Emma sat in her chair.

"Where is everyone?" Derek asked.

"Felicia made Michael go with her to interview the family of Margarite Sanchez. George and Kelly have not returned. And Kyle is in his cave."

"Where else would he be?" Derek opened the file on his desk. He looked at the pictures of all the women. Not one of them looked like the girl he had seen earlier at Charlene's home. His stomach growled. Realizing he hadn't eaten since he had donuts and a granola bar, he made his way into the kitchen.

Scrounging through the cabinets, he found some chips. He opened the fridge and grabbed a soda. Turning around, he yelped, placing his hand on his chest. "Quit doing that."

Kyle laughed at him. "I'm working on my stealth skills."

"You have honed them well."

Kyle wiggled his eyebrows. "I have something for you." He held out a folder.

Derek set his soda on the counter. He stared at 3D images of the music boxes. "How did you get these? I didn't get the photos yet."

"I used the information from earlier on the newest box and found it online. I took the pictures from the older crime scenes that the doctors brought with them this morning and created that one from those." Kyle shimmied on his feet.

Derek stared at the photos. Several depicted the music boxes from different angles. He stared at the latest box. A slight shiver ran up his spine. The music box was identical to the one he saw in the child's room. There was no way to deny that. He lifted his eyebrows at his agent. "These are great. The detail is fantastic."

"I got it as close to the originals as I could. If you look at the first music box, you can see how the man and woman were posed. They were on two different stems that were so close together they looked like one stem holding two figurines." Kyle pointed to the picture. "That's probably why it looked like only one dancer spun around."

Derek squeezed his shoulder. "This is good."

"Thank you." Kyle smiled, showing a big toothy grin. "Hey, I also found something out about the gift registry."

Derek's nose wrinkled. "Registry?"

"Gift. Gift registry."

"Oh, heck. Sorry. What did you find?"

"When someone registers for gifts either for a wedding or a baby shower, or whatever, there is a company called Register Finder. They have several businesses that partner with them. When someone registers for gifts at any of the stores they partner with, you can search the names on their website. It will pull up where they are getting married and the date."

"Were you able to find any information on our victims?"

He sighed, pursing his lips. "No. Not yet anyway. I have put in a call to them to see if they keep any of the records. It is going to be a long shot for the other murders, though. This business didn't start until 2012. I doubt our killer knew about it ten years ago."

Derek paced the kitchen area. "I found out today that our latest victim had a phone call days before the murder. Her sister said they asked about her registry."

Kyle leaned against the counter. "I'm not following."

Derek ran his hand through his hair. "If our killer didn't use this register finder thingy, why would someone call inquiring about our current victim's gift registry?"

Kyle's eyes widened, then his eyebrows squished together. "What?"

Derek stopped pacing. "What—what?"

Kyle shook his head. "I must be tired and hungry; I'm really not following this."

Derek laughed. "I'm sorry. I didn't explain. I went to the home of the current victim today. While there, I ran into the sister. She told me that days before the murder, the victim received a phone call. The caller asked about the victim's gift registry.

"The sister didn't know why, just that Charlene mentioned someone from one store they had registered at had called her. What if the killer wanted to make sure the victim would be around? Maybe they used the registry as a ruse to make sure that the victim would be at the house at a certain time."

"The killer could stalk the victim, follow her. Why call?"

Derek shook his head. "No. See, I also talked to a neighbor. She said a delivery person delivered a package. Then came back later at a different time and walked up to the door. She said it looked like the person carried something that a customer would sign... you know, like for a package."

Kyle opened the fridge and grabbed a soda. Popping the top, he took a long sip. "Your theory isn't making sense. If the killer wanted to use a ruse of the registry to make sure the victim was home, then why did the killer miss her when she delivered the package?"

Derek grunted. "I hadn't worked it out yet."

Kyle laughed at his boss. "I think you're distracted."

"What?"

"C'mon man. We all know about you and Lizzy. And we know how much you hate the congressman."

Derek's shoulders slumped. "It's not what you think."

"It doesn't matter what I think. It matters how the congressman is fucking with you." Kyle looked over Derek's shoulder, then focused on his boss. "Congressman Jackson is mixed up in the Pink Diamond case. We don't know how or in what capacity. But we know he knows all the players. Don't let him use Lizzy to keep you off your game."

"I won't." Derek patted his cheek. "The best thing I ever did was bring you on this team."

"Of course it was," Kyle said as he headed downstairs.

"Don't spend all day down there."

"Yes, Dad."

Derek headed to his desk. He sat and stared at the pictures of the music boxes. He placed them back in the folder and put the folder in his bag. He wanted to show them to Dr. Chelsea.

The clock on the wall said 5 p.m. He double checked his watch. Dr. Chelsea was going to be at his house in ninety minutes. He gathered the other folders with notes and printed copies of photos he had on the whiteboard.

He checked his desk and made sure he had all the files he wanted. Logging into his desktop, he motioned to Emma. "Did a delivery person bring a file from the director?"

Emma shook her head. "No. There have been no deliveries."

No sooner had she gotten the words out of her mouth, the alarm on the door chimed.

Derek saw a man holding a package standing at the door. He pushed a button on his desk phone, unlocking the door. He rose to meet him.

"Are you Agent Reed?"

"Yes."

"I'm Agent Jones, Assistant Director Fretz sent me. He handed him a manilla folder. I need to get a signature from you." He held out a tablet. "Can you sign here?"

Derek signed and studied the tablet before handing it back.

"Thank you," Agent Jones said as he turned to leave.

As he walked out, Derek's agents walked in. "Hey guys. Did you gather any information?" Derek sat on the corner of Michael's desk.

George pointed at the folder. "Is that the case file?"

"Yes," Derek said. "I want to go over it tonight and then we can all go over it first thing in the morning."

Felicia plopped down in her chair. "Man, it is so stinking hot out there."

Michael sat in his chair. "Please tell me winter will bring some cooler air?"

"It will. Trust me." Derek turned towards Felicia and George. "Did either of you find out anything?"

George blew out a breath as he sat. "Betty's sister didn't remember if Betty had a gift registry anywhere. She thought that more than likely she didn't. Between her and her fiancé, they had a good amount of money. She would've asked her family and friends to donate to a charity in their name or give to a local charity what they would spend on a gift."

Felicia yawned. "Scuse me. I got nothing on the registry, either. Margarite's family said they couldn't remember. But her brother remembered Margarite said someone had called about seeing if she needed a wedding planner."

"I'm guessing she didn't need one," Derek said.

"No. Margarite also mentioned that the lady who called was very insistent on coming by. The caller said she thought she could help with the wedding and wanted to speak to her, in person. The brother thought it was odd, because Margarite couldn't figure out how the woman knew her or even knew she was getting married." Felicia checked her computer, making sure she signed off the network.

"Okay. Well, this falls in line with what I learned today." Derek explained to everyone what he had heard from the neighbor and the victim's sister. He also explained the ruse he thought the killer used by calling about the registry.

Kelly leaned forward, placing her elbows on her knees. "I put in a call to my victim's family. I will speak with them tomorrow. Maybe that will yield something."

"Betty's sister mentioned Betty called her the day she was murdered. The last time they spoke, Betty said she had just received a package she thought was from her fiancé. When her sister asked what was in it, she said a nighty and a music box. There was no return address. It had been left at the door. The victim told her sister she spoke with her fiancé, and he said he didn't send her anything.

"Betty's sister said they both laughed and thought he was probably being sneaky. That was hours before her murder." George leaned back, interlocking his hands on the top of his head.

Derek crossed his arms. "There is our pattern. Somehow the killer gets the victim's information, then uses it to figure out when the victim will be at home to deliver the packages. If they aren't there, then they return. How is he getting the information about their weddings?" He pointed at George. "Do you know if the same neighbors still live where Betty lived?"

"Not sure. But tomorrow I will drive out to Betty's old house and knock on some doors." George rose and stretched.

"Don't go alone." Derek stood. "Our latest victim wasn't there when the killer initially delivered the package, so the killer came back to finish the job. Ask the neighbors, if any still live there, if they remember seeing a delivery person. We might get lucky."

Derek snapped his fingers. "If none of the original neighbors are there, maybe Kyle can hunt them down for us. We need to see if anyone remembers a delivery person and how many times they showed up on the day of the murder."

"I will do that first thing in the morning. Is there anything else you need me to do? If not, I would like to go. I have plans." George winked at Kelly.

She laughed. "Plans with what, the remote?"

"Ha ha. No, I have dinner plans. With a beautiful lady." George stuck his tongue out at her.

"Pfft. Lies. All lies." Kelly also stood and stretched. "She looked at Felicia. "Want some company to swim?"

Felicia jumped up. "Heck yeah. Let's order Chinese after our swim."

"Sounds good," Kelly said.

Felicia checked her desk drawer, making sure she had everything. She spun around, facing Kelly. "Wait, you never want to come over and swim. What gives?"

Kelly grabbed her blazer from the back of her chair. "I guess I just don't feel like going home."

A big grin filled Felicia's face. "This is going to be so much fun." They both waved as they left the building.

Emma put the leash on Marc Anthony and packed up her stuff. "I'm leaving too. If that's okay?"

"Of course. See you tomorrow," Derek said, waving as she and Marc Anthony left. He watched the security cameras to make sure she got into her vehicle safely. He turned to Michael. "Why are you still here?"

Michael had been staring at the whiteboard, concentrating on the aerial photos of the victim's homes. "Something is bugging me, but I'm not sure what it is or why."

"Take a break. Clear your head. If you force it, you will never figure it out." Derek picked up the phone on his desk and called down to Kyle's cave.

"Yo."

"We are all leaving."

"I was just on my way up. Give me five."

Derek hung up the phone. "You go. Don't think about it for a while."

Michael rose. "I will. I will try at least." He headed towards the door. He turned towards his boss. "I will say this. I feel like it's staring us in the face. Whatever it is." He waved as he walked out.

Derek stood and walked to the board. As he stared at the photos, he tilted his head. He heard Kyle coming into the main room and faced him. "Ready?" He asked, grabbing the case files from his desk.

"Yup. I'm going to sleep as soon as I eat. I'm beat." Kyle followed Derek and Lola out the door.

When Derek opened the door to his car, Lola jumped into the front seat. "If you need anything, I will be at home. I'll try to keep Lola from bothering you."

"She's never a bother. Plus, the minute I fall asleep, I will be out," Kyle said as he got into the driver's seat of his car.

Derek pulled out right behind him. He rubbed Lola's head. "I miss her too."

Lola whined, curling up in the seat.

CHAPTER FIFTEEN

Derek pulled into his garage just before 6 p.m. When he opened the car door, Lola jumped over his lap and ran to the rear of the car. "Lola, stay in the garage, please." He gathered the files from between the seats and exited the car.

Lola sat at the edge of the garage. She scanned the area, looking for the kids who normally played on the street.

Derek stood at the doorway leading into the house, watching her. He loved having her here. Maybe it was his way of keeping Lizzy close to him. "Maybe I just don't enjoy being alone anymore." He whistled as he opened the door.

Lola ran past him.

Derek braced himself against the wall. "Damn, Lola. Are you trying to break my legs?"

The dog stopped in the hallway and looked at him. She tilted her head to the side, then barked.

"Yes, Ma'am. I will feed you." He followed her to the kitchen, where she sat in front of the cabinet that held her food.

Lola wiggled, spinning around in a circle.

Derek laughed. "You are so silly." He stuck the files under his arm and pulled his phone from his back pocket. Placing an order for a few pizzas and a couple of salads. After filling Lola's bowl, he grabbed a soda pop from the fridge, then headed to the sofa where his laptop and bag sat on the coffee table.

Setting down the files, he pushed the power button on his computer. When it didn't turn on, he dug through his computer bag for the cord. Plugging it in, he let out a sigh as he laid his head back.

The day had caught up to him. He sunk into the cushions, letting his limbs relax. He felt himself drifting off when Lola jumped up next to him. She used her head to lift his hand.

Derek kept his eyes closed as he stroked her soft fur. He heard her snore softly. His breathing slowed as he drifted off again. Just as his body released the stress of the day, his doorbell rang.

Lola bolted off the sofa and ran to the front door. She growled and barked at the voice calling out.

"Derek, you in there?"

Derek shook off the sleep as he stumbled towards the door. He opened it to find Dr. Chelsea standing there with a bottle of wine and a manilla folder. "Hey Doc." He stepped back. "Lola, please move. Let him in."

"Are you okay? You look a little pale." Dr. Chelsea walked past his host, scratching Lola's head as he moved by.

"No, I feel fine. I fell asleep on the sofa. Guess I slept hard." Derek checked his watch. "Wow." Twenty minutes had passed since he sat down. "I must be exhausted."

As soon as he shut the door and headed towards the kitchen, the bell rang. Opening it, the smell of pizza hit him in the face. He took the boxes, signed the receipt, leaving a tip, and closed the door. "Dinner is here. I got a couple of salads."

"Don't tell me you are trying to be healthy?" Dr. Chelsea said, placing the folder he had carried in on the counter. He then opened the bottle of wine.

"Pfft. No. I just knew you would want something healthy. And eating a salad probably wouldn't hurt me either." Derek set the pizzas on the counter. He grabbed a couple of plates and two forks. "Can you eat the salad out of the container, or do you want a separate plate?"

"No. The container is fine." Dr. Chelsea poured two glasses of wine.

"I have bottled water and soda pop. You want one of those too?"

Dr. Chelsea nodded. "Yes. A bottle of water will be great." He carried the glasses of wine and the wine bottle, along with the folder tucked under his arm, into the living room and set them down on the coffee table.

Derek had followed him in with the pizzas and everything else stacked on top. "I don't want to get back up."

"This works." Dr. Chelsea sat in a chair at the end of the sofa. He filled a plate with some slices. Opening the salad container, he emptied the dressing on the greens.

"I wasn't sure what you wanted for dressing. I just got ranch. But I might have something else in my fridge."

"Ranch is perfect." He mixed up the salad. Taking a sip of his wine, he closed his eyes. "This is a merlot. Not as dry as a cabernet, and a slight bit fruitier."

Derek took a sip. "That is nice. I don't drink a lot of wine. But this is nice."

Lola took up residence between the two men. She watched each one. Waiting for her treat.

Derek broke up a piece of pizza and put it on the floor. "Here."

"You shouldn't do that. She will get fat. Plus, it's unhealthy," Dr. Chelsea said.

"Yes, father."

Dr. Chelsea scoffed.

Derek eyeballed the folder on the table. "Is that all your notes?"

"Yes." Ronald slid it over to him. "You have a lot of the photos. There may be a few different ones from other angles. My notes are more in depth. I went through them today."

"I know it's hard, Ronald. You did all you could. You and Dr. Callahan did all you could. The FBI hid this for a reason." Derek pulled out the pictures of the music boxes.

Dr. Chelsea sipped his wine. "I know that. But this case was personal." He wanted to get right into the CT incident and the current murder and how Derek knew things, but he held his tongue and took a bite of his pizza.

"Here. I thought you might like to see these. At least the original music box. Kyle put it together."

Dr. Chelsea looked at the 3d renderings of the music boxes. He studied the original box. "I can see now how I missed the broken piece. They really look like two figurines on one stand."

"That's what I thought. I wanted to alleviate your mind about you missing something."

Dr. Chelsea nodded as he swallowed a bite of food. "Thank you for that."

Derek opened the file Dr. Chelsea had brought and scanned through the photos. Most of these he had. It was the notes he was interested in. He pulled out the notes on the first murder. As he read, he felt the heat from Dr. Chelsea's stare. He bit the inside of his lip. Shifting his position on the sofa, he attempted to get comfortable. He set the folder down and stared at the photo facing him.

Dr. Chelsea watched as Derek avoided his stare. "Can we cut the crap? You can read that folder later. I need to know how you knew about the girl today. She is the girl from the CT scan, isn't she?"

"Why do you ask that? At the time of the CT scan, I gave few details about the girl I saw when I fell asleep. The girl I saw in a dream."

"I saw the look on your face the moment you saw the victim this morning. You recognized her. Plus, you and I know it was more than a dream. Explain. Now."

Derek opened his water and guzzled the cold liquid. He also finished the soda he had opened just before his nap. When he finished, he focused on the backyard.

"Whatever you tell me will stay between us. You know that. But something is different. Ever since you caught Josiah Craig. You have been different."

"Josiah hurt me pretty bad during that case. My actions got a young girl killed. That's all."

"That's bullshit and you know it." Ronald leaned forward. "I'm your friend, sitting here. Nothing you tell me will go back to the FBI. You won't lose your job. I promise you."

Derek knew he could trust the doc. But he worried saying the words out loud would give them power over him. It would be like letting the genie out of the bottle and not being able to get it back in.

Derek tilted his head back. The silence between him and the doc surrounded him like a tomb. "Okay. You won't believe me, anyway."

"Try me."

CHAPTER SIXTEEN

Anastasia parked down the street from the house and watched the next-door neighbor walk to her mailbox. She didn't want to attract attention, but she needed to make sure the woman kept the same schedule. She didn't want to return to the house. Making a second trip put her in danger of being noticed.

She rolled down all the windows, except the driver's side—she cracked it open. The small breeze made the stifling hot air breathable. A small glass butterfly hung from the rear-view mirror. Secured with a small piece of fishing line, it seemed to float in mid-air. The colored glass reflected the sun's rays.

Reaching over to the passenger seat, she opened the glove box. Anastasia closed it and reached into the back seat just as someone knocked on the driver side window. She grabbed her chest, let out a sharp yell, then turned to her left and saw an elderly man with his dog.

"I'm so sorry, miss. I didn't mean to scare you." He glanced around the backseat and then focused on her.

Anastasia leaned away from him. "That's okay. Is there something wrong?" she asked.

"I am part of the neighborhood watch and I wondered why you were sitting out here?" The man's dog tugged on the leash. "Stop it, Fred."

Anastasia flashed a big smile. "I'm waiting for a realtor to show me the home." She pointed to the vacant house for sale. "They must be running late."

The old man looked over his shoulder. He nodded in approval. "That makes sense then. I'm sorry I bothered you."

"No worries. It's nice to see neighbors caring about where they live." She smiled at the man.

"You can't be too careful these days." He stepped away from her vehicle and continued walking his dog.

Her eyes narrowed. She didn't see him carrying anything other than a bag to pick up his dog's poop. Her anxiety skyrocketed. She hadn't switched the license plates for this quick trip. She didn't think it was necessary, and she didn't want to draw the attention of law enforcement.

Anastasia gave herself a few more minutes before she drove off. She pulled her phone out and pretended to take a call. Not wanting to risk someone else noticing her, she started her car, and pulled away from the curb at the same moment Beth Cahill drove into her garage. Anastasia sighed with relief. "Perfect." She made a quick note of the time.

Anastasia watched the young woman get out of her vehicle, and check her mail before heading into her home. Anastasia wished she had brought the nighty and the music box with her. Today would work perfectly.

However, with Mr. Neighborhood Watch on patrol, it was probably be best to wait until Friday evening. Beth came home late on Fridays and the cover of dark would help. The only constraint, the murder had to be done this week. Anastasia couldn't alter the time frame, and she didn't want to wait any longer.

CHAPTER SEVENTEEN

"Quit stalling." Dr. Chelsea filled his wine glass and poured some in Derek's glass. He threw a piece of crust to Lola, who caught it in the air.

"Didn't you lecture me not ten minutes ago about feeding her pizza?"

"Do as I say, not as I do." Dr. Chelsea gave him a sly grin.

"Brother." Derek took a sip of his wine. He glanced at the sliding glass door. The last bits of sunlight filled the sky with bright orange and red hues. He turned back to see Ronald sitting patiently waiting for him to talk. "It started after the Josiah Craig case."

"What started?"

"I don't really know." Derek set his glass on the table.

Lola jumped up and laid next to him on the sofa.

He rubbed her ears. "The nightmares, visions, I don't know."

"Tell me about the first one."

"It happened when I was on medical leave. I kept seeing the dead girl."

"The one Josiah Craig raped and murdered in the carnival tent?"

"Yes. Chrissy. At first, it was only her. She kept showing up. Talking to me." Derek took a deep breath. "I figured it was because I felt responsible for her death."

"You shouldn't. She was dead the minute that man abducted her."

Derek frowned. "That's what she says."

Ronald lifted an eyebrow at him. "She says? You mean she's still talking to you?"

Derek dragged a hand down his face. "Yes. She pops up at weird times. I thought I was losing my mind. That's why I started self-medicating."

"And that is also why you asked for the CT scan?"

"That and I kept having these horrible headaches. The visions are more intense." Derek picked up his water bottle.

Lola sighed at the movement.

He rubbed her belly. "During the last case, the Billy Edmond murder, I had a lot of crazy dreams. I would see fragments of things that didn't go together. They didn't always make sense."

"Fragments? What do you mean by that?"

"Bits and pieces of a movie in random order. As clues started coming out, the pieces made more sense. Sometimes I would see something from the past, sometimes events that hadn't happened yet."

Derek paused, taking another sip of his water. "During that case, I heard someone in my closet in my bedroom. I thought it was a wild animal that got in or something. The door closed behind me and the light flickered, then went off.

"I had the sensation of dying in the closet. An intense burning in my chest. I smelled urine, I felt myself slowly dying like I was suffocating. We later found out that a young girl died in a closet after having an asthma attack." Derek looked at Ronald. "It was like I experienced what she felt when she died."

Ronald swirled his glass. The wine sloshed against the sides. "Do the visions seem to happen only when you're working a case?"

Derek shifted around. "I guess. Maybe not. I don't know. I'm always working a case. No. I don't think they happen only when working. They happen when I'm stressed and that's usually during a case. But Josiah Craig pops up as well."

"When did he start showing up?"

Derek shrugged. "When I was on medical leave."

"About the same time as Chrissy?"

"Yeah, I guess so. He never looks good. I mean, he is always decaying with bugs and rotten flesh."

Dr. Chelsea took a sip of his wine. "How does Chrissy look?"

Derek smiled. "She always looks pretty. Young. Happy." He pointed to his neck. "She always wears a ribbon around her neck to hide the wound from when Josiah Craig slit her throat. But sometimes it bleeds. She says it has something to do with me."

"Do you think she is right?"

"I have no fucking clue."

Dr. Chelsea set his glass on the table. "Have you been having the headaches more frequently?"

"No. Sometimes. If I do, they happen right before a vision or dream... hell, I don't know what they are called. I just know I don't like them."

"Tell me about the girl in the CT scanner. You hadn't seen her before?"

"No."

"Nowhere? Not at a store, at a restaurant, on the street?"

Derek shook his head. "No. I have never seen her before I had the dream during the CT scan. Unless you count this morning."

"Have you seen anything else about this case?" Ronald focused on his friend.

Derek glanced at the hallway that led to the second bedroom. "Before I got the call for the case this morning. I had an incident."

"What kind of incident?"

"I woke up and heard noises. When I went to investigate it, I saw a girl." Derek pinched the bridge of his nose. "She wore a night gown and held a music box."

Ronald reached out and touched his leg. "It wasn't the girl from this morning?"

"No. It was Margarite Sanchez."

"The third victim. Have you seen anyone else? Is there going to be another victim?"

"I don't know. I mean maybe." Derek stood and walked to the glass door. "I went back to Charlene's house. A girl grabbed me from under the bed. I've never seen her before."

Ronald followed him. "Derek, can you describe her?"

Derek turned around. "What the hell? Describe her to who? The fucking news? Maybe they can run a story. We need a young woman with pale blue eyes to contact the FBI."

Dr. Chelsea grabbed his arm. "I promise. All of this will stay between us. But you have to let me help you."

"Help me how?" Derek stared out at his yard.

"We can use hypnosis to help you relax. Maybe the visions will be clearer. You can use what you see to solve this case." Ronald grabbed him and spun him around. "I can't let this killer get away. I've carried these murders for too long."

"These visions are scary as fuck. Sometimes they seem so real." Derek pulled away from his friend. "During the last case, I would see a vision and felt like it was happening to me. Like I was feeling what the victim's felt. I saw a car crash. A vehicle went over a cliff. I was in the car. Felt the impact. I thought every bone in my body shattered. I hate them."

"You mentioned the girl Chrissy, from the Josiah Craig case still visits. What does she say to you?"

"She's annoying as hell. But that has to be just me reasoning with myself, right? Like my subconscious."

"She's real, Derek. Even if only to you. Tell me what she says."

"She tells me to let them talk to me. She says I'm keeping her around because of my guilt." Derek walked back to the sofa. Lola had stretched out, taking his spot. He moved her over and sat. He leaned his head back and closed his eyes.

"Derek, there are people who have injuries like the ones you received from Josiah who wake up from comas and can speak in another language. I've told you the brain heals itself in mysterious ways. That you seem to have these visions when you are dealing with a case can be your brain's way of healing." Ronald paced in front of the sofa. "Your intensity when you are working on a case could be what sets the visions in motion."

Ronald stopped pacing. "You were having headaches before the visions. That can also be an indication there may be an injury we haven't found yet."

Lola lifted her head. She cocked it to the side. Listening. She jumped off the sofa and went to the winged back chair in the corner. She sat in front of it, staring. Her tail wagged and she whimpered.

Ronald watched the dog and then turned towards Derek. "What is she doing?"

Derek opened his eyes. Chrissy sat in the chair. His shoulders slumped. "Ah, hell."

Ronald shifted his gaze between Derek and the chair. "What is she looking at? Who's here?" he sat on the edge of the coffee table facing the chair. He spun his head around, looking over his shoulder at Derek. "Lola sees these visitors too?"

"Yeah. How you going to explain that? She hasn't had a brain injury." Derek stared at Chrissy. She wore a new dress. The ribbon around her neck was clean. No blood dripped this time. "Where's the blood?"

Chrissy brought her knees up to her chest. "No blood today. I see you told him."

"He forced me too."

Ronald's head swiveled around like an owl. "Are you talking to her now?"

"Chrissy, meet Dr. Ronald Chelsea. Ronald, this is Chrissy." Derek's head fell forward. His chin rested on his chest. "I can't believe this. I'm losing my fucking mind."

"What is she saying to you?"

"I like him. He seems like a good man. I know you are fond of him." Chrissy reached out to touch his hand. She frowned when he didn't react.

"Stop Chrissy."

Ronald stared at the chair. "What is she doing?"

"She's messing with you. She was just reaching out to touch you." Derek finished the last of the wine in his glass. He grabbed a piece of cold pizza and took several bites.

Ronald rubbed both arms. He stared at the chair.

Derek watched as Lola rested her chin on the cushion of the chair.

Chrissy scratched Lola's ears. Or tried to.

Derek's brow wrinkled. He didn't look at Ronald when he spoke to him. "Yeah, so you think I'm crazy?"

"Not at all. I don't think you are crazy at all."

Derek looked sheepishly at his friend. "I saw something else today."

"What?" Ronald asked.

"When I was driving. I saw a little boy in the back seat of a truck that was later involved in an accident. When I went to the car, the boy was gone."

Ronald sat up straight, shifting his weight. "Have you had a case with a little boy?"

"No. No children. Except the young girl from the last case." Derek sighed. "I also saw Josiah Craig in the truck. When I pulled up next to it, he was driving."

"Do you see Josiah Craig most times when you have these visions?"

"I'm not sure. I never thought about it." He remembered what happened in the garden earlier that afternoon. He should've told Ronald about that, but decided not to. "Still think I'm not crazy?"

Ronald shook his head. "You are not crazy."

"Then why am I seeing these things? I'm not psychic. I have never seen dead people before. So why now? And why am I talking to a dead girl?"

"I don't have the answers. I think something happened during the Josiah Craig case. You came close to dying. You watched the man blow his brains out in front of you, with your gun. You watched him rape and kill Chrissy. I think the guilt you carry has made you susceptible to things we don't have answers to."

Ronald's eyes narrowed. "Just because I don't have a scientific explanation doesn't mean what you are experiencing isn't real. Maybe the dead are reaching out to you. Maybe it is your subconscious taking the clues you see and giving you an insight into the case no one else has.

"Lola seeing things makes me think there is more to this than just an injury. Animals have always been in tune with the spiritual world. They hear and see things we humans don't." Ronald stood and moved back to his original seat. "I also think our emotional state makes us vulnerable, or a better word is receptive. In your case, I think all these things are playing a part.

"Either way, I think you should listen to Chrissy. She seems to guide you. Even if it is your subconscious, you are using her to make sense of what you see. I also think you should allow the others to reach you."

"Why don't I just hang a sign outside that says the dead are welcome here? How do you explain the dead girl from this morning as being the same one from the dream in CT? This makes no sense. I'm not a spiritual guy."

"Like I said, you can't always get answers. Again, this doesn't mean it isn't real."

"If I am seeing people before they die, and I can't stop it, what good is this gift or curse? Now I'm going to feel responsible for murders that haven't even happened yet. This is no way to live."

"This is where I think hypnosis may help you to handle the visions and keep the fear factor at bay, allowing you to use the visions instead of fighting them."

Dr. Chelsea leaned closer. "You will not be able to stop something from happening. I don't think that is what the visions are for. You have to remember that. You know, it could be your brain is seeing connections we don't. The visions are a guide to help get the killer quicker. To solve the case sooner. Saving others. Tell yourself whatever makes it easier for you to deal with this."

"This is too much." Derek said, standing gathering the pizza boxes. He stacked the empty salad containers on top and headed towards the kitchen.

"Listen." Ronald followed him with the empty wine glasses and bottle. "Think of it as a tool. A tool to help you solve cases. Nothing more. I won't tell anyone about this. I will not report it to the FBI."

"I never thought you would," Derek said, leaning against the counter.

"Derek, I need you to use this to help stop this killer. I will help you anyway I can. I will find a study regarding brain injuries and try to get you some answers. Medical answers. But this is going to happen whether you want it to or not. If the dead are trying to reach you, it means something. Let them."

Derek placed the remaining pizza in the fridge. He cleaned up the kitchen. "I don't want my crew to know. They will think I'm crazy and they will report me as unfit to command this unit."

"No one would turn you in. I bet if you told them, they would help you. But you can handle it the way you see fit. I want to set up a hypnosis session. See if we can get some clues who this killer is."

"Can we do it here?"

"Absolutely. Wherever you are most comfortable." Dr. Chelsea moved closer to Derek. He gripped his shoulder. "I will be there for you. You call me whenever you have a vision. Just call me."

He turned to head towards the front door. "You know, when I was a kid, I used to see my dead grandmother. I would tell my mother about it. She thought I was making up an imaginary friend. Until my grandmother gave me a message for her. Something only my mother would know."

"What happened?"

"Eventually I quit seeing her. I probably told myself there was no such thing. I wish I had never done that. She made me feel safe. Even after she died."

Ronald patted his pockets, making sure he had his keys. "You go through my notes. Keep them. I made you a copy. Let's plan on getting together this week sometime to get some answers."

"I will." He stood in the front doorway and watched his mentor drive off. He turned to see Chrissy standing in the front hallway. As he closed the door, he smiled at her. "Well, I guess you're happy."

She let out a loud laugh. "Finally, someone told you to listen to me. This is going to be great!"

CHAPTER EIGHTEEN

"Don't even start." Derek sat on the sofa. He watched as Chrissy seemed to float to the chair across from him. He ignored her as he opened the case file from the previous murders.

The photos of the crime scenes were the same in Dr. Chelsea's file. He laid those to the side, more interested in the agent in charge's notes, Derek scanned all the reports.

Agent McDougal didn't take the greatest notes on this case. As Derek read through them, it became clear the agent had no interest in solving the murders. "He just wanted to get done and get out."

"Why?"

Derek peered up at Chrissy.

Lola sat at her feet. Sprawled out on the floor.

"Why what?"

"Why wouldn't the other investigator do his job?"

He sighed. "I'm not sure. I know Dr. Chelsea and Dr. Callahan tried to give some input, and he wasn't interested. He probably wanted to retire and not get caught up in this case.

"Where does that leave you and your team?" Chrissy bent over to try to pet Lola. Her hand touched the dog's fur. "I wish I could pet her."

Derek stared at her. He felt a piece of his heart break off. She died so young. No chance to experience life. He couldn't help but blame himself. "I'm sorry, Chrissy."

She looked up, smiling. "You have nothing to be sorry about." She sat back, smoothing out her dress. "How are you going to approach this case? It seems like you need the past case to solve the recent case."

"That's it exactly." Derek read through a few more pages. He stacked some notes on top of the photos. Flipping through the pages, he found three papers stapled together. "What do we have here?" He read through two police reports. He went back to the first page, then studied each of the other pages. "What the hell?"

"What is it?" Chrissy asked.

Derek didn't look at her. "Something isn't right." The first page had a few notes, but nothing related to the police reports. The two police reports came in days before the first two murders.

The first one reported a car which had parked a few doors down from the victim's home. Neighbors had reported a suspicious vehicle. The police report stated the vehicle had tinted windows and they did not recognize the driver. There was a license plate number. There was no follow up report.

Derek checked the second report. The vehicle description matched the first vehicle, but the license plate numbers were different. He double checked the reports. "How did no one follow up on this?" Jotting down a few notes on a piece of paper in the folder, Derek wrote the description of the car and both plate numbers.

"You corrected your mistake." Derek stared at the police reports. Days before the first two murders, witnesses saw the killer. Which meant the killer stalked the victims.

He ran his hand through his hair. "You needed to learn their habits." Derek searched the notes on each victim. Interviews of coworkers at each place of employment turned up nothing.

No jealous co-workers. No affairs or jealous lovers. One woman had a nine-to-five job. The others worked odd hours. Derek tapped out a few commands on his laptop. He entered the National Crime Information Center (NCIC) and ran the plate numbers. They didn't come in the wanted files of the FBI. Tomorrow, he would have Kyle check the DMV.

Derek pulled a pad from his bag. He jotted down some notes, including what he had scribbled earlier regarding the license plates. "If the killer is stalking the victims, how is the unsub picking the victims?" He tapped his pen on the pad.

Lola sat up and growled.

Lost in his work, he hadn't noticed when Chrissy left. He glanced around the room and didn't see anyone.

Lola jumped up and ran through the doggie door.

Derek stood and followed her to the sliding glass doors. He peered out into the backyard. Nothing out there but no-seeums—those unseen creatures that dogs bark at and chase.

He thought of Lizzy. Glancing at his watch, he debated on whether to call her. He removed his phone from his pocket and texted her.

Hope you are enjoying yourself. Lola is doing fine. We miss you.

He didn't expect her to text back. At least not right away. But that didn't keep him from hoping. He stared at his phone for a few moments before deciding to head to the shower. He pushed the button on the wall and made the glass frost over. He never liked blinds or drapes, and had this system installed a few months back.

Checking the front door and the side garage door, Derek locked everything tight, flipped on the floodlights, and set his home alarm. He did not have the doggie door connected to the alarm system. Lola's collar allowed her and only her to enter the through the door.

He walked past the spare bedroom. He stood at the cracked door. Derek reached out for the knob, about to walk in. He pulled the door shut and continued to his room.

Undressing for the shower, he thought about how the conversation with Ronald Chelsea went. He had to admit he felt better having shared what was happening to him. The only other person he thought he could tell was George.

Derek had a feeling his agent already knew. At least based on their last conversation during the previous case. Turning on the hot water, he waited for the steam to rise.

Stepping in, he let the weight of the day and the entire case wash away. Placing his hands against the tile, the thumping of the jets helped release the tension from his muscles.

His thoughts drifted to the night before Lizzy left. They had showered together and then spent the night eating in bed and watching old movies. He loved that about her. Hell, he loved everything about her. Even though they had a great night, she seemed distant. He didn't ask her about it. Figured if she wanted to tell him, she would.

Washing his hair, he tempered down the anger. As much as he loved her and wanted her, he wasn't sure if this relationship was the best thing for him. She owed him nothing, and he would never back her into a corner.

She loved her job. Most of her clients didn't have sex with her, but there were a few. Although those jobs were few, he still didn't like it. As the water pelted his skin, he thought of the congressman.

He balled his fists. "I hate that man," he growled, thinking about him. Not only for his involvement with Lizzy, but for his involvement in the Pink Diamond case. A case with corruption at the top of the FBI and State Department. A case that put Lizzy in danger because of her involvement with Congressman Jackson.

Derek rinsed his face one last time, then turned off the water and stepped out. He grabbed a towel from the rack and dried off. Wrapping the towel around his waist, he stepped into his bedroom. But it wasn't his bedroom. "Oh fuck. Not now. Please."

CHAPTER NINETEEN

Patrick Weatherby stood and stretched. "Well, that's finished," he said as he turned towards his wife. He pointed at the finished crib. She had fallen asleep in the rocker. Lucy looked peaceful. They had tried for several years to have a child. After going through several miscarriages, they tried IVF. This time it worked.

All the other attempts had taken too much of a physical and mental toll on them. They both agreed, if this pregnancy didn't take, they would stop. Yet, through a miracle, they conceived. Wanting to be surprised at birth, they decided not to learn the sex of the baby.

The television news interview they did would air Friday during the morning shows. He didn't want to do it, but Lucy had convinced him. She wanted to help others who were struggling with getting pregnant to know there was help.

He sat on the floor and watched her sleep. Patrick had wondered if his past sins had kept him from being truly happy. Maybe this is his punishment for what he did.

He closed his eyes and remembered Annie. She was a good woman. And would make the best wife. Just not the best wife for him. He didn't mean to hurt her. Patrick wrestled with the guilt even now, years later.

He didn't plan what happened. Although he didn't cheat on her, he wounded Annie and that was never his intention. His heart had different ideas. He leaned his head against the wall. Regret about the way he handled the situation blanketed him. But now, with his baby on the way, he needed to let go of the guilt he carried.

He stood and placed a blanket from the side table over his wife, gently touching her head. She was all he ever wanted. All he would ever need. The birth of his child, boy or girl, it didn't matter. This child would start a new chapter in their lives.

And although this should be one of the happiest times in his life, he couldn't shake the feeling of doom. The feeling that something lurked in the shadows, waiting to steal his joy right out from under him.

CHAPTER TWENTY

Derek held onto the towel. He closed his eyes and took a deep breath. He would be an observer. "Relax. It isn't real." He breathed out a few times before opening his eyes. He stood in the kid's room. Rays from the sun shone through the window. They bounced off the glass butterflies hanging from tiny threads of unseen string.

Derek hadn't noticed them before. They were tucked in between the airplanes that hung from the ceiling. He walked through the room. This time, he moved to the other side, where a small desk sat against the wall.

He wanted to open the drawers and search for something, anything to help him understand why he needed to see this. But when he pulled on the drawers, they didn't budge.

On the top of the desk sat a picture. Derek tried to lift it, but it wouldn't move. He bent down and stared at it. The young boy held a trophy. The engraving on the trophy was ineligible. But behind the boy, he could see a banner. Like what hung in a cafeteria of a school.

The tiles above the desk were in the shape of an arc. The letters on them were fuzzy, making it hard for Derek to make them out. He turned to look at a shelf. The same one that held the pinned butterfly and the music box.

Suddenly he felt nauseous. His stomach rolled. He tasted the pepperoni as the pizza he had for dinner crept slowly upwards. He swallowed, pushing the food back down.

Derek wiped his brow. A cold sheen of sweat covered the surface of his skin. "What the hell?" as he turned back towards the door, he heard muffled cries coming from under the covers on the bed.

The bed had been empty when he entered the room. He leaned back away from it as he moved towards the door. Whatever was under the blanket moaned. Derek saw something moving under the cover as if it wrestled an unseen force.

Derek stood a few feet away from the door. He took another step and reached for the doorknob. As he turned, the crying stopped. He kept his head down, averting his gaze. *I don't want to be here.*

He wanted to run through the door, but his desire to look under the cover kept him there. Maybe it would give him answers. Answers he needed to solve these cases. Reaching over, he placed his hand on the edge of the blanket. He took a deep breath and yanked it back.

A young boy laid curled up. His skin was red and swollen. Blisters distorted his face and peeling skin, as if he suffered second-degree burns. Sores on his arms oozed. He had sunken eyes and a gaunt face. He looked thin, malnourished. An IV needle stuck out from a vein in his arm.

The boy opened his eyes. He stared directly at Derek. "The medicine burns. I can't do this much longer. Let me go. Let me go with the *ba-buchka*."

Derek stepped back. He had a sudden loss of breath. A tightness in his chest squeezed his ribs. A deep sadness crept over him. He reached out to touch the little boy.

"It hurts, Mommy."

Derek didn't know what to say. He searched for words that would help, but he didn't know what to tell the boy. "It's okay. It will be okay."

The child smiled as he let out a long breath. "I love you, Mommy. I love you." His breathing labored for a few moments until the last hiss of air escaped his lungs.

Derek's eyes filled with tears as he hit the floor of his room. His knees and hands broke his fall.

Lola jumped off the bed and ran to him, licking his face.

He couldn't catch his breath. His chest shuddered as he tried to inhale. He held onto Lola's neck, burying his face in her fur. He squeezed her tighter as she leaned against him.

The tidal wave of sadness lessened. His breathing returned to normal. He steadied himself as he stood and gave himself a minute for his shaky legs to hold his weight. Using the wall, he got his bearings. Making his way to the bed, he removed the towel and collapsed between the cool sheets.

Lola jumped up and laid next to him, whimpering as she nuzzled him.

Draping his arm around her, he closed his eyes. He forced himself to push the vision of the boy dying out of his mind. He didn't want to deal with it now. Tomorrow would be soon enough.

He pulled the dog closer to him and drifted off to sleep as exhaustion overtook him. "I'll be okay, girl. This can't go on forever, right?"

CHAPTER TWENTY-ONE

Wednesday morning 7 a.m.

Lola burst through the door of the Legacy Unit. She searched every-where, then came running back to Derek.

"I told you in the car, he wouldn't be here this early." He dropped his computer bag on his desk and walked to the kitchen. After starting the coffee maker, he grabbed a breakfast burrito from the freezer and heated it in the microwave.

Clear-headed this morning after one of the most restful sleeps he has had in a long time, he wanted to analyze what he experienced last night. He leaned against the counter waiting for his food and black liquid crack.

Thinking back to the other day, he pictured the kid's room when he first saw it. He noticed the same music box left at the latest crime scene. Derek couldn't be sure what he saw was even connected to this case. Hell, he couldn't trust what he saw. His brain jumbled everything to-gether. Yet, a nagging feeling told him this was all connected.

The microwave dinged at the same time the coffee maker beeped. He took the biggest cup from the cabinet and filled it. His phone rang as he headed towards his desk. He dug it out of his bag on the last ring. "Derek."

"What day should I come to your house?" Dr. Chelsea asked.

"Good morning to you."

"Sorry. I have an early appointment this morning."

"How about tomorrow, Thursday?" Derek asked.

"That will work. Say 6 p.m.?"

"That's fine. See you then." Derek hung up. He glanced up looking at the security screen. George stood outside. He watched as the agent scanned his thumbprint and input the code.

"Why are you here so early?" Derek asked as he sat behind his desk.

George put his weapon in his desk drawer. "I couldn't sleep."

"I actually slept well last night. First time in a long time."

George nodded. "Hold that thought." He hustled into the kitchen and came back with a cup of coffee. "Did you go through the old case file last night?"

"I did. I want to go over it with everyone today. It looks like our killer made a mistake."

"Really?" George sipped his drink. The warm caffeine helped remove the fog around his brain.

"Yeah. There were two police reports, both described the same car, and both had license plate numbers. Here's the weird thing. There were two different plate numbers."

George's coffee cup stopped short of his lips. "How is that possible?"

"I'm not sure. I'm hoping Kyle will give us some answers." Derek looked at the clock on the wall. He figured he had roughly thirty to forty minutes before the others showed up.

George opened the file he had left on his desk. He searched through some of his notes, mapping out the best time to scout the neighborhood where Betty Shore lived. Since Derek wanted to discuss the case with the team, he scrapped the idea of getting there before people left for work. He made some notes on a pad of paper. His stomach growled as he drank the last of his coffee. "I need some more and I need to eat something."

"There are some breakfast burritos in the freezer. Help yourself," Derek said.

"Thanks. I think I might do that." George headed into the kitchen.

Derek moved the aerial photos to one side of the whiteboard, placing them under a magnet. He wrote some notes on the board. His mind focused on the things he had discovered about the case. Like the boy, the butterflies, and the music box, he wanted to bring them all up, but it wasn't the time.

As George walked back to his desk, Emma and Marc Anthony walked into the unit.

Lola jumped up from her bed and ran to greet her best buddy.

"Good morning, Miss Lola," Emma said as she released her dog from his leash. The dogs ran around the main area like a couple of toddlers high on a sugar rush.

Marc Anthony stopped at both George's and Derek's desks.

"I wish I could wake up with their energy," George said.

Emma laughed. "You and me both. I have to get something from my car."

Derek raised an eyebrow as he watched Emma retrieve several containers from her car on one of the security screens. "That looks like food."

George's head whipped around. "Hot diggity. I hope it's something good."

"If it's homemade, I bet it's fantastic." Derek walked to the door to help her as she came in. He reached out to lift the containers. "What do we have here?"

Emma puffed out a breath. "Thank you. I thought I would make us lunch today. I know these cases require a lot of phone calls and legwork, so I thought I would bring us some goodies."

She followed him into the kitchen. "Let's put all those in the fridge. I will put them in the oven around 10:30 to get them baked by lunch."

"What is it?" Derek tried to sneak a peek under the foil lids.

Emma closed the door. "A few different dishes. Now get." She shooed him away.

He reached into the fridge to grab a soda and laughed when she eyeballed him, making sure he didn't peek. "You better put a note on them so no one goes snooping or snacking."

She snapped her fingers. "That's a great idea." Emma headed off to her desk.

Back at his desk, Derek opened the files on the computer. Emma had downloaded everything into one folder. He scanned the notes his agents had made on their cases.

Nothing was breaking open yet. He scribbled a few notes on a pad of paper. Derek looked up when the door opened. He watched as the rest of his crew walked in.

"I need you guys to get your drinks, coffee, whatever, and let's meet in here in about thirty minutes," Derek said.

Kelly put her purse and gun in the bottom drawer of her desk. "You got something?"

"Not sure. We will discuss everything shortly." Derek motioned to Kyle as he headed towards his lair. "I need you to do something. Can you gather a list of all the neighbors that lived next to or across from the first four victims? With current phone numbers? I think our quickest way to get ahold of these people would be through the phone."

"Yeah. I think I can. I will need to do some digging."

"Can you do it in thirty minutes?"

"Maybe." Kyle turned to head downstairs.

"Do the best you can. And thank you, Kyle."

CHAPTER TWENTY-TWO

"Everyone, gather around." Derek stood at the board. He pulled his phone out and texted Kyle. "I'll leave these aerial shots here on the board. In case any of you need them."

The agents moved their chairs closer. Nodding in response.

Michael ran into the kitchen and grabbed a granola bar and a soda. "Anyone else want something?" he called out.

"Soda," George yelled back.

"Ooh, I want a snack," Felicia said.

George pointed at everyone.

Kelly shook her head.

"Bring several items," George yelled out.

Michael entered the room carrying a handful of sodas and a few different snacks. "I grabbed a few things."

Kyle ran up the stairs carrying some papers and hustled into the room. "Sorry."

Derek ogled him. "What's up?"

Kyle smiled. "I may know how the killer is picking her victims."

Everyone turned towards him.

Derek crossed his arms over his chest. "Spill."

"I ran a web search. I don't know why I didn't think of it before." Kyle handed Derek a few pieces of paper. "I was looking for archived social media posts. A local newspaper article popped up when I searched for April's name. That made me search local newspapers for the other victims."

Derek read each piece of paper. "Holy shit. Great job."

"In the newspaper?" Kelly asked. "Why?"

Kyle turned towards her. "They all had wedding announcements in the paper."

Felicia smacked her forehead. "Why did I not think of that?"

Michael's brow wrinkled. "I don't get it. Why would a paper run a wedding announcement?"

The girls turned towards him.

Emma laughed. She winked at Felicia and Kelly. "He has no clue, does he?"

The two women laughed.

"Nope," said Felicia. "One of the best things about getting married, especially in a bigger city, is you get your wedding day announced in the paper. It usually has a picture, and they always list where you registered for gifts."

Kelly took one soda.

"I thought you didn't want anything?" Felicia asked.

Kelly rolled her eyes at her. "I changed my mind. I'm allowed to do that, you know. Anyway, my cousin had her wedding announced in the paper. She got a bunch of extra gifts and cards. Friends she hadn't spoken with in ages reached out to her."

"In some towns, it's a big deal," Emma said.

Derek placed the papers on his desk. "This gives us a new way to come at these cases." He studied the whiteboard and erased everything he had just written on there. "Let me tell you guys what I found in the original case file."

He faced Kyle. "I need your help." Derek explained the police reports about the car. "Kyle, I need you to find those license plate numbers. Let's see if the killer took them off other cars and placed them on theirs. Also, run the description of the car through every database you can get into."

Kyle jotted down the license plate numbers and the car description. "I will hunt this information down."

"I have concluded our killer stalked the victims, and the police report confirms that. If witnesses reported the killer's car as suspicious, then I think our killer had to nail down the times when the victim would be at their home." Derek paced in front of the board.

George spoke up. "I think this confirms our theory that the killer is posing as a delivery person of some sort."

Felicia nodded. "This really makes sense."

"Wouldn't the victims be suspicious when a delivery driver shows up without a delivery truck?" asked Michael.

Derek sighed. "You would think so. However, I think her being a woman is disarming. And she probably has some kind of excuse. We have to assume she is dressing like a delivery person. Maybe even has a badge."

"Several companies have people use their own vehicles to make deliveries. This isn't a far stretch at all," Felicia said.

Kyle held up a few more papers. "I found the names and numbers of one or two neighbors that lived next to the victims." He handed them to Derek. "I don't know who has which victim."

Derek handed the papers to George. "Pick whom you're covering and pass them down."

George took the paper with his victim's name and passed the papers to Felicia.

As each agent took a sheet of paper, Emma took notes. She lifted her hand. "Kyle, could you send me all this information? I want to put it in the case folder on the system."

"I sure will, as soon as I get downstairs," Kyle said.

"I want everyone to get on the phone and call these neighbors. See if any remember seeing a vehicle or the delivery person. I found nothing in the notes of the file," Derek said.

"I can't believe this agent didn't do his job." George chugged the rest of his soda.

"I don't understand it either. But there is nothing we can do about a botched case from ten years ago. Let's focus on what we have." Derek moved the aerial photos from under the magnet and spread them across the board.

"Here are the areas surrounding each house." Derek took a marker and highlighted the streets around the houses. "The killer would have taken the easiest route in and out of the neighborhoods."

Michael sat quietly. He ran through everything they had so far.

Derek noticed his youngest agent. "Michael, what are you thinking?"

"I'm not sure." He looked around at his fellow agents. "We are all on the same page. This killer is a woman. We now know she has been targeting women who are getting married, and she has found them through the papers."

Everyone nodded in agreement.

"It's the why that I don't get," Michael said. He looked at Felicia. "You mentioned her fiancé dumped her. She is super angry, jealous, and hellbent on... what? It's not revenge."

Derek rubbed his chin.

Michael placed his elbows on his knees. "I'm not sure what I'm even trying to say. Never mind."

Felicia sat closest to him. She rubbed his shoulder. "Women can do some crazy things when they are in love. Are you hung up on the brutality of her actions? Is that causing the questions concerning the reason?"

"No. That's not it. I get why she killed the first four women because her fiancé left her at the altar, and she wants to spare them the same hurt. But what is the reason now? This is what's bothering me." Michael stood and went to the whiteboard. "May I flip this?" he asked Derek.

"Yes. Do whatever you need to."

Michael flipped the board to the other side showing the pictures of each victim. "Here are the four victims from ten years ago. Gruesome as they are," he said, pointing to the newest victim. "This one is worse."

Michael looked at each colleague before focusing on his boss. "What is she trying to protect them from now? What happened in the last ten years that made her not only start killing again, but killing with such brutality? It's as if she wants to obliterate these women. Yet, preserve them somehow."

He looked back at the board. He sat on the corner of Derek's desk, facing everyone. "We know she isn't killing because of the breakup. That time has passed. Whatever is driving her to kill now has to have an endgame. I think that's what's truly bothering me. What is the endgame?" Michael faced his team. "Something is staring us right in the face, but I can't see it."

CHAPTER TWENTY-THREE

The agents sat in silence as they thought about what Michael said.

A knot formed in Derek's stomach. It felt like a band of pressure squeezed his chest, constricting his breathing. "Let's not get ahead of ourselves. We don't want to make conjectures about what we think the killer might be doing. Let's focus on what we have." Derek crossed his arms. "Each of you make calls. After lunch, we will look at everything we have and see if we are getting anywhere."

He walked to his chair and sat. "I know we are under a lot of pressure to solve this and do it fast. But we need to do it right by letting the evidence speak to us."

Emma glanced up at the clock. "Oh, I need to get lunch in the oven."

Felicia spun her chair around. "Put lunch in the oven?

Kyle stopped on his way back to his cave. "Lunch? You brought lunch?"

Emma smiled as she walked past everyone. "Yes, I did. I brought a bunch of food. This seemed like the best day to do it."

Michael rubbed his hands together. "I can't wait."

"Me too," Kelly said. She punched George in the arm. "How was the date?"

George pretended to zip his lips. "I can't tell you."

"Why not?" she asked.

"I don't want to jinx it." George chuckled at her expression. "It went well. We met for dinner at a local restaurant. It was nice to sit with someone and not talk shop."

"I bet." Felicia spun around in her chair. "I hate talking shop. That's why I like to date non-law enforcement." She stopped and sighed. "But that rarely happens."

"Why?" asked Michael.

"Once I describe an old case and the dead body that goes with it, my dates usually get scared away," Felicia said.

"I thought you just said you don't like to talk shop," Kelly said.

"I don't. But sometimes there is nothing else to talk about."

"You are dating the wrong people," Kelly responded.

Derek sat behind his screen. He started looking for any reports of dead kids. He didn't even know what to search for. Using a few key-words, he searched the internet.

Scanning story after story, he felt that knot in his stomach get bigger. He couldn't ask Kyle for help, and he couldn't mention it to anyone. Plugging in the term cancer, child, and chemo, he hoped something would pop up.

The results he kept getting were articles on childhood cancer and the latest cures. "C'mon. There has to be something here." Peeking around the side of his monitor, he made sure nobody heard him.

He continued to type out keywords he thought might bring about some answers and he kept coming up empty. He leaned his head back and rubbed his temples. Twisting his head from side to side, he needed a break.

Grabbing his coffee cup, he headed into the kitchen. There wasn't enough in the pot for a full cup. He made another pot and leaned against the counter. The aroma from Emma's dishes cooking filled his nostrils. His stomach growled.

He rummaged through the snack drawer and pantry, looking for something to eat. Granola bars and chips were about all he found. Open-ing the fridge, he found a pack of English muffins.

"Ooh." He checked his watch. It would be at least another hour or two before lunch was ready. He placed one into the toaster. Grabbing a plate, he took some butter and jam off the shelf in the fridge.

As he waited, he moved towards the back door and stared out the window. The garden was beautiful. Even in the Arizona heat, the plants thrived. The toaster dinged. He buttered the muffin and put some jam on one side.

Walking back to his desk, he had an idea. He took a big gulp of coffee and a couple of bites of his English muffin. He typed out butterflies, get-ting results that pertained more to flowers. "That was a stupid idea."

Derek pulled out the information Kyle had given him about Char-lene. She and her fiancé had been engaged for over a year. They dated in high school. She worked for a local retail store as a manager.

He scanned the details but found nothing. Nothing that would help point to her killer. Derek glanced up, gazing around the room. All of his crew sat on the phones or searched for information on their computers.

Taking a few bites of his muffin, he licked the jam off his fingers. He sipped his coffee. *What the hell am I missing and how the hell am I going to stop this killer?* His phone vibrated on the desk. "Derek."

"Derek, it's Dr. Callahan. We found nothing on the box. No prints, fibers, nothing. We found a partial fingerprint on the lid of the music box. But it was too damaged to be viable."

"Crap. Do you have anything else?"

"The ribbon used is not the same as the one used in the previous murders, but it is similar."

"What does that tell you?" Derek asked.

"Nothing. Someone could buy this ribbon anywhere. Craft shops to fabric stores. It isn't fancy. That's about all I have. Simple everyday ribbon."

"You're killing me. Don't you have any good news?" Derek pulled on the ends of his hair.

"Maybe. I ran some tissue samples, and the chloroform used was homemade. Which means...."

"Which means our killer looked on the web for instructions."

Dr. Callahan laughed. "Bleach and hydrogen peroxide. It isn't hard to make."

"Do you have anything else?"

"I am still waiting for some other lab results. But it isn't looking like there is much in the way of forensics."

"This isn't what I wanted to hear." Derek took another sip of his coffee.

"I did email you some of the crime scene photos. I'll keep you posted on the rest."

"Thanks, Doc." Derek leaned back in his chair and rocked back and forth.

"Did the doc have anything?" George asked.

"Nope. Nada. Zilch. Do you have anything?" Derek asked, finishing his muffin. Checking his email, he looked at the photos of the crime scene. Nothing much different than what he already had. He scanned over the music box.

"Betty's fiancé said no one had it in for her. She was well-liked and had a lot of friends." George shuffled around some papers. "I spoke with a neighbor. She no longer lives in the same house, but she remembers the day of the murder.

"She said it was hard to forget. Betty came home from work she thought around 4 or 5 p.m. The neighbor remembered because Betty rarely got home that early."

Derek frowned. "Did the neighbor remember why she came home early?"

"She thinks she remembers Betty said she expected someone. Her memory is spotty, but she is sure Betty mentioned something about the wedding." George picked up his paper. "The neighbor, her name is Miranda, said early that day someone dropped a package off at Betty's door."

Derek perked up. "Did she see the delivery person?"

George shook his head. "No. But she was driving out of her garage when the car pulled up. A person in a baseball hat set something behind the post on Betty's porch."

"Please tell me she saw the car." Derek rested his elbows on the desk.

George smiled. "She did. Her description matches the ones in both police reports."

Derek rose and moved to the whiteboard. He shuffled the victims' photos around, making more room. "Okay. We have three witness reports about a dark blue or green vehicle with tinted windows." He flipped through the folder on his desk. "A four-door compact car. It looks like it may have been a Camry or something similar."

He made a note under Charlene's name and photo. "At the latest murder, a small dark SUV was spotted. Maybe black, blue, or dark green." Derek stepped back from the board. He glimpsed Emma walking into the kitchen. He heard the oven door open and close. The smell of Italian food wafted into the main room.

Everyone stopped what they were doing when Emma called out that lunch was ready.

The dogs perked up from their beds and raced the agents to the other room.

CHAPTER TWENTY-FOUR

George inhaled. "Emma, this smells fantastic." He walked over to the oven and looked over at her. "Can I remove the foil?"

"Yes. It's ready." She lifted a cookie sheet with several loaves of Italian bread on it. She motioned to Michael. "Can you slice the bread for me?"

"Yes, I sure can." He stepped up to the counter and began slicing.

Lola whined. She nudged her way to the counter and sat ready for her own plate.

Marc Anthony barked and wiggled his way next to Emma.

She patted his head. "I have a treat for you and Lola. Quit fussing." She scratched Lola's ears.

Felicia grabbed a stack of heavy-duty paper plates from the cupboard, but real silverware from the drawer. She squinched up her nose. "Can't use plastic ware."

"No kidding," Kelly said. "I hate using plastic forks and knives."

Emma stepped aside, letting everyone fill their plates. She watched each person scoop out a serving of lasagna, rigatonis, and Caesar salad. She had made fresh bread and a surprise for dessert.

"I can't believe you made all this food for us." Derek leaned over and kissed her cheek. "This is really nice."

Kyle ran up the stairs. "Is there any left?" he asked, grabbing a plate.

"There is plenty," Emma said. "I have a surprise for dessert," she called out loud enough for the ones who were already in the main area. She followed Kyle through the food line and filled a plate. She filled a glass of water and walked to her desk.

Emma held her chin high as she walked past everyone. She watched her coworkers, gaging their reaction and trying to figure out if they liked the way the food tasted. A grin filled her face when she heard the moans of delight.

"Oh, my gosh! Emma. This is so good." Kyle stuffed his mouth with a bite of bread.

"I'm so glad you like it. I just wanted to do something for all of you. Each one of you has made me and Marc Anthony feel at home." She sat at her desk.

Marc Anthony sat at her feet.

Emma reached into her bag and pulled out two large, meaty bones. "Lola," she called out.

Lola sat up and tilted her head towards Emma.

"C'mon, girl. I have a treat." Emma held up the bone.

Marc Anthony barked and wiggled, waiting for his treat.

Lola bounded at full speed to Emma.

"Whoa, girl," Emma laughed at both dogs. When she gave them their bones, they ran to their beds.

CHAPTER TWENTY-FIVE

The dogs ran from person to person, looking for morsels of food.

"Where is everyone at with phone calls?" Derek asked, taking a bite of lasagna.

George gulped a glass of water. "I don't have much more than what I shared earlier."

Kelly held up a finger. "Hang on." She lifted her plate, looking for her notepad. "I talked to a neighbor of Lana Berkshire. She didn't remember much, unfortunately. I'm still trying to get a hold of the second person Kyle found information on."

Felicia shuffled her notes on her desk. She lifted folders and pulled out drawers.

The other agents stopped eating and watched.

Kelly snickered and placed her hand over her mouth, trying not to laugh.

Kyle leaned towards her desk. "Do you need some help?"

Felicia slowly turned around. All eyes stared at her. "I hate all of you."

Kelly laughed so hard she couldn't catch her breath. "How are you so put together with your outfits and your makeup, but you can't keep your desk organized?"

"Two different things." Felicia took a bite of food. "Now shut up. I found it." She held the paper up, shaking it. "Okay. I've got Margarite Sanchez. One neighbor said she saw a dark blue, almost black car on the day of the murder. She was watering her bushes when the car pulled up.

"She saw a person carry a box to the door. When Margarite answered the door, the visitor went in. The neighbor assumed she was a friend, and didn't pay attention the rest of the evening."

"Did the neighbor, by chance, see when the person left the house?" Derek asked.

Felicia shook her head. "Not the exact time. The neighbor came out to place her trashcans at the curb and that was around 9 p.m. By that time the car was gone."

Derek made a note on a pad of paper. "The neighbor saw the murderer. Too bad she didn't pay more attention. Leaving us with nothing new to go on."

Kyle sat with a smirk on his face. He wiggled his eyebrows at Kelly. "Looks like I'm the best agent in the room, then."

"Oh brother," Kelly said.

"Spill it, Kyle." Derek pointed at him.

"I ran those two license plate numbers. They weren't registered." Kyle finished his bread and threw his plate into the trash.

"I'm not sure I understand? What do you mean they weren't registered?" Derek asked.

"The numbers didn't come up in any database. I called a local tag agency and inquired what that meant. They do not register license plates until the moment they assign them to a car and driver." Kyle opened his mouth to finish when Michael cut him off.

"Wait, what does that mean?" Michael asked.

"In a nutshell, if I worked at the tag agency, I could steal a license plate or two." Kyle rolled his chair over to Derek's desk. "According to a worker, it would be very easy to take a plate from the agency. They are not on a list anywhere. They sit in a pile until they are assigned to someone."

Derek stood and threw his plate into the trash.

Emma rose from her desk. "Before you start your discussion, who wants dessert?"

Everyone raised their hands.

"I'll be right back," Emma said.

"Okay," Derek narrowed in on Kyle. "Is there a way for the average person to get a license plate?"

Kyle shook his head. "Nope. You have to either own a tag agency, or work for the tag agency, or DMV. I think it would be harder to walk out with a plate from the DMV, though."

Derek picked up a marker and moved over to the board. "This is great." He jotted down the information on the board, off to the corner, under the photos. "Kyle, what about the car? Do you think based on what we have, we can narrow in on our suspect's car?"

"Oh boy. I can start a search. If I had the make and model, I could get a list pretty quick." Kyle spun around in his chair.

"We know the car driven ten years ago was a dark blue or green Camry-like car. Does that give you a start?" Derek asked.

"Sure. There are probably a few thousand registered," Kyle laughed. "What about the car the killer drives now?"

Derek pursed his lips together. "It looks like the killer upgraded the car from a compact sedan to an SUV. But we have even less to go on concerning the SUV."

"I can start a run looking for registered Camry owners. If I could get tag agencies to give me a list of employees dating back ten years, I could cross-reference those names with names of Camry owners." Kyle flicked his collar. "I mean, I am a stud, but I don't think I'm a magician."

Derek tilted his head back. "Shit. We can't get a warrant for every tag agency. Can you get a list of the owners of the tag agencies?"

"That's easy. It's public record," Kyle said.

"Okay. Get me that list to start." Derek ran his hand through his hair.

George snapped his fingers. "I have an idea." His voice trailed off when Emma walked in with a tray.

"Tell me that isn't tiramisu?" Kelly asked.

"Yes, it is." Emma set the tray on the closest desk and handed everyone a plate. "I hope you like it. It was one of my husband's favorite dishes."

Felicia stood and gave Emma a hug as she walked past. "Your husband was such a lucky man."

"Oh, stop it. No mushy stuff." Emma motioned towards the tray. "One of you can put that back in the kitchen. I'm going to walk the dogs."

"I'll take it," Michael said as he ran to the kitchen.

George took a bite and savored the dish. "This is so good." He swallowed and then continued. "Back to what I was saying." He took another quick bite and then pointed to the board.

"We have the aerial shots of the victim's neighborhoods. Let's assume she works near where she lives. How many tag agencies are in the area around the crime scenes? We can start there and work our way out."

Derek checked the other side of the board, then flipped it. He repositioned all the aerial photos. "The crime scenes are in a contained area, but not a tight one. We know our killer is choosing the victims via the newspaper announcements, but other than that, I don't see a connection with distance and placement of the homes."

"Damn," George said.

Derek put a number above each victim's house, representing the order in which they died, then tapped the pen against his lips. He finished his dessert while he thought about what they had.

Kelly spoke up. "Can you put the months of each victim's murder above the houses? I know Lana was murdered in September."

Derek wrote the month of each murder above the houses. "Okay. Where do we go from here? We know the date was the sixteenth of the month." He stood with his back to the agents.

"That's it," Michael said.

"What's it?" Felicia asked.

"It's been nagging me." He turned towards Kelly and Felicia. "You two and Dr. Chelsea thought the date meant something to the killer for the previous murders, and you also agreed that she was more than likely dumped and the wedding was canceled."

He looked at Derek. "We know the killer chose the victims from announcements in the paper. We also know the killer murdered the victims on the same date. It wouldn't be a stretch to think the date represented either the day she was dumped, or if we're lucky, the day she was set to get married."

Derek smiled. "It wouldn't be a stretch at all. Good work."

"There's one more thing," Michael said.

"What is it?" Felicia asked.

Michael faced her. "Couldn't she have had a wedding announcement in the paper as well?"

Derek's jaw slacked. "Holy shit." He scribbled on the board, making a note.

Kelly stared at Michael. "I never even thought of her having announcement."

Derek turned to Kyle.

"You don't have to say anything. I'm on it. I'll scan the newspaper announcements for weddings scheduled on the sixteenth of the month," Kyle said. "I'll check that year and the next as well. If I don't find anything, I will go out a year on either side. I will get the list of tag agency owners first."

Felicia snapped her fingers. "What if I call a few wedding venues and see if they keep records that far back? I can inquire if they had any weddings scheduled for that day in any month that were canceled. I can also ask about all our victims."

Kelly grabbed her pen and pad. "Once we get some names, we can start cross-referencing dates, names, and venues."

"Kyle, I can do some searches, too. Just let me know what you need," Michael said.

For the first time in this case, Derek thought they had a chance. A chance at stopping this killer. He just didn't know if it would be before someone else died or not.

CHAPTER TWENTY-SIX

By 5 p.m. Derek's eyes hurt. Everything he looked at blended together. "Okay," he said, twisting his neck. "Let's come back to this tomorrow. We are going to have a lot of information to go through."

He stood, stretching. "Have all of you put your notes and everything you have so far into the computer?"

Everyone but Felicia nodded.

"Felicia? Where are you at?" Derek asked.

"I'm putting in everything I have found out so far. I have about eight wedding venues sending me what records they have." Felicia typed out a few last sentences.

"Kelly, what did you get?" Derek said as he packed his laptop into his bag.

"I've been helping Felicia. We hit all the wedding venues in the area. I'm waiting for a few more to contact me back and let me know what records they have. I've had one say they needed a warrant." She held up the name. "I figured if we need it, Kyle could always work his magic."

Derek chuckled. "Let's start with what we have first."

George nodded in Michael's direction. "He and I have been calling the tag agencies. Several of them have been very helpful. I too have a list of agencies that want a warrant. More than I had hoped for. We should have enough to go on by tomorrow. And if we can't get anywhere, then we can look at getting warrants."

"Warrants will open the floodgates and we will have to explain why. The news will catch wind of that for sure. Before we do that, call back the ones who want a warrant and see if they remember a woman who worked there ten years ago that canceled their wedding.

"They might be more apt to help you find just one person and not need their entire roster of employees." Derek pulled his phone from his pocket. "I know Kyle is still working on searches. He might come up with something too." He texted him to wrap up and get upstairs. He also texted Dr. Chelsea.

Instead of Thursday, can you come tonight?

Derek sat back down and leaned his head back, closing his eyes. He listened to his crew wrap up their work. Knowing damn well most would take it home with them. "Don't take it home."

George cocked his head to the side. "Come again?"

Derek opened one eye. "Don't take the work home. Tomorrow, we will all be putting this information together. I need you guys to be fresh."

"No complaints from me. I'm exhausted," George said.

Derek's phone pinged back.

Yes. I can be there tonight. I will bring dinner. I don't want pizza.

Derek laughed.

That's fine. Come when you want. I will leave soon.

See you in a bit.

Kyle came upstairs. Running into Emma in the kitchen. "That lunch was fabulous. Thank you."

She patted him on the cheek. "I packaged it all up. There are tons of leftovers for lunch tomorrow. Enough for everyone." Walking into the main office, she let the others know about the leftovers.

"Yay for us!" Kelly said, grabbing her gun from her desk.

Derek stood and followed his crew out the door.

Lola whimpered as Marc Anthony walked away.

"You will see him tomorrow." Derek opened the car door.

She jumped in and sat in the front passenger seat.

Derek started the car, blasting the AC and the seat coolers. "You are getting spoiled." As he drove out, he realized he hadn't spoken with Lizzy since she left.

He dialed her number. "To hell with the congressman." The phone rang through the Bluetooth. After five rings, her voicemail answered. Instead of leaving a message, he hung up. Derek scratched Lola's head. "Maybe we will get to talk to her tonight."

Lola sighed, resting her head on the middle console.

Derek reached for a pack of gum. Realizing he was out, he thought about stopping for a multi-pack. As he came up to a gas station, he decided against it. He kept biting the inside of his lip as he thought about this hypnosis session.

He had never been hypnotized before. He wasn't sure he even wanted to go through with the procedure. But he had a sense of urgency come over him this afternoon. He felt as if time was running out. Time, he didn't have before something bad happened.

CHAPTER TWENTY-SEVEN

Anastasia stood in her son's room. She needed to pack up his things. She couldn't leave them for someone else to go through. She had arranged for her mother to take them.

Once she was gone, her mother could do what she wanted with them. It seemed too hard a task for Anastasia to give them away. As she packed up his clothes and a few toys, she stopped.

She used the palms of her hands to wipe her face. The tears didn't stop. She pressed the heels of her hands against her eyes. Her airway tightened as the sobbing took over.

She kneeled on the floor, clutching her son's toy. "This isn't fair. He was an innocent boy." Anastasia buried her face in a stuffed animal. She rocked back and forth as the sobbing returned.

She rolled onto her side and curled up in the fetal position. The sobs turned into whimpers. Several minutes later, Anastasia took a deep breath. Her breathing slowed as she sat up. "I have to do this. I have to finish what I started."

She rose slowly and continued packing. An hour later, she had cleared most of his clothes and toys. Anastasia slid the boxes to one wall. She shifted her attention to the hanging planes. She carried an empty box to the middle of the room and began pulling them off the strings, holding them in the air.

A weak smile tugged at the corners of her mouth as she stared at the last one they had hung together. "You loved making these." She let her fingers follow the outline of the plane. Anastasia pulled the remaining planes from the ceiling and then set to work on the butterflies.

She wrapped each glass butterfly in tissue and laid it inside the box with the planes. When she had finished, she closed the box and set it next to the others. There wasn't a lot left in the room, but what remained could wait until another day.

Anastasia closed the door behind her and leaned against it. She inhaled slow, deep breaths. "I have to leave the sorrow here. If I take it with me, I can't help the others. They need my help." She stepped away from the door and smoothed down her shirt. She tidied her hair, pushing the loose strands behind her ears.

"I will join you soon, my sweet son. And we will both be with the *babuchka*. But first, I need to help the others. I need to save them from the heartbreak they will suffer if they go through with their plans."

CHAPTER TWENTY-EIGHT

Wednesday 7:30 p.m.

Dr. Chelsea cleared the plates. "That was much more civilized than pizza on the sofa."

Derek finished his glass of wine while sitting at the small table in the kitchen area. "I like pizza on the sofa." He poured the last of the wine into his and Dr. Chelsea's glasses. "However, I enjoyed the steak and potatoes."

"Not the carrots, though?"

"I don't like carrots. They have no flavor. And they are orange. Never trust an orange vegetable."

Dr. Chelsea sat in the chair next to him. "That is by far the most ridiculous thing I have ever heard."

"I made it up." Derek fiddled with the stem of his glass. "Will this hypnosis thing hurt?"

Dr. Chelsea almost spit out his sip of wine. "Are you drunk?"

"I don't mean hurt—hurt. I guess what I mean is, will this mess with my mind and make things worse?"

"No. Not at all." Dr. Chelsea stood. "I want you to sit in your most comfortable chair."

Derek rose and walked to the living room.

His favorite spot was taken by the dog. Lola was sleeping on the sofa. The second most comfortable spot was his recliner. "Here." He pointed to it.

"Okay. I need you to sit and relax." Dr. Chelsea reached into his bag and removed a metronome. He placed it on the table next to the recliner.

Derek looked at it, raising an eyebrow. "You going to sing to me?"

Dr. Chelsea laughed. "You never want me to sing to you." He turned on the metronome.

Derek watched the wand bounce back and forth.

"I want you to lie back and just get comfortable," Dr. Chelsea said.

Derek shifted around in his seat. He wiped his hands on his pants, wiggled and reset his arms.

"Are you done?"

He cracked an eye open. "I'm getting comfortable."

"No, you aren't. You're fidgeting." Dr. Chelsea touched his leg. "Breathe in and out through your nose."

Derek settled back into the chair. He breathed in and out slowly through his nose.

"I want you to concentrate on the ticking sound of the metronome. Let that noise lull you into a relaxed state." Dr. Chelsea removed a pad and pen from his bag. "How are you feeling?"

"Apprehensive."

"That's normal. Try to pay attention to the ticking sound. Let that feeling of apprehension roll off your shoulders. There is nothing to be worried about and there is nothing to fear."

Derek slowed his breathing and focused on the sound of the metronome.

"I want you to think of one thing that brings you joy and happiness. Picture it in your mind. Front and center." Dr. Chelsea watched as Derek face slacked and the crease between his brows smoothed out.

"Do you have a picture in your mind?"

"Yes."

"Whenever something seems real or fear becomes overwhelming, I want you to focus on that picture."

"Okay."

"Let your body sink into the chair. You can feel the heaviness of your limbs."

Derek let all the stress go. Each limb felt weighted and heavy.

"What was the last vision you saw?"

"A little boy's room."

"Have you seen this little boy before?"

"No."

"What happened before you saw the room?"

"I was in the shower and I got out. I walked into my bedroom, but it wasn't my bedroom. It was his room."

"What did you see?"

"Planes and butterflies hung from the ceiling. Then I heard the cries."

"What cries?"

"The little boy was under the covers. He started crying."

"Did you lift the covers?"

"I did. He looked sick. Like he had cancer or some other illness."

"Did he speak to you?"

"He did. He told me he was hurting. He talked to me like I was his mom and he kept saying he loved me. The boy spoke to me as if I was his mom. The boy kept saying another word *bobushka*."

"Do you mean *babushka*?"

"I'm not sure. The boy said he wanted to go be with the *bobushkas,* or something like that."

Dr. Chelsea made a few notes. "What were you feeling?" He pulled his phone from his jacket pocket and texted someone.

"Sadness. An overwhelming sadness. I couldn't help him. I couldn't' do anything to ease his suffering." Derek wiped the moisture from his cheek.

"You're safe. It's okay to feel the emotions."

Derek breathed slowly. He released the pain and sadness.

"Why do you think you saw the little boy?"

"I'm not sure. I don't know who he is. The current case has something to do with him, I'm sure of it. But I don't understand why or how?"

"What makes you think the boy is related to the case?"

"The butterflies and the music box."

"How do the butterflies fit with the case?"

"The music box has the butterflies on it. And the boy's room had a pinned butterfly. Like in a museum. Like the entrails of the latest victim."

Dr. Chelsea made some more notes. "Derek, think about the boy's room. Did you see anything that might tell you about his identity?"

As Derek sunk deeper into a hypnotic state, his body felt as if it floated. He thought back to the room.

Dr. Chelsea leaned forward. "Derek, you have just walked into the room. What do you see besides the butterflies?"

"I see a desk on the far side of the room. I can see a picture in a frame."

"Who is in the picture?"

"The boy."

"What else is in the picture?"

Derek shook his head. "It's fuzzy. He's holding a trophy, but I can't read the engraving."

"What else do you see?"

"It looks like a cafeteria in a school. I can see a banner, but the letters are fuzzy as well."

"Tell me what else is around you."

Derek stood in the center of the room. He glanced up and saw letters on tiles hanging above the desk. "I can see tiles with the letters of his name, but I can't make them out."

"Concentrate on the tiles. Take each one and focus on it."

Derek started with the first tile. D was the first letter. As he stared at the rest of the tiles, they became fuzzier. The room spun. Derek gripped the sides of the recliner.

Dr. Chelsea noticed Derek's body stiffen. He tried to bring him back from being under. "Derek, I want you to listen to me as I count from one to ten. When I get to ten, you will open your eyes."

He waited for Derek to respond. "Are you ready?"

Derek's face tightened. His eyes moved rapidly under his eyelids. His hand balled into fists.

"Derek? I need you to respond."

Derek felt the weight of his body. He felt as if he was being pushed into the recliner. As the room spun, a loud howling noise filled the room. He screamed out as he covered his ears, shielding himself from the high-pitched whirling noise.

"Derek, I need you to open your eyes." Dr. Chelsea shook his shoulders. "Derek!"

Blackness filled the boy's room. Derek's breath came out in a shallow hiss. "What the hell?"

"Derek?" Dr. Chelsea called out to him.

Derek now stood in the foyer of a large home. A chandelier hung from the twenty-foot ceiling. He looked up at the dazzling lights. As his eyes adjusted, he heard the screams coming from another area.

He ran through the home. Running down the hallway, it seemed to stretch out in front of him. His breathing became labored as he struggled to reach the end. The screaming intensified.

Derek reached out to grab the wall and brace himself. His hand slid to the side, causing him to fall. When he looked down, he sat in a pool of blood. The crimson fluid seeped from under a door. He got on his feet. Reaching out, he turned the knob.

Stepping into the room, he saw a man hunched over a woman. "Hey,"

Derek yelled. "Stop that!"

The man quit crying.

It was then Derek noticed the woman's stomach had been ripped open. The shredded flesh left a gaping wound.

The man looked over his shoulder. His eyes narrowed into slits. His face was puffy and his eyes were swollen. "How could you do this?"

Derek shook his head. "I didn't do anything. I'm here to help."

"How could you kill them both? What did I do to deserve this?"

Derek didn't understand. There was one body. One dead woman. His pulse raced; he kept shaking his head. "I didn't hurt anyone. I'm the FBI, I'm here to help."

The man's face contorted as he slowly turned around. "You let this happen. You didn't stop her. You killed my wife. You killed my family."

Derek tried to step back, but he was frozen in place. As the man turned around, he held something in his arms. "No. No. I didn't do that." He pointed at the man. "I didn't do that."

"Yes, you did. You didn't stop her. She did this, and it's because of you." The man held out his dead baby. Ripped from the mother's womb, the umbilical cord dangled to the ground.

"No. I tried." Tears streaked down Derek's face. He recoiled, shuddering, as he stepped back from the gruesome sight. "I'm so sorry. I tried. I tried to find her."

The man took several steps towards Derek. He held the baby boy out. "This is your fault." At that moment, he threw the bloodied, dead child at Derek.

Screaming, Derek leaped back. His hands swatted the at the air as he tried to keep the baby away. He fell over the side of the recliner.

Dr. Chelsea reached down to help him. "Derek, you're safe. It's me."

Derek continued to swat at the doctor's hands. "Get that away from me."

Dr. Chelsea lifted his hands. "Derek, it's okay. I don't have anything in my hands. Look." He lifted them high, flipping the palms over so Derek could see they were empty. "I need you to take a breath. You're okay."

Derek's eyes were wide with white showing around the entire iris. The veins in his neck bulged. "Where's the dead baby?"

Dr. Chelsea stepped closer. "It's just me. No dead baby. Take my hand, Derek."

Lola jumped off the sofa when Derek began yelling and sat at his side. She licked his cheek.

Derek shook off the visions. He held onto to Lola's neck. "I'm okay, Doc. I'm okay." He made no move to stand.

Dr. Chelsea sat in his chair, pulling it a little closer to Derek. "When you're ready, I need you to tell me about the vision."

Derek nodded slowly, standing. He sat in the recliner but thought twice and sat in Lola's vacated seat. He grabbed a bottle of water from the coffee table and took a long sip.

"Talk to me. You were in the kid's room before all hell broke loose. Do you remember?"

"Yes." Derek stroked Lola's fur. She nuzzled next to him on the sofa. He pulled her a little closer to him. "I was looking at the photo, then I stared at the tiles with the letters."

Dr. Chelsea picked up his pad. "You said you could see the first letter of the boy's name. What was it?"

Derek took another sip of his water. "D. I couldn't see the other tiles. I thought the name was about to come into focus when there was a howling noise and the room went black. When I opened my eyes, I was in another house. I could hear screaming. More like wailing coming from another area."

"Did you recognize the home? Have you ever seen it before?"

"No."

"Was there anything familiar to you?"

"No. I made my way down a hallway. I reached out to steady myself using the wall and my hand was covered in blood. I fell or slipped; I don't know. When I looked at my jeans, they were covered in blood."

"What happened next?"

"I went into a room and a man was holding a woman." Derek huffed out a breath.

"Take your time."

"I'm okay. A little rattled. Someone had ripped the woman's stomach open, but the man blamed me. He said I caused it to happen, then he turned and held a dead baby boy."

Dr. Chelsea wiped his brow. "I'm lost. What dead baby boy?"

"A dead baby which came from the dead woman. He kept saying I did it. I didn't stop her and because of this, his family is dead. He kept blaming me." Derek sat on the edge of the sofa, resting his head in his hands. "Something bad is going to happen if I can't find this killer."

The doctor's mouth hung open, digesting what he heard. His phone vibrated. He glanced at the text. "Earlier you said the boy mentioned the word *babushka*?"

"Yeah, it sounded like that."

"I think he said *babuchka*."

Derek's brow wrinkled. "Is there a difference?"

"According to my friend, very much so. If you make the ch sound you are saying butterfly. If you make the sh sound, you are saying grandma. The boy was saying butterfly in Russian. *Babuchka*."

"Then that means this kid is definitely connected somehow to this case. It can't be a coincidence that he is saying butterfly and has a shit ton of butterflies in his room." Derek laid his head back. "I have to stop this killer."

"Think about the banner in the picture. You said it reminded you of a school cafeteria."

"Yeah. Like a school science fair. They always have them in the cafeteria or gym. This made me think of a cafeteria."

"Did you see any of the letters of the school's name?" Dr. Chelsea jotted some notes.

"I couldn't make out anything."

"If he won a trophy, maybe we can use that to find the boy. Maybe a picture of him winning the trophy at the science fair."

"How am I going to tell Kyle to look for that? What excuse am I going to give him for how I know to look for some kid who may have won a science fair and seems to be Russian?"

"Tell him the truth. You trust him, don't you?"

Derek trusted Kyle and needed him to hunt down information. He just didn't think he knew him well enough to tell him this kind of stuff. Derek's head fell forward.

"Tell Kyle the truth. He won't say anything. Tell him you have been having crazy dreams and you just want to see if it is your self-conscious telling you something."

He shrugged. "I don't even know what all this means. Is the woman dead already? Will she be murdered? Is this even related to this case or something else?" Derek had to figure out what this vision meant, and he had to stop it. He couldn't be responsible for dead person, especially a baby.

CHAPTER TWENTY-NINE

Thursday morning 8 a.m.

Derek sat, watching his crew settle in for a long day of research. They munched on the donuts he brought and the chatter slowly died off as they went to work.

He peeked out from around his monitor. Several times, he wanted to say something about what happened. Opening his mouth then stopped himself. *They will think I'm batshit crazy.*

Picking up his cup of cold coffee, he walked into the kitchen. He stared out the window at Emma and the dogs playing in the small back-yard. Lizzy still had not responded to his texts. Something was different. It wasn't just her not being able to respond. It felt as if she didn't want to respond.

Maybe it was this case bleeding over into his personal life. She had no obligation to contact him. However, he couldn't help but think some-thing didn't feel right about the whole situation.

He shook off the thoughts of her and the congressman. "I have too much going on here to let that distract me." Moving to the counter, he reached for the coffee pot, then changed his mind and grabbed a bottle of water from the fridge.

Back at his desk, he observed his team following through on yester-day's information. He could ask Kyle for some help, but then he would have to explain how he knew certain things. Derek wasn't ready to do that just yet.

He turned on his desktop computer, then changed his mind and opened his laptop. "Let's start with the boy," he said under his breath. Typing out a few commands, he searched for science fairs in the last three years.

From the picture of the boy, and the time frame they were looking at for the murders to have started back up, Derek assumed the boy had to be in either the fourth, fifth, or sixth grade when he was in a science fair.

First, he typed in school science fairs in Phoenix. "Wow," he said, staring at the computer. He glanced up over the top of his laptop, making sure no one heard him. He narrowed his search to science fairs over the last three years.

That brought the number down. Still not manageable. He typed in winners school science fairs Russian. This gave a much smaller number. However, the list now had literally Russian science fairs.

Derek pulled up each listing and scanned through the pictures. After ten, his brain shut down. He leaned back in his chair, running his hand through his hair. "Felicia, what have you come up with? Any leads on the wedding events?"

Felicia held up her finger as she finished her call. When she hung up, she turned around. "As of now, I have a list of fifty-five canceled weddings. Some of these were from months before the killings started and some were from months after the killings stopped. Not sure about how far to go back before the killings started."

"I think it's safe to set aside everything with a date after the killings stopped. Keep what you have for before the murders. We can see where that gets us." Derek rocked back and forth in his chair.

"I'm still waiting for a few." She threw a wad of paper at Kelly. "Where you at? Finished your list?"

Kelly threw the paper in the trash. "I have about the same amount. Most are from before the murders started, so maybe we will get lucky."

George spoke before Derek could say anything. "I have a pretty good list of women who worked for the tag agencies ten years ago. I had Michael call some again, asking specifically for a young woman who had their wedding canceled."

Michael smiled. "I must have a better-sounding voice. Several gave me information." He looked at his list. "I have twenty-five women who worked at a tag agency ten years ago. The kicker, no one remembers a person having their wedding canceled." He laid the paper on his desk. "I am waiting for one return call. From a guy who has run an agency for fifteen years."

Derek sat up straight. "How long will it be until he calls you back?"

"Hopefully by the end of the day today. He is out of the office," Michael said.

"Let's get our lists together. Michael, give your twenty-five to Felicia and Kelly. Let's cross-check to see if any of the names match theirs from the wedding venues." Derek finished his bottle of water.

He pointed at George. "Cross-reference your list with them as well."

"I can do that," George said.

Derek pulled out his phone to text Kyle, then decided against it. He thought the break away from his desk may give his brain a refresh. "Emma, I'll be downstairs if you need me."

She waved at him as he walked out.

Lola and Marc Anthony followed Derek down the stairs, knocking him into the railing.

Derek tried to grab the rail. His foot slipped out from under him as he tumbled down the steps. He screamed out as he hit the concrete floor below.

Hearing the scream at the same time the dogs ran into his office, Kyle jumped up and ran down the hallway. "Oh shit. What did you two do?"

Upstairs, George heard the cry first and ran to the kitchen. From the top of the stairs, he could see Derek crumpled in a heap at the bottom. He ran down the small flight of steps, taking two at a time.

Michael followed.

Kyle met them at the same time. "Shit."

George kneeled down. "I don't want to move him yet." He checked for a pulse. "He is alive. Thank God."

"Derek? Derek, can you hear me?" Michael asked.

Emma ran halfway down the steps and called out. "Here. There are smelling salts in this kit. See if that will wake him."

George caught the kit in the air. He searched the bag and found the small breakable pod. Cracking it open, he held it under Derek's nose. "C'mon, wake up." He moved the pod away from Derek's nose and then back, hoping the smell would wake him up.

"I'm calling an ambulance," Kelly said. As she turned to go grab her phone off her desk, Derek moaned.

"Wait," George called out. "Derek? Derek, can you hear me?"

After his eyes fluttered open, he closed them again.

"I don't like this," Kyle said.

"Call for the ambulance," George said, looking at Kelly. "I don't want to move him until he is conscious or until the paramedics get here. I'm not sure what his injuries may be."

Derek moaned again, but he didn't wake.

Lola moved between the men and sat next to him. She whimpered, looking at Kyle.

He kneeled next to the dog. "It's okay girl. He's going to be okay."

Michael used a penlight to check Derek's eyes. "I don't think he responded to the light," he said, glancing up at George.

The doorbell chimed.

Kelly turned around and ran to the front door. "He's at the bottom of the stairs." She stepped back, pointing towards the kitchen, as she let them in.

"What happened?" one asked as he followed the other.

"The dogs ran down the stairs with our boss, and knocked him down." Kelly was right behind the EMTs. She stopped at the top of the landing.

The paramedics moved next to Derek. Before they moved him, they checked his vitals and placed a brace around his neck.

"We need the backboard." The paramedic turned towards the men. "Can you guys help us get him up on the board? I don't want to put him in a sitting position until they check for neck or spinal injuries."

"We can help. Whatever you need," Kyle said.

The one paramedic nodded to the other, who ran to get the backboard and gurney from the ambulance.

Within minutes, they had Derek strapped to the board, and the five men lifted him up the stairs.

Once at the top, they placed Derek on the gurney.

One paramedic glanced at George. "Is anyone riding with us?

George looked at his coworkers. "One of us should go."

Michael raised his hand. "I'll go. Someone will need to pick me up from the hospital and bring me back here."

"Just call me and let me know when. I want updates," George said. "Once we know what is going on, you won't need to stay there."

Michael followed the two paramedics to the ambulance.

Emma watched as they wheeled him out. She turned to the crew. "I will call the director and let him know."

George pressed his lips together. "Can you call Dr. Chelsea as well?"

She nodded, sitting at her desk. Quickly scanning the list of numbers, she dialed the director. "Assistant Director Fretz, this is Emma from the Legacy Unit."

"Yes, Emma. What can I do for you?"

"Derek fell down the stairs. Looks like he tripped. He's been taken to the hospital."

"Okay. I'm on my way over there. Call Dr. Chelsea for me."

"I was about to do that."

"Listen, tell George I want him to take over. Keep working on the case. Did anyone go with the paramedics?"

"Yes, sir. Agent Finch rode in the ambulance."

"Okay. I will keep you updated."

Emma glanced at the silent phone. "George, the director wants you to take the lead here. He said to keep working the case."

George nodded, turning to the crew. "Okay. Derek is in excellent hands, and I'm sure he will be all right. We will check on him later. Let's go over these names and see if we can narrow this list to a few."

"I need to check the searches I ran. They should be finished. I will bring that list of names up." Kyle turned on his heels and ran to his office. Mindful of the dogs as he rushed down the stairs.

CHAPTER THIRTY

Michael took the bag containing Derek's personal effects from the paramedic as they exited the ambulance. "Thank you."

"No problem. Just follow us." The paramedic led the way into the ER.

Michael showed his credentials to the nurse, then followed her and the paramedics as they rolled Derek into an open room.

The nurse took Derek's vitals.

Michael stood in silence as the paramedics explained to the nurse what happened and what fluids they administered during the drive over. He watched as the nurse hung the IV started by the paramedics and checked the fluid levels.

Derek stirred as they moved him from the gurney to the bed. He moaned but didn't wake up.

Michael moved closer to one side of the bed.

A doctor came in and read through the chart. "Let's get a CT scan with contrast. And put a catheter in. Not sure how long he may be unconscious."

"Yes, Doctor." The nurse stood at a computer and typed in the requests for tests and the catheter. She looked at Michael and smiled. "Is he a coworker or boss?" she asked. She removed his clothing, placing his clothes in a plastic bag, then dressed him in a hospital gown.

Michael attempted to help. "I think I'm more in your way than anything," he said as he took the clothes from the nurse. "He's my boss. And my friend," Michael said, setting the bag down on the floor next to him.

"Those are some of the best bosses. I understand a couple of rambunctious dogs tripped him up."

Michael chuckled. "You could say that. They got a little excited and rushed down the stairs."

A tech came in to take Derek for the CT scan.

"If you will just wait here, they will bring him back when they're finished," the nurse said as she followed the tech out.

"No problem." Michael sat in a chair. Derek's phone buzzed in the plastic bag with his other items. Before he could answer it, the phone stopped. "Crap."

The door to the room opened and in walked Assistant Director Fretz.

Michael stood. "Hey, Director."

"Agent Finch, do you have any information on his condition?"

"No, sir. They took him for a CT scan. He was still unconscious, but he stirred before they wheeled him out." Michael set Derek's belongings on the tray table against the wall.

"How does this guy knock himself out so many times?" AD Fretz paced the room. He glanced at his watch. "Did they say how long the test would take?"

"No, sir, they did not."

The door to the room slid open and the tech wheeled Derek's bed back into place. He nodded as he exited.

The nurse walked in and checked that Derek was hooked up to the machines. She studied the director. "And who might you be?"

"I'm Assistant Director Fretz of the FBI. I'm his boss," he said, pointing at Derek. "Do you have any information yet?"

"No. As soon as the doctor gets the results of the CT scan, we will have a better idea of where we are at and what we need to do." She made a mark on Derek's chart before leaving.

Assistant Director Fretz moved to the side of the bed. "Derek? Agent Reed?"

Derek stirred, but didn't open his eyes.

Michael hid his concern. As more time passed, without Derek waking, the more complex the situation became. "Hey Derek, it's me Michael."

Derek moaned, still not opening his eyes.

Assistant Director Fretz leaned over the bed rail. "Can you hear me, Derek?"

Derek didn't respond.

The doorway opened again and this time, Dr. Chelsea walked in with an untucked shirt and crooked bow tie. He rushed to the side of Derek's bed. Taking in his condition, he turned towards Assistant Director Fretz and Agent Finch. "Do we have any answers yet?"

Michael shook his head. "Waiting on CT results."

"Tell me what happened," Dr. Chelsea said.

Michael recounted the incident to both of the gentlemen.

"Smart idea not to move him." Dr. Chelsea patted Michael's shoulder. "I'm sure there isn't...." he stopped himself when the ER doctor entered the room.

"I'm Dr. Talley."

"I'm Assistant Director Fretz, FBI." He pointed to Dr. Chelsea. "This is Dr. Chelsea. He is friend of Derek's and he handles the psych evals for our agents."

"Nice to meet both of you. The CT results don't show any damage. Your agent has one hard head." He turned the computer monitor towards the men in the room and pulled op the image of the CT scan. He pointed to the back of the skull. "This is where he conked his head on the concrete floor.

"Besides having one heck of a headache, he should recover with no issues. I can see bleeding but at this time it looks like a hematoma just under the surface of the skin. I'm not seeing any cranial bleeding. At least not at this time. I would like to move him to a room upstairs and keep him for one or two days. I would like for him to wake up." The doctor made a few notes in the file on the computer.

"No bleeding, you're sure? Nothing else?" Dr. Chelsea asked.

"No. The CT scan was uneventful. Which is both a blessing and a curse. Why he hasn't woken yet is a little concerning. However, I can't find a medical explanation why he hasn't. I bet he will regain consciousness on his own within the next hour. Of course, if he doesn't wake on his own, we will run another round of tests. A brain injury can show hours later," Dr. Talley said.

Assistant Director Fretz nodded. "Thank you, doctor."

The physician logged off of the computer and made a note on the chart at the end of the bed, then left the room.

Assistant Director Fretz motioned towards the two men. "I would like someone to be here when he wakes. I have a meeting or I would stay."

"I don't mind staying," Dr. Chelsea said. "I'm betting you rode with the ambulance."

"I did," Michael said.

"Well, there is no need for all of us to hang around. Why don't you give him a ride back to the unit? I will keep you both updated," Dr. Chelsea said to the director.

"That's a good idea." The director turned to Michael. "Do you have Dr. Chelsea's number?"

"No, sir." Michael removed his phone from his pocket.

Dr. Chelsea told him the number and placed Michael's in his phone. "When you get to the unit, let whoever is in charge know that I will update them. You can text me their number or I can just keep you as a point man."

Michael saved the doctor's number. "George is actually in command. I will give him your number. I'm sure several of us will come by tonight."

"I'll be here." Dr. Chelsea turned towards the director. "Don't worry about Derek."

"Do you think he will take a few days off?" Assistant Director Fretz asked.

Michael smirked, hiding his laughter.

Dr. Chelsea barked out a laugh. "No. Of course, he will not take time off. I hope we can get him to stay in the hospital for twenty-four hours."

Assistant Director Fretz stared at Derek, who rested on the bed. "I know why he didn't crack his skull open. Agent Reed is one of the most hard-headed men under my command." He headed towards the door. "Agent Finch, let's go."

"Please keep me posted, Dr. Chelsea," Michael said.

"I will, son." Dr. Chelsea watched them leave. He dragged over a chair and sat near the side of the bed.

A nurse came in. "We have a bed upstairs." She unhooked Derek from the machines and moved the IV bag from the stand to the holder connected to the bed. "Grab all of Agent Reed's things and follow me."

Dr. Chelsea collected the plastic bag holding Derek's items. He gave a quick scan of the room before exiting and following the nurse.

CHAPTER THIRTY-ONE

Derek felt as if he floated. His eyelids fluttered. Flashes of bright light flew past him. He attempted to lift his hand and shade his eyes, but he struggled to get his muscles to work together. Relying on his other senses to figure out his surroundings, he focused on the unfamiliar sounds and voices. However, the more he concentrated on them, the more distorted they became.

"Stop struggling. You're in the hospital."

Derek heard her voice. "No. I don't want to be here. Go away."

"I can't go away. You took a pretty good smack on the head. You need me." Chrissy held onto his hand.

He tried to look towards her voice, but his muscles wouldn't cooperate. "My head hurts."

Dr. Chelsea bent over the top of the bed. He strained to understand Derek's garbled mutterings. "Derek, Derek, can you hear me?"

Chrissy squeezed Derek's hand. "He's worried about you."

"Quit yelling at me." Derek moaned. "Why is it so loud?"

"I'm not yelling at you. Your auditory senses are on overdrive," Chrissy said.

Dr. Chelsea stared at Derek as they moved him from the ER bed to the bed in the room. The agent moved his mouth as if he spoke, but all he heard were grunts and moans. "Derek?" Dr. Chelsea set his things down. "Derek?"

"I will bring some water and crackers. When he wakes, he may need something for nausea. The doctor doesn't want him to have anything that will induce sleep." The nurse checked his IV. "I will also replace this bag."

Dragging a chair from across the room, Dr. Chelsea pulled placed it where he could see Derek and the TV in the corner. His phone rang. "Hey. Yeah, I won't be back in the office today. Just move everything to another day. I will be in first thing in the morning. Okay. Thank you." He placed his phone back in his jacket pocket.

The nurse returned with two large water jugs with straws. "I figured you may want some water. I filled one of these for you." She held up the large cup.

"Thank you. Can he eat when he wakes up?"

"Yes. He doesn't have any restrictions. We can have a tray brought up for dinner." She made a note on a board that hung near the door. "My name is Sarah. I'll be his nurse until 11 p.m. If you need something, just call for me." She handed him a controller connected to the bed. "This controls the TV and you can call us on this or the button on the side of the bed."

"Thank you, Sarah." Dr. Chelsea took a long sip of his water. He was thirstier than he realized. He pulled out his phone and dialed the Director. After updating him, he called Michael.

"Dr. Chelsea, how is Derek doing?" Michael asked.

"He's been moved to a room. They want him to stay here for twenty-four to forty-eight hours for observation to make sure there is no delayed swelling."

Michael relayed the message. "That's great. Look, I'll bring Derek's bag with his laptop. George will also swing by to fill him in on where we are in the case. Before I leave, I will call you, Dr. Chelsea, and see if you two would like something to eat."

"Thank you. The nurse is putting Derek on the dinner delivery this evening. I can grab something from the cafeteria later."

"Well, I will call anyway. Just to make sure. Thank you for the update. We will see you in a few hours," Michael said as he hung up.

Dr. Chelsea touched Derek's shoulder. "Derek?" he gave him a slight shake. He heard Derek moaning. He watched his friend's face. Derek's brow wrinkled as if he was in deep thought.

"Derek," he called out. He touched his hand. "Derek, this is Ronald Chelsea. Can you open your eyes?"

Derek heard a voice, but it sounded as if someone spoke to him through a wind tunnel. "What? Who is that?"

"Dr. Chelsea is trying to get you to wake up."

"I am awake. I'm talking to you," Derek said.

"I can hear what's in your head. You are not awake." Chrissy sat on the edge of the bed.

"Why can't I open my eyes?"

"You're out cold. Knocked yourself out. Actually, the dogs helped. Do you remember what happened?"

Derek concentrated. He pushed his brain to cooperate. He could see snippets being in the kitchen, but after that, a fog encases him. "I remember the kitchen at the office. I don't remember what happened after that."

"You fell down the stairs. Cracked your head on the concrete."

"Oh no. I'm in a hospital, aren't I?" Derek asked.

"Yup. I just told you that. Got your own room for a night or two."

"No. No. No. I don't want to be in the hospital." Derek grabbed the blankets. His hand balled into a fist.

Dr. Chelsea saw Derek's hand clench the blanket.

"Chrissy, help me wake up. Please." Derek pleaded with her.

"How can I help you wake up?"

"I don't know. You always pop up. Surely you can help get me out of this."

"Why can't you relax? Enjoy the quiet. Your head needs a break."

"I don't like it. Someone will try to talk to me. They always sneak into my dreams. If I can't wake up, they will bother me." Derek struggled to move.

Dr. Chelsea touched the back of Derek's hand. "If you can hear me, you're okay, Derek. You fell and hit your head. You need to rest. But you also need to wake up. Can you open your eyes?"

Derek heard Dr. Chelsea. "Ronald?"

Dr. Chelsea waited for him to answer. "Derek, can you hear me?"

"Ronald, can't you hear me?" Derek tried to move his head from side to side. It felt as if it was in a vice grip. "Chrissy, help me."

"Derek, I don't know what to do. How do I wake you?" Chrissy moved from sitting on the side of the bed. She tried to touch his cheek. "Can you feel that?"

Derek's body tightened. "No. I felt nothing. I'm so tired, though." His eyelids felt heavier than they did a few moments ago. His limbs pulled him into the bed. "Chrissy, I feel like I'm sinking. I'm tired."

"Let go, Derek. Your body needs to heal. I will try to keep the others away. I promise. They won't bother you.

"Do you promise?" he asked.

Dr. Chelsea heard those words clear as day. "Derek? Derek, what do you want me to promise?"

As he slipped into the blackness, he didn't hear Dr. Chelsea.

Chrissy stayed at his side. She would do her best to keep the others at bay.

CHAPTER THIRTY-TWO

Derek blinked, focusing on the quiet room. Dr. Chelsea was asleep in a chair next to his bed. He lowered the bed rail and swung his feet over the edge. He reached over, shaking Ronald's shoulder, but couldn't wake him.

He padded across the room in his hospital gown and turned on the light. It flickered and then went out. The hair on his arms stood on end. Derek reached for the door handle. Stepping into the empty corridor, it was eerily quiet. Emergency running lights along the floorboards cast a soft hue down the hallway.

"Hello?" he called out. "Nurse? Anyone?" Derek noticed his feet felt tacky. Looking down, he saw why. He wore the yellow socks hospitals give their patients. He wiggled his toes. "These are hideous."

He glanced up when he heard something from down the corridor. He followed the noise. "Hello?" Derek walked past two empty rooms. The third door was cracked open. He peeked in. A young pregnant woman laid in the bed.

She smiled at him. Rotten teeth jutted out from decaying gums. She held up her hand and waved. "Hi, Derek." The flesh on her fingers had peeled away from the bone and hung like flaps of fabric.

Derek shook off what he saw. "I'm imagining this. This isn't real." The scratching noise sounded closer. At the T-hall, he turned and followed the sound down the new corridor. He passed a room, but came back to it, when he heard the same noise on the other side of the door.

He pushed the door open. A stench hit him in the face. Derek covered his mouth, swallowing the bile lingering at the back of his throat. A small lamp in the far corner of the room cast a creepy glow, giving life to the shadows as they danced across the walls.

The covers on the bed were disheveled. The blanket had fallen over the side. Each breath he inhaled burned. His chest felt tight, constricted. He took a deep breath, expanding his lungs. When he blew it out, wispy smoke hung inches from his mouth. Derek shivered. The temperature in the room had dropped to near freezing.

He heard whimpering coming from the area near the bed. He took a hesitant step closer. Within arm's length, he bent over as he took another step. "Hello? Are you under there?" Derek bent a little lower. He could see someone sitting on the floor. He squeezed his eyes shut. "Relax. This isn't real. It's just a dream." As the words left his mouth, he lifted the blanket.

The woman from the other night smiled at him. Her stomach ripped open. Reaching inside the wound, she pulled out a dead baby boy. She rocked him in her arms. Lifting her head, she gazed at Derek. "This will be your fault if you don't help us." She threw the baby towards him. The bloated, discolored body landed at his feet. Its eyes popped open.

Derek stood frozen in mid-movement. He recoiled, stepping back as spider-like legs burrowed out the sides of the baby's body. Each one growing quickly until the legs were long enough to support its weight. He took another step back, away from the bed.

"You have to stop her. We don't have much time." The lady leaned forward. Her body twisted as she got on all fours. Her bowels hung from the gaping wound, dragging on the floor as she moved closer to Derek.

He scrambled back, falling on his butt. The spider creature crawled towards him. As Derek moved closer to the door, the baby followed his every movement. Derek glanced over his shoulder to see how far he was from escaping.

The door was a few feet away. He tried to stand, to get on his feet. But he wasn't fast enough. Something grabbed his leg. He looked back to see the woman holding his foot in both hands.

"Save my baby, please. Don't let her kill my boy."

He kicked at her until she released him.

The creature scurried quickly. It ran up his legs, perching himself on Derek's stomach. The baby twisted his head from side to side.

Mesmerized by the baby's eyes, Derek stared into the pools of molten black.

The baby's expression morphed into a sad pout just before the creature lunged.

Derek snapped out of his daze as the baby landed on his chest. A large mouth-like opening widened. Sharp fangs lined the blackened gums. Derek screamed as he reached out to stop the creature from ripping his face off.

Dr. Chelsea jolted awake. "Derek." He stood and grabbed Derek's hands.

Derek struggled against the creature.

"Derek!" Dr. Chelsea yelled at him, as he shifted his hold from Derek's hands to his wrists. "Nurse!" Dr. Chelsea called out.

A nurse ran into the room. Derek sat clawing at the tubing, trying to pull out his IV. She grabbed his arm. "Agent Reed." She pushed a button, calling for help.

"Nurse's station."

"Martha, I need help in 402. Bring the hand restraints. She struggled to keep Derek from ripping out his IV.

A second nurse entered. She wrapped one restraint around Derek's wrist. She secured it to the side of the bed, then moved to the other side, and repeated the process.

"Hand restraints?" Dr. Chelsea asked. "Do we need that?"

"Until he fully wakes up. I bet he is having a bad dream, and it seems very real to him." The nurse checked the IV in his arm. "He didn't pull this out. That's good."

Dr. Chelsea let out a deep breath as she left the room. "Derek." He patted his cheek. "Derek?" He pushed out a long breath as he held onto Derek's hand.

Sitting back in his chair, Dr. Chelsea held tight to his friend's fingers. "You're going to be okay." He took in deep breaths and let them out slowly, calming himself down.

Derek squirmed on the bed. He attempted to open his eyes, but he couldn't budge his eyelids. He smacked his lips together. Derek attempted to lift his hand, but he couldn't.

Dr. Chelsea heard Derek stir. He rose from the chair and moved closer to his side. "Derek? Can you hear me?"

"Ronald?" Derek turned his head towards his friend. He yanked on his hand, trying to raise it. "I can't move. What's going on?"

"It's okay. I need you to relax. You are in a hospital." Dr. Chelsea pushed the button to call the nurse.

"Nurse's station."

"He's awake. Please send in the nurse." Dr. Chelsea squeezed Derek's fingers. "Do you feel that?"

"Yes." Derek struggled to open his eyes. "I can't get my hands to move or my eyes to open."

"They strapped you to the bed. Just relax and hang on for a minute. Don't panic."

The nurse scrambled in and took his blood pressure. "Agent Reed, you are in the hospital. Do you know how you got here?"

Derek searched his memory. "I fell."

"Yes, you did. We had to strap your hands until you woke up. You were trying to pull out your IV. I need you to relax. When you are fully awake, we can remove your restraints."

Derek nodded. "I'm sorry."

"No need to be sorry, Derek."

"I'm thirsty," he said, smacking his lips together. "My throat is so dry."

Dr. Chelsea held the straw near his lips. "Here is some water. Use the straw to take a sip."

Derek took several gulps of cold water.

"Not too much. Slow down." Dr. Chelsea set down the cup. "We need to make sure you don't vomit it back up. Can you open your eyes?"

The nurse stood next to the bed. Waiting.

Derek squeezed his eyes shut. He tried to open them. They felt as if a sticky film coated them. Blinking several times, he got them to open. Everything he looked at had a haze around it. He blinked again. "My eyes aren't focusing."

"It's okay. Take your time, Agent. You've been unconscious for several hours," the nurse said.

Derek stared at the young woman. The haze disappeared, and both she and Dr. Chelsea came into focus. He went to lift his arm again. "Can you remove these?"

The nurse smiled. "As long as you won't rip your IV out."

He frowned at her. "I didn't mean to do that."

She unhooked the first one. "We only it did for your safety."

"I'm sorry." He looked at Dr. Chelsea. "I didn't mean to cause problems."

The nurse unhooked the second restraint. "It's okay. You were disorientated." She stuck the restraints in a drawer. "I need to go let the physician know you are awake."

Dr. Chelsea slid the tray table over the bed. "If you want some more water, it's here." He watched as Derek closed his eyes. "What did you dream?"

"What? Why do you ask that?"

"You screamed out, then tried to pull out the IV. What did you see?"

Derek opened his eyes. "The dead woman from the other night and her dead baby, who turned into a creepy spider baby."

Dr. Chelsea shook his head. "Wow. That would scare the shit out of me."

"Tell me about it. When you were grabbing my hands, I was trying to get the creature off me." A faint smile filled Derek's face. "Sorry."

Dr. Chelsea laughed. "Nothing to be sorry about. I'm just glad you finally woke up." He glanced at his watch. "You've been out for close to five hours."

"Shit. I don't like that." Derek's fingers skimmed the back of his head, where the pain pounded against his skull. "Ouch. Crap that hurts."

"You hit the concrete pretty hard."

"Can you call Kyle? Or hand me my phone. I need him to take care of Lola."

Dr. Chelsea dug out his phone and texted Michael. He told him Derek was awake and wanted Kyle to take care of Lola. "Michael texted me back. He will tell Kyle about Lola. And they will all come see you later."

"Text him back and tell him to bring the case files."

"Seriously? Can't you take a break?"

"I'm stuck here. I might as well have something to do."

Dr. Chelsea did as he asked. Maybe having his work would keep Derek in the hospital for at least one day.

CHAPTER THIRTY-THREE

Thursday evening.

Anastasia pulled into the driveway. She assumed the woman who left was Beth's mother. Not that it mattered. She had planned on doing this Friday night, but she didn't want to wait. A sense of urgency seemed to nag at her ever since the other night.

Anastasia exited her car, carrying the package with her. She glanced up and down the street. Empty. No neighborhood watch patrol. Knocking on the door, she looked over her shoulder. Double checking the street was still empty. It was the dinner hour. That should give her enough time.

She had driven out to the neighborhood earlier that day. A driving force pushed her to change her plans. Her desire to be with her son had made her rethink her timeline and planning.

She had seen Beth come home early, and it all seemed to fall into place. "Why not?" she had said to herself. The timing couldn't have been better.

"Hello? May I help you?" Beth Cahill asked.

"Hi, I think I got your package by mistake. I moved in a few days ago." Anastasia held out the package.

Beth didn't notice the gloves the stranger wore. She looked at the package, reading the address.

A car pulled into the driveway.

Anastasia froze. She pulled her ball cap down lower on her head. She turned and waved. "Nice to meet you," she called out as she got in her car and drove off.

Beth's mother looked at her daughter. "What was that about?"

Her brow drew together. "Some new neighbor." Beth held up the package. "Said this was outside her door. I guess the mailman delivered it to her by mistake."

The mother took the box. "Who is it from?" She flipped it over. "There is no return address."

Beth took the package back. "Let's open it and see what's inside."

Anastasia's eyes drifted to the rear-view mirror. She kept watching to see if anyone followed her. Tightening her hands around the steering wheel, her forearm muscles bulged. "Shit, shit, shit." She hit the steering wheel with an open palm.

Panting as she drove away, she rocked back and forth. "I can't believe it. What if I was in the middle of killing her and her mother showed up? Shit. This is not good. This is not good."

Driving a little too fast, she forced herself to slow down. Anastasia concentrated on her breathing. "Calm down. No one paid attention to you. It's okay." She slowed her breathing, attempting to calm herself.

She drove home and pulled into her garage. It wasn't until the door was down that she relaxed. Anastasia grabbed the screwdriver from her passenger seat and switched the plates back.

"What the hell was I thinking? I am so stupid." She stomped on the floor of her garage. "Why didn't I just keep with the plan? Friday night. I will just have to do it Friday night."

CHAPTER THIRTY-FOUR

Late Thursday evening

"I can't believe you knocked yourself out. Again," George said, taking a piece of pizza.

"I can't thank you guys enough for bringing pizza. The food here is awful." Derek guzzled the last of his soda. He reached for his big cup of water.

"How's the head?" Felicia asked.

"It hurts. Man, laying back on the pillow is painful. But the doc said there was no damage." Derek grabbed the last piece of pepperoni pizza.

George pointed at the files. "We gathered all the names and we are still going through them. Cross-Referencing them. You have all the names in there. Most are listed by both the bride and the groom's names. Some are listed by just the bride's. And a handful were listed by the groom's name only."

Derek nodded while he chewed his bite of food. "I will go through this. I have a feeling sleeping here will be rather hard."

Michael gathered the trash, then took the remaining pieces of pizza and placed them in one box. "Do you want these?" he asked, pointing to the boxes.

Derek frowned. "I don't have a refrigerator. Don't know how long they will last before they make me sick. One of you should take them home."

Michael motioned around the room. Everyone else passed on the pizza. "I'll just throw them away."

Kelly stretched. "Lola wanted to come with us. Kyle said he had food at his place. He was going to keep her with him tonight so she wouldn't be alone all night. He's going to bring her back to the unit tomorrow."

"I'll call him soon. I'm proud of you guys." Derek lifted the file. "You gathered a lot of names. If we can't find our killer in this batch, I'm not sure we will find her."

Dr. Chelsea stood. "Do you want me to stay with you tonight?"

Derek shook his head. "Absolutely not. You go home and rest." He smiled at his agents. "All of you, rest. I'm hoping they will let me go tomorrow. I will call one of you to come get me."

Felicia raised her hand. "I can."

George placed his chair back against the wall where it had been when he entered the room. "Any of us can get you. Whenever they let you out."

Derek snapped his fingers. "Did Kyle get any more information on his searches?"

"He did," George said. "He has about ninety-five names of women who had their weddings scheduled for that date and canceled. He used an eighteen-month window for both that and the newspaper announcements. I haven't gone through it. His searches finished just before we left the unit. I put the results in the file as well. Also, he has the list of agency owners in there."

"We will cross-reference all the names first thing in the morning," Kelly said.

Dr. Chelsea patted his pockets. "I think we should go. I know visiting hours are almost over." He focused on Derek. "And you need to rest. Sleep. Please don't stay up all night doing research."

"I won't. Thank you for bringing my laptop and for getting it set up on the tray for me. Bending over is not the best position for my head." Derek laughed at Dr. Chelsea's look. "I promise I won't work all night."

"Okay. Good night, Derek. I will call you in the morning." Dr. Chelsea stood at the door as the other agents said their goodbyes and filed out. He looked one last time at Derek. "Rest. You need it."

"Yes, Dad." Derek watched as his team and good friends left his room. He wondered if he should take the doctor up on his offer to stay with him, but Derek had no intention of sleeping. "I don't want any bad dreams while I'm here. They will most definitely lock me up."

He slid the tray table closer to him. He checked his phone. Still no message from Lizzy. His mind raced. Bouncing around from one explanation to another. He feared something horrible may have happened to her. Or worse yet, he feared something horrible was about to happen to her and he wouldn't be able to stop it. He texted her a message. "Maybe she will respond."

He texted Kyle.

Hey, thanks for taking care of Lola. Is she giving you any trouble?

A picture popped up on his phone screen. Lola sat curled up with him and his cat Squeakers on Kyle's sofa.

Nope. She's fine. Don't worry about her.

Thanks. Hopefully, I will be out of here tomorrow.

Derek opened the file containing all the names they had found. He started with Kyle's lists. He took the names of wedding announcements and slowly cross checked them against the list of canceled weddings.

Within thirty minutes, his head pounded. Not sure if eye strain caused the pain or if the bump was the culprit. Either way, he needed a break.

He turned on the TV looking for a distraction. Flipping through the channels, his eyelids fluttered. He didn't want to go to sleep. He didn't want to dream, but his body wasn't listening to him. Derek gave in. He settled back against the pillow, easing his head down.

As he relaxed, the throbbing in his head subsided. He didn't fight it. Just this once, he would listen to his body. He hoped no nightmares would show up. No dead people. He wanted to rest. Nothing else.

CHAPTER THIRTY-FIVE

Friday morning 5 a.m.

Derek jolted awake.

"Good morning." The nurse smiled as she took his blood pressure. "I bet the doctor releases you today."

It took him a minute to register where he was. He realized he slept through the night with no bad dreams. "Uh, that's great. When? And who are you?"

She pushed the blood pressure machine back against the wall. "The doctor won't make rounds until nine. Usually, patients get released by lunchtime. My name is Catherine. I'm your nurse for the day."

"Getting out sounds great and nice to meet you, Catherine." Derek wrestled with the IV. "I need to go to the bathroom."

"Oh, you don't need to get up." She pointed to his gown. "You have a catheter. You were unconscious until late yesterday. We can't remove it until the doctor gives the orders."

Derek stared at the nurse. "I just pee? While I'm laying here?"

The nurse held up his urine bag. "You've been doing it since they brought you into the hospital."

"This is weird." Derek frowned. "Can you see if we can at least remove that?"

Catherine laughed. "I will call now and see if he will give that order."

Derek watched as she left the room. His bladder felt as if it would explode. He fought the urge to urinate, but his body didn't listen. He sighed in relief once his bladder emptied. "Wow. I dislike this."

He used the controls on the bed to raise his upper body to a more comfortable position. Derek reached over and pulled the tray across his lap. The file remained open on the tray where he had left it, but his computer was now in his satchel.

Glancing at the file, he saw his notes in the side margins. He inspected the papers. Nothing looked amiss. He started where he left off the night before and began going through the names. He had made a fairly good dent in the lists when Catherine entered the room. "Hey did someone move my laptop last night?"

She smiled at him. "I did. I came on shift early this morning. You were asleep. I didn't want you to hit the table and knock it off. I thought it would be better in your satchel." Catherine held up her hands. "I didn't touch anything else."

"I didn't think you did. I was just making sure I didn't sleep walk or something."

"You did not sleep walk," she said, looking at the bag hanging on the side of the bed. "I see you used the bathroom." Catherine put on a pair of surgical gloves and unhooked the bag from the tubing and emptied the urine into the toilet.

"I don't enjoy peeing this way. You know, going to the bathroom in bed. It feels really weird." Derek watched her as she threw the bag into a bin marked biohazard material. His eyes widened. "Does that mean you are going to remove it?"

"Yup." She lifted the covers and then his gown. "This tape is very sticky. I'm going to rip it off quickly. It hurts less." She lifted the edge of one corner and peeled it back. "Take a deep breath."

Derek squinted at her. He gripped the covers in anticipation of pain. The moment he took a deep breath, she ripped off the tape. "Wow. Crap. That hurt."

Catherine giggled. "Wait until I pull out the cath."

"Seriously?"

She laughed at his expression. "No. I'm kidding. The tape hurts the worse. I have just a little bit more tape to remove." Catherine continued slowly removing the tape on the inner thigh until the tubing moved freely.

Derek winced as the last of the sticky tape came free. Pulling every hair out with it. "Man. You would think they could use something less painful in that area."

"It has to stay put. If we didn't use very sticky tape, you could risk kinking the catheter or tugging on it." Catherine inserted a syringe into the end of the catheter tubing. "I am deflating the balloon that is used to hold this in place."

Her soft touch did nothing to relieve his embarrassment as she moved his penis to the side. He looked away, staring at the wall.

"Now. I want you to take a deep breath when I say so. I will then pull the Foley Catheter out. You will feel discomfort, but it isn't painful."

Catherine maneuvered into position. "Okay. Take a deep breath and exhale slowly."

Derek followed her instructions. When she pulled the catheter out, he winced. "A little more than just discomfort."

"There. All done." The nurse put the tubing in the biohazard bin. "You have to pee on your own before you can leave. I suggest you drink a lot. What can I get you?"

"A beer?"

"Cute. How about a soda?"

"Yeah. Diet if you have it."

"I will bring that and some fresh water," she said, taking his large cup out with her.

Derek breathed easier with the catheter gone. He rubbed the inside of his thigh and glanced under the gown and checked out his penis. It looked normal. "Not sure what I thought I would find."

Catherine returned and set the water and soda on the tray. "Breakfast will come around in about an hour. Maybe ninety minutes. Would you like some graham crackers?"

"No thank you. I'm fine until breakfast." Derek watched her leave before he started going through the files again. He popped open the can of soda. Guzzling half of it, he burped several times. "Oh man, that felt good."

He settled in and went over the names. For every name that matched Kyle's list of wedding announcements and Felicia and Kelly's list of canceled weddings, he circled them. He had about sixty-five names left to go through on Kyle's list when someone walked into his room carrying a tray of food.

He closed the file and set it on the bed next to his side. "Thank you," Derek said as the worker placed the food on the table tray. Lifting the cover off the plate, Derek smiled. "Pancakes and eggs." His mouth watered. They smelled edible. But he didn't have too much hope for hospital food.

Removing the plastic cover off the cup of coffee, he inhaled the aroma. "Ooh, please let this be good." He took a sip. Strong and good. "At least they make a good cup of coffee. He poured syrup over the pancakes and settled back.

He turned the TV up and searched for something to watch. He scrolled through all the channels and finally settled on one of the local morning shows. They ran through the weather for the week and then the sports.

The sports analyst talked about the Arizona Cardinals and how good they were expected to be this year. "They better be with all the money they are paying the quarterback."

Not a huge fan of sports, Derek did enjoy football. Both college and pro. He wasn't a diehard, having to watch every game, but a beer and a game on TV was a nice way to spend a weekend.

Derek watched as the local feel-good story came on. The camera zoomed in on the newscaster. He listened as she talked about IVF and how many women needed this procedure to have a chance at having a baby.

He took a sip of his coffee and lifted his piece of bacon. As the camera view moved out to a wide-angle view, Derek's hand stopped an inch from his mouth. His jaw hung open. "Oh, shit. Oh, shit." He scrambled for the remote and turned up the volume.

The couple on TV spoke about the treatment they went through trying to get pregnant. And when they were about to give up, the procedure worked. The wife spoke about the reasons this treatment was important for couples who can't have children without intervention.

Derek searched for his phone. He found it under the tray of food and dialed Dr. Chelsea's number.

"Good morning, Derek. I was going to come see you."

"Ronald, I know who the couple is from my dream?"

"What? How?" Ronald's voice cracked with excitement.

"I'm watching them on TV."

CHAPTER THIRTY-SIX

Anastasia sat at her dining room table. Yesterday's debacle threw off her timing. "Don't veer from the plan again, Stasi...stick with what you know." She still couldn't believe how close she came to getting caught. She did not want to be in that position again. The task had to be completed. It had to be the same number. Four the first time, four this time. Then she could be with her son.

Beth Cahill would get home late tonight. She would bring another nighty and music box, but she hoped she could recover the first ones. "Nothing I can do now but wait." Anastasia hummed as she sipped her coffee.

The oven dinged. Grabbing a pair of oven mitts, she lifted out the breakfast casserole. The bacon, onion, and eggs smell filled the kitchen. "Oh, this looks fabulous."

She took a plate from the cabinet and poured a glass of orange juice before she sat down. Turning on the TV she found her favorite news channel and waited for the morning show to continue.

Anastasia filled her coffee mug and dug into the casserole. She watched the newscaster talk about IVF. She felt sorry for women unable to have children. Even though her marriage never happened, her ex-fiancé gave her the best gift. Her son.

She watched as the camera panned over. Her phone pinged. She responded to her friend's message, telling her she couldn't meet for lunch after all. Anastasia lifted her glass of orange juice and took a sip.

When she glanced at the TV, the glass slipped from her hand and orange juice spilled across the table. Anastasia paid no attention to the mess. She stared at the screen.

"I don't believe this." There on the TV sat the man she should've married. The man who canceled her wedding. "You bastard." The words spewed out with venom. "I don't fucking believe this."

Patrick Weatherby sat next to his wife. The woman he left her for. The woman who ruined her life. She had let all the anger and hurt go when she had her son. Her entire body trembled. She balled her hands into fists, digging her fingernails dug into her flesh. She turned up the volume and listened to their pathetic story about the struggles to have a child.

She smirked at the pain in their voices. "At least I had your son, you bastard." Anastasia took great delight in knowing Patrick couldn't have kids with the woman of his dreams.

As she sat and listened to how successful they had become as a couple and how empty they felt at not being able to have a child, Anastasia laughed. "I am so glad you suffered. The icing on the cake would be if you couldn't have kids at all."

The moment she said the words, she knew. She knew what to do. She pushed her plans for Beth Cahill to the side. "This is so much better than killing more women." Anastasia's laughter overtook her. Tears flowed as the plan unfolded. She stood and danced around the kitchen. "I prayed for something to make me whole again and this is it."

She couldn't believe how her life was coming full circle. This time it would be she who inflicted the pain. It was her time to take from Patrick the one thing he wanted more than anything in the world.

Anastasia squealed with delight. "You are about to have your world ripped out from under you." She pointed the remote at the TV pausing it. She glared at the couple. They looked so happy. Anastasia couldn't wait to rip that happiness away. "Karma is a bitch. And it's about to smack you in the face."

CHAPTER THIRTY-SEVEN

Derek took his tray of food and set it on the foot of his bed. He slid the top of tray table away from him, exposing another smaller tray underneath. He leaned over and grabbed his satchel off the chair and placed his laptop on the tray.

His foot twitched as he waited for it to boot up. He took out the secure hotspot connection and hooked it into the Wi-Fi. Derek typed in the man's name from the TV.

Several stories came up. When Patrick Weatherby's business took off, there were stories about how he met his now-wife, Lucy Wilcox. And how he canceled his previous wedding.

Derek's heart raced as he read through story after story. They all referenced his previous engagement, but none listed the woman's name. He searched article after article. Derek found no mention of his former fiancé's name.

About to give up and start a new search, Derek found one article in which the author referenced Patrick's prior engagement and asked about the breakup.

Derek read through the story, skimming most of the breakup details. Until he came to a name. Anastasia Parker. There. The name of their killer. He was sure of it.

He pulled up another search window and typed Anastasia Parker. Sweat beaded on his hairline. His breakfast churned in his stomach. In a story about childhood leukemia, Anastasia sat next to her son's bed in the hospital. Another picture showed the young boy in the hospital cafeteria. The banner in the back had science fair scrawled across it in big block letters. From his vision, Dimitri stared back at him.

The story explained how sick her son was and how working at the hospital had been a blessing for her. She had cut her hair in solidarity, so both had shaved heads. She could spend time with her son and still maintain the job that helped pay his bills.

Anastasia talked about how not all parents were as lucky as she was. She and her family immigrated from Russia after her father died and her mother later remarried. They had a lot of businesses, so Anastasia had support that other parents didn't have. Plus, her job at the hospital allowed her to work and see her son.

Anastasia had been working with parents to start a foundation that would help other parents in the Phoenix area with bills and critical needs while their children received treatment. She explained how her son's passion for butterflies had given her the name of the foundation. Metamorphosis.

Derek dug through the file. He searched the list of names Kyle had gathered. Anastasia Parker and Patrick Weatherby were on his list of canceled weddings. Scanning through the list Felicia had worked on. He found Anastasia's name on the page for canceled venues.

His mind raced. He needed to get them to act on her name, but how the hell would he explain the way he knows beyond any doubt that this was their killer? He fumbled through the papers and found the list of workers at tag agencies. Her name wasn't on this list.

He knew George and Michael were still working on it. That meant there was a big possibility that they could still find her name. Derek knew from the visions that Anastasia would target Patrick and Lucy. Whether that was her end game when she started, this was her end game now.

He remembered the list of tag agency owners. Derek searched the file on the tray. When he found it, he saw one name. Jeffrey Parker. He searched the internet for everything he could find on Anastasia's family. "Hot damn." Derek slapped the tray with his hand. Jeffrey Parker was Anastasia's stepfather. And that explained how Anastasia got the plates.

Derek laid his head back. He thought of how he could manipulate the information. He snapped his fingers and searched the names on Kyle's list that he hadn't gone through yet. He matched them with five other women that had canceled weddings.

"Okay. This could work." He mulled around the way he could approach this. He grabbed the list from George and Michael. None of the names matched theirs. "That could benefit me more. This idea might work."

Derek scribbled a few notes on a blank piece of paper. He wrote all the other names down and then wrote Anastasia's at the end of the list. This was going to work. Sliding her name in with the few he found, would allow for someone else to find the information about Patrick and

Lucy.

Catherine walked in. "How was your breakfast?"

"Good. Thank you."

"I need to get one more set of vitals. The doctor is on the floor and he should come in shortly." She placed the blood pressure cuff around his arm. As the machine ran through its steps, the nurse's brow wrinkled. "Your blood pressure is a little high."

Derek laughed. "Oh, I talked to my friend, Dr. Chelsea, this morning. I was excited about some news he told me. I bet that is making it fluctuate."

"That may be. It isn't high enough to worry about. Just different from what it has been these last twenty-four hours." The nurse finished up when the doctor walked in.

"Good morning, Agent Reed." He lifted the chart from the end of the bed. "How are you feeling?"

"Great. I am hoping you will let me go home."

"I will let you go, as long as you go home and not to work. You should have one more day of rest. And since it's Friday, that will give you maybe three days to recuperate." The doctor placed the chart back on the hook at the foot of the bed.

"I can agree with that," Derek said.

The doctor squinted at him. "I'm not sure I can believe you."

Derek held up his fingers. "Scout's honor."

"Were you actually a scout?" the doctor asked.

Derek laughed. "No. But if the Nurse Catherine tells Dr. Chelsea when he picks me up, he will make sure I don't do anything. He is a nag."

The doctor turned towards the nurse. "Make sure you tell him when he shows up."

She grinned. "Yes. Doctor."

"Okay. You can leave as soon as your ride gets here." He left the room.

The nurse lifted the food tray. "I will draw up the discharge paperwork. Call your ride. Have you peed yet on your own?"

"No, but I have to."

"There is a cup in the toilet. Urinate in that so I can see you did it."

"I will. First, I will call my ride." Derek dialed Ronald's number.

"I'm rearranging my schedule. Are you being discharged?"

"Yeah. Take your time. Well, not really. Get here as quick as you can."

"I'm working on it."

The line went dead. Derek sat on the side of his bed. His feet rested on the floor. He removed the yellow socks and stood, making sure he had his balance before he walked to the bathroom. He steadied himself as he filled the bowl like thing in the toilet.

Once his legs were stable, and he was sure he wouldn't fall over, he made his way to the shower. He found a toothbrush, toothpaste, shampoo, and conditioner. Waiting for the water to get hot, he pulled off the gown and stepped in. The hot water felt fantastic.

Standing under the pelting drops, he thought about the next moves in this case. There was no way he was ready to let his team in on his ability. Curse was a better word. Derek turned off the water and grabbed a towel hanging from the hook. Brushing his teeth, he stepped out into the room with a towel wrapped around his waist.

Catherine walked in. "Oh, I'm sorry."

Derek waved her off. "You pulled a tube out of my dick. Nothing to be embarrassed about now."

She hid her smile. "I've never had anyone say it quite like that."

"Should I have asked to take a shower?"

"No. You're fine." She pointed to the bag on the sofa. "That has your clothes."

Derek spun around. "Oh. I was wondering where they were." He walked to the small sofa. Looking through his things, he pulled out his jeans and underwear.

"I thought FBI agents had to wear suits." Nurse Catherine grabbed his wet towels and placed them in the dirty linen bags.

"I run a special unit. It's more laid back than most offices." He frowned at her. "To the dismay of my boss, I have never worn a suit. I don't even own one." He pulled his underwear up under his towel, and then did the same with his jeans. Once on, he removed the towel and draped it over a chair.

She scribbled on a piece of paper and handed it to him. "If you ever want to go out for dinner."

He took her number and stuck in it the front pocket of his jeans. "I just might take you up on that offer."

"I hope you do," she said as she left the room.

Derek checked his phone. Still no message from Lizzy. "This isn't like her." Putting on his shirt, he pushed the worry out of his mind. Right now, he had to stop a killer.

CHAPTER THIRTY-EIGHT

Friday 1 p.m.

Derek sat in the front passenger seat of Dr. Chelsea's car. "Thank you for picking me up."

"Promise me you won't stay at the office the entire day." Dr. Chelsea stopped at a light.

"I promise. I have to pick up Lola and my car. I need to show them the names I want them to look at. This will give me the perfect cover. See, I'm going to take it easy and let them find the connection."

Dr. Chelsea looked over at him. "What are you going to do? Can't you just arrest her?"

"We have a few steps before we can do that. However, we can question her. We can put heat on her. That will more than likely get her to make a mistake." Derek shifted in the seat. "It could also let her know we are onto her and she stops all together and goes underground. And that would suck."

"You can't let her kill this couple."

Derek stared out the side window. "I don't think she wants to kill the couple."

"I don't understand," Dr. Chelsea said.

"I think she wants to hurt Patrick. And the best way to hurt him would be to kill his wife and the baby. Then he would have to live with the pain of losing the child he had tried for years to have." Derek looked at his friend. "That would be the best way to hurt him."

Dr. Chelsea pulled into the Legacy Unit parking lot. "That makes sense." He parked and turned towards Derek. "I can't believe we are so close to closing this case. I've carried it with me all this time."

"I know that feeling. I know what this means to you. You need to not do anything on your own, Ronald."

"I would never do anything to jeopardize this. I promise you." Tears filled his eyes.

"Ronald, I know you never would. I'll call when I get home. You can come over and I will tell you everything we find out."

"I would like that. Call me later. I'll bring dinner."

"Chinese. Bring Chinese." Derek exited the car. He watched as his good friend drove away. Placing his thumb on the scanner, he stepped into the building.

Emma jumped up and greeted him at the door, and hugged him. "How are you feeling?"

Before he could answer, Lola ran out from the kitchen, followed by Marc Anthony.

Derek braced himself as the chocolate boxer barreled towards him. "Hey girl," he laughed as she wiggled against him. He scratched her ears and rubbed her back.

Marc Anthony wanted to get in on the action. He nudged him with his head and whimpered when he neglected to pet him.

"I love you, too." Derek scratched his back and let him give him a big dog kiss.

Everyone had followed the dogs over.

Felicia hugged him. "I'm so glad it was nothing serious."

"Seeing you on the floor at the foot of the steps was something I don't want to see again," Kelly said.

Michael took his bag from him. "Let me get that for you."

"I'm not dying," Derek said, following him to his desk.

Michael put his satchel down. "I know. But I bet you aren't supposed to be doing anything but resting, right?"

"Aren't you supposed to be at home?" George asked.

Derek sat in his chair. "Yes. But we need to go over something. Did you guys find any more names?"

Felicia sat at her desk. "We were just about to go through all the names."

"That's what we need to talk about. Someone needs to get Kyle for me. After this briefing, I will head home." Derek pulled the file from his bag.

Kelly headed towards the kitchen.

Derek could hear her call out to Kyle.

When she came back in, she brought a soda for him. "Here."

"Thank you. How'd you know?"

"I didn't. I just assumed." Kelly moved to hug him, but patted his shoulder instead. "I'm glad you're okay."

Derek bit his upper lip, hiding his smile.

Kyle walked in from the kitchen, munching on some chips. "Boss man, how you feeling? How's your head?"

"It's okay. A little sore."

"If you keep hitting it, you may end up permanently damaged. Maybe you need one of those cranial helmets." Kyle laughed at the evil stare.

Derek sat in his chair. "I want to go over something with you guys." He opened the file. "I found a few names this morning."

Everyone took seats.

"I went through the names in the files. I started with matching Kyle's list to Felicia's and Kelly's." Derek stood at the whiteboard. He spun it to the side with the aerial photos and removed those. Then wrote the six names he found on the two lists. He put Anastasia's name in the middle of the others. "I have not found these names on the list that George and Michael are working on. Is your list complete?" Derek asked.

George leaned back in his chair. "I think we have it as close to finished as we may get it."

"Have you added any names since you gave me this list last night?" Derek asked.

"A few more," George said.

"Go through those and see if you can find these names. I'm not too worried about not having the names on all the lists. There could be many reasons her name isn't coming up via the tag agencies." Derek took a sip of his soda. "Check the list of owners of the tag agency as well. Maybe a relative owned the agency. This could be how our killer got the plates."

"We have several tag agencies that want us to get a warrant," Michael said.

"Let's hold off. I don't want to do that until we have to. I want us to search these names. Find out everything you can about each woman. Maybe we can figure out whom one of these women was supposed to marry," Derek said.

He turned to face Kyle. "I know I ask so much of you, but could you focus on these six names? Gather everything you can on each. And give the information to these guys and me. See if you can find out about their families. This way you can see if a relative may have owned the agency."

"Absolutely. I can have the searches done pretty fast. How long are you going to stay here?" Kyle asked.

"I promised the doctor I wouldn't overdo it. That is the reason he let me go home today," Derek said.

"Then you need to gather your stuff and get home," George said. "I can make sure we go through these names. How about if I come over later and give you our results? We can come up with a game plan and how we need to move forward if one of these women is our killer."

"Why don't we plan on meeting here tomorrow as well?" Kelly asked.

"Yeah. We should do that." Michael looked at the other agents and said, "we can't let this killer get any further ahead of us."

"We need to be here. What time?" Kelly asked.

"How about 9 a.m.?" Derek asked.

"Perfect." Kyle stood. "I'll run the names."

"Emma," Derek called out. "You don't need to be here tomorrow."

"Thank you. I appreciate that," she said.

Derek stood and placed the file in his bag. "I will call the director on the drive home. George, when will you be over?"

"Let's say 6 p.m."

"Okay. I'll bring donuts in the morning." Derek reached into his desk drawer and retrieved his gun. He wasn't wearing it when he fell down the stairs. Clipping it to his jeans, he stopped. "I appreciate you guys. I know this isn't a nine-to-five job. But I know we have been pretty lucky to have nights and weekends off."

George stood. "This is the best unit I have ever worked for. I sure as hell don't mind putting in long hours."

Derek smiled at his crew. "Thank you. George, I'll see you tonight." He whistled for Lola as he walked towards the door. Stopping at Emma's desk, he scratched Marc Anthony's head. "Emma, can you update all the files on the network? This way, I can go through the files while I'm at home."

"No problem at all, Derek." She typed out a few commands on her computer. "I will make sure the crew updates their files."

"Thank you. You are the best." Derek held the door, waiting for Lola. He watched as she gave Marc Anthony a dog smooch. "Lola, let's go."

She sulked out to the car.

"When we get home, we will take a nap on the sofa. Okay?" Derek rubbed her head.

Lola sighed as she curled up in the front seat.

Derek put his bag in the backseat, then dialed the director. His phone connected to the speakerphone.

"Derek, how are you feeling?"

"I'm doing better. I promised the doctor and Dr. Chelsea that I wouldn't overdo it this afternoon. I'm on my way home now."

"That's good. What's going on with the case?"

"We have six names. We are running them now."

"You're kidding me?"

"No sir. Six women. Kyle is running searches on them now. George will bring everything he finds to me this evening. We are going to come up with the best way to proceed."

"Whatever you need from me. If you need search warrants, you just let me know. I know the Bureau will do whatever they can to stop this killer."

Derek turned onto his street. "I will keep you posted. We are going to be at the office in the morning. If I need a warrant, I will call you then."

"Okay. Judge Reinhold will be more than willing to give us what we need."

"Even on a weekend?"

"Of course. I'm playing golf with him tomorrow morning. If I let him win, he would give me a search warrant for his own mother's house."

Derek laughed as the line fell silent. Pulling into his garage, he received a text. He grabbed his bag as Lola jumped out of the car. When he unlocked the door from the garage to the house and pushed it open, Lola ran past Derek. He heard the doggie door open as she headed for the backyard. After he placed his bag on the kitchen counter, he checked the text message.

We need to talk.

Lizzy. Derek's heart thudded against his chest. His gut told him this would not be good news.

Phone or in person?

In person would be great. Can I come over?

Of course, Lizzy. I'm home. Come now.

I'll be there shortly.

Derek placed the palms of his hands on the counter. He rocked in place. "This can't be good." He glanced at his watch. Walking to the sofa, he stopped and watched Lola play in the yard.

That stupid dog had become an important part of his life. Not just his connection to Lizzy when she wasn't around. Lola meant way more to him. Derek had a sinking feeling in his stomach. A wave of nausea rolled over him.

"I can't deal with this now," he said as he walked towards the sliding glass door. He fidgeted with his watch, glancing at the face. He jumped when the doorbell rang.

Lola ran through the doggie door, beating him to the door.

He opened it to find Lizzy standing there. Her long hair cascaded over her shoulders. "Hi."

"Hi." She kneeled down and gave Lola hugs and kisses. "How's my girl?" She rubbed her belly when she laid on her back. "I missed you."

Lola whined and gave her a wet kiss.

Lizzy stood and wrapped her arms around Derek. "I missed you."

"When did you get back?"

"Two days ago. I needed some time." She walked to the living room, as Lola ran out the doggie door. "She loves it here, doesn't she?"

"I think she would love being wherever you are."

"No. The moment she met you, I think she became your dog. It just took me a few years to realize that." Lizzy wrapped her arms around her waist. She turned to face Derek. "You know how much I love you, right?"

"I know you think you love me. I know on some levels you may feel obligated to love me." Derek sat on the coffee table. "Why are you here, Lizzy? Why did you get back two days ago but didn't bother to call or return any of my texts?"

Lizzy sat on the chair across from him. "Jackson asked me to move in with him."

"Are you going to?"

"Yes. I think so."

"That's great, Lizzy. If he makes you happy. That's all that matters to me." Derek stared at her. He saw the pain in her eyes. "It's okay, Lizzy. I understand."

Tears crested over. They rolled down her cheek. She wiped her face. "I want to stop what I'm doing. I think it's time. I don't want to be everyone's girl."

Derek stood and moved towards the glass door. "You don't need him to stop. He just makes it easier to do."

She wrung her hands in her lap. "That's a fair statement. He does make it easy. Am I so wrong for wanting easy?"

Derek turned around. "Not at all. I want you happy." He turned back to the glass. "I'm sure Lola will love his estate."

"I was hoping you could keep her. She loves it here. You take her to work with you and she needs someone who can give her the attention she needs." Lizzy stood. She moved to stand next to him.

"If that's what you want. I would love to keep her. I have fallen in love with her." He chuckled. "It's kind of hard not to."

"I'm sorry Derek. I know you wanted us to be more of a couple. I thought it might work. But I don't fit into your world."

"My simple world." He turned towards her. He wiped the moisture from her face. "I know I don't run in the circles you are used to. That's okay. You want more than I can ever give you."

Lizzy took his hand and kissed the palm.

He slid his hand behind her neck and pulled her close to him. He wrapped his arms around her. "I love you, Elizabeth. I will love you until the day I die."

She clung to him. Burying her face in his shirt. "I'm so sorry."

"Shh. You have nothing to be sorry for. Nothing at all." He lifted her chin. "I need you to know something. If you ever need me. I don't care why. You call me."

"I know I can always call you."

"No. You don't understand. If you ever feel threatened or scared. If someone ever comes after you, you need to call me."

"Derek. No one is going to come after me. Jackson is a congressman. Not the mafia."

"Just remember what I have said. Okay? Promise me?"

She looked up at him. His eyes narrowed on her. A darkness filled them. "I promise. I swear." She stepped back. "I don't want Lola to see me leave. I'm going to sneak away. I'll bring her bed and other toys from my condo and leave them on the porch."

"Okay." Derek followed her to the door.

Lizzy turned around. She took his hand in hers and placed the key to his front door in it. "I can never thank you enough for what you did for me all those years ago."

"I didn't do anything special."

"You did. I got my life back. You helped me get out of that world and that brought me here." She reached out for the door. "You are a good man, Derek. And I love you. I will always love you."

He watched her leave. Staying in the open doorway until he no longer saw her car. He slowly closed the door. Sitting on the sofa, his head rested in his hands. He squeezed his eyes shut. But the tears snuck out.

His heart broke into a million pieces. He'd never felt this type of pain before. He'd done a good job of shielding himself from letting his heart get to this point. A tingle ran down his spine. He took a deep breath. "Not now."

Chrissy sat in the high-back chair. "I'm sorry. I never thought she would do that."

"I wish I could say I thought the same thing. But I'd be lying to myself if I said that."

Lola ran through the doggie door. She ran through the house, looking for her Lizzy. She came back to the living room and stared at the chair.

Chrissy reached out to pet her. "She'll be happy with you."

Derek snapped his fingers to get the dog's attention. "I hope so." When the dog came to him, he pulled her close to his body. He rubbed her ears and kissed her nose. "How do you feel about living with me, huh, girl?"

She wiggled her butt and snuggled up against him.

"She's going to be fine, you know? Lola deserves to be with you. Besides, she sees the dead too. You were meant to be together. You need each other."

Derek leaned back against the sofa. He scratched Lola's belly. "I need her." He raised his eyebrows, glancing at Chrissy. "Lola. I'm talking about Lola."

Chrissy giggled. "You're going to be okay, Derek. I know that." She fiddled with the hem of her dress. "You know who the killer is."

"Yeah. I feel bad, I tricked my crew. I didn't tell them I know the name. I made it so they would figure it out."

"That's not the worst thing you could do. Don't you think it would be easier to tell them?"

"No. Are you crazy?" Derek laid his head back. "That's all I need. It's bad enough Dr. Chelsea knows." His brow furrowed. "It's not like I can conjure up the images. Or that I can figure out the lottery numbers. Half the time, the visions make little sense." He sighed. "Sometimes they are so fucking real I can't take it. I know they are visions, and not happening to me. But shit, they are so vivid."

"This is your calling. It's your job to speak for the dead. You're their last hope to not be forgotten. You're their last hope to be released from the binds that keep them tethered to the living." Chrissy's eyes filled with tears. "You're their only hope."

Derek's breath hitched. "I wish I could've stopped him from killing you. You don't deserve this."

"It's not your fault. You'll realize that at some point." Chrissy stood. "I need to go. You need to rest."

Derek's eyes were heavy. "Chrissy, where do you go?"

"Nowhere. I can't leave yet. I see others go. But I can't go yet."

"Is that my fault? Am I keeping you here?"

"You're part of it. But there is something else keeping me here. It has to do with you. However, it's not because of you or anything you've done."

"Can you tell me what it is?"

"I have no clue. I just know I have to stay. I have to be here for you." She stood. "I'll be around."

He watched her vanish. His eyelids felt heavy. He shifted his body. Stretching out on the sofa.

Lola laid half on him and half on the sofa.

He draped his arm over her. His breathing slowed as he let go of all the pain and the anger. Lizzy came into his life and made it all the better. He would cling to that until he couldn't.

CHAPTER THIRTY-NINE

6 p.m. Friday evening

Derek opened the door. "Hey, Ronald."

Dr. Chelsea shut the door behind him. "What's the matter?" he asked, following Derek into the kitchen.

"I don't want to talk about it right now." Derek turned around. "It involves Lizzy."

"Say no more. When and if you need to talk, I'm here."

"Thank you." Derek unpacked the food. "I forgot to tell you George was bringing the results of the searches on the names." Raising an eyebrow, he smirked. "I think you have enough food."

Dr. Chelsea laughed. "You can never have too much Chinese food."

The doorbell rang. "That's George." Walking to the door, Lola ran past him. "Seriously dog, do not trip me again." Pulling open the door, he stepped back. "Hey George. Dr. Chelsea is here too. I hope you are hungry."

"I'm always hungry. I brought beer." He raised the twelve pack.

"Nice." Derek closed the door. "I'm guessing you're staying here?"

George lifted a bag. "Yup."

Derek laughed. "Good man."

They walked into the kitchen.

Ronald had emptied all the cartons onto plates. Glancing up, he motioned for the men to join him. "Let's eat."

Derek grabbed two beers, the half empty bottle of wine he had in the refrigerator, and a wine glass.

George put the other beers in the fridge after grabbing two more for the table.

"I got us all some bottles of water too," Dr. Chelsea said.

As they loaded up their plates, Lola sat at Derek's feet. "I forgot to feed you, didn't I?"

Lola ran to the cupboard.

Derek filled her bowl and then sat back down.

They all ate in silence for a few moments.

George moaned. "Why is this tasting so good?"

"I know. I must have been craving Chinese food and didn't realize it." Derek chomped on an egg roll.

"This place has the best egg rolls. I got a dozen," Dr. Chelsea said, dipping his into some sweet and sour sauce.

Derek turned to George. "What did you guys come up with after I left?"

George took a pull of his beer. He rose and walked to the kitchen counter, where he left his bag. Digging through it, he pulled out the folder. "Out of the six names, two rescheduled their weddings for later dates."

"I think we can set them aside for now." Derek drank some water.

"I do too. That leaves us with four." George pulled the top woman's sheet, handing it to Derek. "Lorna Thomas. She had some issues after the cancellation of her wedding." George continued to eat, letting Derek read the sheet.

Ronald leaned into Derek so he could read over his shoulder. "I'd say she had some issues. She had a psychotic break."

Derek read through the report that Kyle found. "I don't even want to know how Kyle got this report."

"Public record. She went to trial for beating the shit out of her ex-fiancé. Lorna did a number on his truck and his body." George pointed to something lower down on the paper. "She spent two years in a psych ward. He refused to press charges and ended up being a witness for the defense. Looks like he blamed himself." George laughed.

Dr. Chelsea raised an eyebrow. "What is so funny?"

"His new wife, mind you, this isn't the woman he dumped Lorna for. His new wife, was the nurse that watched over Lorna at the hospital." George shook his head. "Some men are idiots."

"That's extremely suspect," Dr. Chelsea said.

"Not against the rules. They met during Lorna's stay, but they didn't actually get together until a year after they discharged Lorna." George poured some of the sweet and sour sauce on his plate as he took another egg roll from the platter.

Derek scanned the next few pages of information on Lorna. "Do you think she is a viable suspect?"

George shrugged. He took a sip of beer before he answered. "Not sure. She showed no other anger towards random people. Just the boyfriend. She left the hospital and has maintained a steady job."

"I think we should interview her. Tomorrow, we can call her and two people can go see her." Derek finished the first beer. He poured the last of the wine into Dr. Chelsea's glass. "I think I have another bottle in the fridge."

Ronald waved him off. "I don't want any more. Thank you." He lifted his bottle of water. "This will do."

George handed Derek another few sheets of paper. "This is a very viable suspect. Her name is Sarah Bancroft. This lady was dumped at the altar. He bailed at the I-dos. And I mean, when the preacher said do you take, he said no and ran out."

Derek smirked. "That would make me furious and out for blood if I was a girl."

Ronald took the sheets from him. "Let me look." He read through her information. "For someone left at the altar, she didn't retaliate with violence." He handed the papers back to Derek. "She stole his money."

Derek set them down on the table. His concentration wasn't there. Lizzy kept popping into his thoughts. "Tell me what you think," he said to George.

"None of these four women, except for Lorna, had any violent tendencies. However, they all had the means to do this. They were all rejected on one of the most important days of their lives," George pointed to Sarah's information.

"Sarah, never married. She dropped out of college but later went to nursing school. She would have the skill." George took the paper and set it aside. He ate a few bites of food.

Opening the file, he removed the third woman. He sat back and read the file to refresh his memory. "This is Anastasia Parker."

Derek maintained a stoic expression. He snuck a peek at Ronald. His friend didn't bat an eye at the name. "Tell me about her."

"She didn't work at a tag agency. However, her stepfather owned one. She had every opportunity to take the license plates. This skyrockets her to the top of my list. Her work history shows she started working at a hospital. But that didn't happen until two years later."

"What did she do in the meantime?" Dr. Chelsea asked.

George faced the doctor. "Nothing that we could find. There is no work history until the hospital. She lived with her mother and stepfather. Her mother brought the family over after their father died. They are Russian immigrants. She met the stepfather here and remarried. They had several major businesses, including the tag agency. I doubt Anastasia had to work."

"Do you know why the wedding was canceled?" Derek asked. He popped the top on another beer.

Dr. Chelsea finished what was on his plate. He drank the last of his wine and sat back. Catching Derek's eyes, he quickly pointed to the food. "Do you want any more?"

Derek patted his stomach. "I think I'm stuffed."

"You two keep talking. I will put up the food." Dr. Chelsea gathered the dishes and listened while he shuffled around the table.

George finished his egg roll and pushed his plate to the side. "Dr. Chelsea, that was nice. I will treat next time. Thank you."

"I'm glad to do it. I would just be sitting at home alone. It's nice to eat dinner with friends," he said as he finished cleaning up.

Continuing, George read Anastasia's information. "The fiancé canceled this wedding. Patrick Weatherby. He didn't wait until the last minute, though. He did it months in advance."

"Do you know why?"

"It seems he fell in love with his now wife, Lucy Weatherby. Formerly Lucy Wilcox." George opened another beer. He shuffled through a few pages. "When Patrick canceled the wedding, Anastasia disappeared."

"Until she resurfaced at the hospital?" Derek asked.

"Yes." George placed his forearms on the table. "There is one thing. Anastasia had a baby."

Derek sat back. "A baby?"

"Yes." George sipped on his beer. "There is no evidence that the baby was Patrick's. Nothing legally anyway. And Anastasia could have had a fling after the breakup and got pregnant."

"Why does Patrick's name sound so familiar to me?"

"He has a rather large and profitable advertising agency. Here is the sad part, and why she is at the top of my list. Her son had a rare leukemia. He became sick. During this time, Anastasia started a foundation. Get this, called Metamorphosis."

Derek frowned. "Why is that so important?"

"When a caterpillar turns into a butterfly, it is called metamorphosis." George chugged the last of his open beer. He walked to the refrigerator and grabbed another one. "You want a beer?"

"Yes, please."

Derek feigned surprise. "Holy shit. I know why his name is so familiar to me." He took the beer and popped the top. "In the hospital this morning, while I was eating breakfast, there was a news report on him and his wife." He pulled his phone from his pocket. "Here. They are doing IVF and they talked about the procedure. This is their first kid."

George's beer stopped short of his lips. "Come again?"

"What?"

"You said her ex-fiancé is having a baby with the woman he left Anastasia for? And they were just on the news?"

Derek's face slacked as his shoulders slumped forward. "Oh, shit." He dragged a hand down his face. "Are you thinking what I'm thinking?"

Dr. Chelsea came around from the kitchen. He stood between the two men. "I think if she is the killer, this will push her over the edge."

"Maybe she doesn't know." Derek looked at George and Ronald.

George searched his phone. "She had to see it. I'm looking at every major news channel. This couple made the rounds on most of the morning shows locally and," he held out his phone. "They were on one nationally syndicated show."

"Fuck." Derek stared at Dr. Chelsea.

The doctor came around the table and sat down.

"Are you okay, Ronald?" Derek asked, squeezing the man's shoulder.

"I am. Can you go arrest her?" he asked the two men.

George shook his head. "We can't arrest her. But I think with this connection, we should break up into two teams. Let Kelly and Michael handle the other women. And you, me, and Felicia can handle Anastasia."

Derek didn't want to waste time on the other women. He knew Anastasia was the killer. Beyond any doubt. And on the off chance he was wrong, then they could come back to the others. "No. I have a better idea."

George drank his beer. "Yeah? What is it?"

Dr. Chelsea leaned in closer to Derek. "What is it, Derek?"

"I think it's time for an undercover sting."

CHAPTER FORTY

Lucy padded through the house on her bare feet. The baby had been active most of the day. Her due date was just under three weeks away. She placed her hand on her belly. "Calm down, young child."

"Who are you talking to?" Patrick asked, stepping into the living room.

"Your child. I'm almost sure this is a boy. Girl or boy, he or she is kicking the hell out of my ribs."

Patrick leaned down and placed his mouth next to her belly. "Listen, child of mine, this is your dad. Stop kicking your mother." He stood up. "How's that?"

She lifted her chin to one side, waiting. "I think it might... oops no, it did nothing."

"Is this any sign of whether our child will listen to me?"

"If he or she is anything like you, they won't listen to you." She sat next to him on the sofa. Their phone had been ringing all day after they did the interview rounds. This was the first time it sat silent.

"I never thought people would be so interested in our journey with IVF," Patrick said, pulling her into the crux of his arm.

Lucy snuggled in. "With all that is happening with Roe v Wade, this is another part of the hot topic. I hope this cause isn't overshadowed by the political aspect."

"Let's not worry about that tonight." Patrick turned on the TV.

"You're going to watch the Friday night game, aren't you?"

He laughed. "I can watch anything you want."

"How about a scary movie?"

Patrick was about to push for something else when the phone rang.

"I'll get this one, then we are unplugging it." She reached behind them and lifted the house phone from the cradle. "Hello?"

"Hello, is this Mrs. Lucy Weatherby?"

"Yes, it is."

"Hi, I'm Angelica Carter, I work for the Phoenix Woman's Coalition. We would love to interview you for our podcast. We here at PWC were so moved by your interviews on TV. Many of the women we work with don't have access to these kinds of services. We are hoping you might bring some much-needed attention to them and their needs."

"I would love to. When did you want to do this?"

"I would love it if I could come tomorrow."

"I'm sorry. The earliest I could do anything would be, hang on," she covered the mouthpiece. She poked her husband. "Are we doing anything on Sunday?"

Patrick shook his head. "No, but don't make it too early."

She went back to the phone. "The earliest I could do something would be Sunday evening. Around 4 p.m."

"That would be great. Is your address 1425 North Woodland Drive?"

"Yes, it is."

"I will be there at 4 p.m. With my crew. How far along are you?"

"I have about three weeks to go."

"Are you having a boy or girl?"

"We chose not to find out."

"How wonderful. You must be so excited. Your husband must be very excited as well. I know his first engagement didn't end so well, so this must really be a blessing."

"What do you mean?"

"Oh, please forgive me. I had to do some research so my boss would sign off on the podcast and I saw an interview he did regarding his first engagement."

Lucy bit her bottom lip. "I see."

"I will be there around 4 p.m. I can't thank you enough. See you Sunday."

Lucy sighed. "That was the women's coalition. They work with underprivileged women."

"I think that should be the last interview for a while." Patrick rubbed her belly. "I don't want you stressing over things like this. After the baby is born, sure. Do as many as you want."

Lucy kissed his lips. "This is why I love you."

CHAPTER FORTY-ONE

Derek and George moved to the sofa after Dr. Chelsea left.

"I think this case overwhelmed him. He has been waiting ten-plus years to put those murders to rest." George was on his fifth beer. He stretched out on the sofa and watched the Friday night college football game.

Derek sat at the other end of the sofa. He propped his legs up on the coffee table. Lola sat at his side. "I am still full."

George laughed. "Me too. How long is Lola going to be staying with you?"

Derek's body tensed. He didn't want to talk about this. He also had enough lies and deceit for one day. "Forever."

George sat up. "Is Lizzy moving in with you?"

Derek saw the glint of excitement in his eyes. "No. She is moving in with Congressman Jackson."

George sat up. His legs swung over the edge. "Hold that thought." He jogged to the kitchen and grabbed four more beers. When he sat back down, he lowered the sound on the television. "Explain," he said as he set the beers on the table.

Derek sat up. Opening one beer, he took a long gulp. "I had been texting and calling her the last few days. She had been ignoring me. She came over earlier today. Told me the congressman asked her to move in."

"What did you say?"

"What the hell am I going to say? No? I told her I wanted her to be happy."

George pointed to Lola. "She didn't want her?"

"She knew how much I loved Lola. Lizzy gave her to me so I wouldn't lose my shit because she was going to live with asshole number one." Derek scratched the dog's ears. "This dog and I have a weird bond. This was the best thing Lizzy could have done for me."

"Well shit. Are you okay? I mean, really, okay?" George ogled his friend's face. "Don't lie to me either."

A faint smile tugged at Derek's mouth. "I will be. I've known Lizzy for a very long time. She doesn't owe me anything. Do I love her? Yes.

Ever since the day I met her. But I can't give her what she wants. My life is too simple."

"I'm sorry, Derek." George looked around. "You got any cards?"

Derek flinched back. "What?"

"Cards. A deck of cards?"

Derek laughed. "Yeah, in the drawer there." He pointed towards the television stand.

"Let's play while we hash out this undercover sting." George grabbed the deck and shuffled. "Rummy?"

"Yeah. That sounds good." Derek repositioned himself. "I'm a badass player. You ready to lose?"

"Fuck you, buddy. I'm about to wipe the floor with you." George dealt the cards. "Okay, how are we approaching this?"

Derek arranged his cards. "We need to contact Patrick and Lucy Weatherby. We need to see if Anastasia has contacted them."

"You think she will contact them?"

"Not sure. But I bet within the next day or two she will try to either contact them or get into their house."

"Are we going to camp out on their porch?" George laid down two sets. "Gin."

"Shit. You cheated."

George's laughter filled the room. "Okay. Sore loser."

This time, Derek dealt the cards. "Tomorrow, I want to call the director when we are all together. I think we need to go to the Weatherby's home and tell them what we know."

"We don't have actual proof." George drew from the deck. He discarded and rearranged his hand.

"If you go out again, I will shoot you where you sit."

"Whoa, you are a violent man."

Derek laughed. He finished his beer and opened another. "We're not going to want to get up in the morning."

"Nope."

"I think in the morning, we go there to see them. We call the director from there if we need to. We explain what we know and what we believe."

George laid down his cards. "Gin."

"You motherfucker." Derek threw his cards on the table.

George laid back laughing. "I told you I was going to wipe your ass."

"You cheat. Man, I know you are cheating."

George dealt again. "What if Anastasia doesn't show on her own?"

Derek shuffled his cards around and then drew from the deck. He looked at George and wiggled his eyebrows. "Gin."

"Crap." He added up the points. "You are within striking distance." George shuffled the cards but didn't deal. "What if she doesn't show on her own?"

Derek sighed. He finished his beer.

Lola jumped down and ran out the doggie door.

"Then we make her come to us." Derek smiled at his agent.

"And you think you can do that?"

"I do." Derek looked over his shoulder and watched Lola run around the yard.

"How do you plan on making her come to us?"

Derek turned to face George. "We dangle the carrot."

"What's the carrot?"

Derek stood. He picked up the empty beer cans. A salacious smile spread across his face. "We use the one thing she wants more than anything to hurt Patrick"

"And that is?" George asked.

"We give her the opportunity to be alone with the mother and baby."

CHAPTER FORTY-TWO

8:00 a.m. Saturday morning

Derek left George in the shower to go get donuts for the team. Lola sat in the car beside him. For the first time, he felt like he might have the upper hand. He parked in front of the donut shop, ran in, and picked up his order.

Once he was back in the car, he called the director. He explained his plan and got the go-ahead to tell the Weatherbys about the case.

"Are you sure this Anastasia is the killer?"

"Yes. I would bet my career on it."

"If you are wrong, you won't have a career."

"I'm willing to risk it. Normally, I wouldn't focus on the obvious. But it fits. It fits too perfectly to not be the right choice."

The director growled into the phone.

"Did you just growl?"

"Shit. If you're wrong, not only will you not have a career, you, me, and your team will be looking for new jobs."

Derek laughed.

"I don't think this is funny, Derek."

"We could always start our own detective agency." Derek broke out in a howl.

"What the fuck is wrong with you?" The director tried not to laugh.

Derek laughed so hard he couldn't see the road. "Wait, stop." He continued to laugh. "I have the perfect name too." Derek thought he might pee. "We can call ourselves Fretz's Follies."

"You're a fucking idiot." The director laughed. "Shit. I don't know why, but I trust you."

Derek wiped his face. "Damn. That felt good. It's been a shit week."

"I heard about Lizzy."

"Crap. How did you hear about that?" Derek gripped the steering wheel, his knuckles turned white.

"It's kind of a big deal. Congressman moves in with his mistress, who was a former call girl."

"Damn. I hate that for her. That's not what she is."

"Look, you can't control what others think. Most everyone respects Lizzy. She is well liked and Congressman Jackson will keep her protected. At least from rumors. I'm just sorry you're getting the shit end of the stick."

"It is what it is." Derek glanced over at Lola. "I got Lola. That makes it easier."

"Okay. Set up the plan, then go see the Weatherby's. If I need to be there, I can." The director paused. "Derek?"

"Yeah?"

"I am sorry. I'm here for you. Whenever you need me. I know the Pink Diamond case has you worried about Lizzy and her safety. Just know I will do whatever we need to in order to keep her out of danger."

"I appreciate that. I'll keep you in the loop. Fretz's Follies signing out." Derek hung up before he could hear the director curse him out. As he pulled into the parking lot of the Legacy Unit, Derek pushed down the fear Lizzy was getting involved in something he couldn't protect her from.

The one thing Derek knew for sure, if anything happened to Lizzy, because of the congressman, they would never find the asshole's body. Ever.

CHAPTER FORTY-THREE

Lola rushed in first, and checked every nook and cranny.

"It's Saturday. He won't be here." Derek set the donuts on the table against the wall. He walked into the kitchen and started making coffee. George and he had worked out a fairly good plan of attack, and the director gave the go ahead.

"Only a million things could go wrong." Derek leaned against the counter. The aroma of the coffee lifted his mood. Not as hung over as he thought he would be, he still couldn't wait to get a cup.

When the coffee maker beeped, he poured the hot liquid into the carafe and started on the next pot. Opening the refrigerator, he grabbed a soda pop. From the cabinet, he picked up several coffee mugs and walked to the front office. He set the mugs next to the donuts and the soda on his desk.

Back in the kitchen, the second pot of coffee was complete. He poured it into the carafe and sealed the cover. There were still a ton of paper plates. He grabbed a handful and a bunch of napkins and headed into the main office.

The front door opened up. George walked in with Felicia and Kelly.

"I need coffee," George said, following Derek to the table.

"How did you sleep?" Derek asked

"We will discuss that later."

Derek raised an eyebrow. "I don't think I like the sound of that."

George patted his back. "It's not bad. I spoke with my grandmother late last night. It was weird."

Derek turned to face him. "How old is your grandmother?"

"She is ninety-five years old. Acts like she is in her fifties."

"Wow." Derek took a sip of his coffee. "I don't want to live that long."

"Shit, neither do I," George said.

Kyle walked into the unit. "Good morning."

Michael came in right after. "I'm so hungry," he said looking at the donuts.

"Hey," Felicia said, walking to the table. "Didn't you eat breakfast?" she asked Michael.

"No. I literally woke up an hour ago."

Kyle joined her. "I want to come over and go swimming."

Felicia smiled at him. "Tomorrow?"

"Perfect. I'll bring beer and snacks."

Kelly walked up next to the two. "I want in."

Felicia pointed at her. "You need to bring actual food."

"I will bring a bunch of food." Kelly filled her cup with coffee and placed a few donut holes on her plate. She scanned the various flavors of donuts and settled on two crème filled varieties.

Derek set his plate on his desk. He watched as his crew sat at their desks and settled in. "You guys ready?"

They nodded.

Kyle gave a thumbs up since his mouth was full.

"Okay, last night George, myself, and Dr. Chelsea went over the list of women. We agreed to focus on one." He lifted a piece of paper. "Her name is Anastasia Parker."

"Why are we focusing on her?" Kelly asked.

"Anastasia hits on all three lists. And while I was in the hospital, I saw a special on the morning shows. A couple, Patrick and Lucy Weathersby, spoke about IVF." Derek took a sip of his coffee.

George took over. "Patrick is the man who left Anastasia at the altar. And Lucy is who he left her for."

"Wow," Felicia said.

Kelly looked at George. "We have five other women. What else makes her the killer?"

Derek raised his hands. "We can't say with one hundred percent accuracy she is the killer, but we have a few things that put her at the top of the list." He sipped his coffee. "First, she had a son. From the records, it seems he was born roughly four months after the killings stopped.

"Second, her son died a couple of months ago. He had a rare form of leukemia. Shortly after his death, the killings started again." Derek pointed to a picture on the board. "That music box has butterflies around it and our killer spread the victim's entrails out in a pattern that resembled butterfly wings."

Derek lifted his cup of coffee but didn't take a drink. He snapped his fingers. "And when I interviewed Darla Stevens, a neighbor of Charlene, she said she thought the delivery person was a man.

"Anastasia shaved her head to support her son. By the time she killed

Charlene, her hair would have grown out. Under a baseball cap, from the back, she would look like a guy. Anastasia also created a foundation. George, do you want to explain that?"

George nodded. "Anastasia created the foundation while her son was alive. And it helps families in this area when dealing with children and childhood illnesses. The name of the foundation is Metamorphosis."

Kyle shook his head, holding up his hand. "I don't understand why that is important."

Derek faced him. "When a caterpillar turns into a butterfly, that process is called metamorphosis. There were several pictures that showed the young boy's room and he had lots of butterflies hanging on strings. Anastasia and her son often referred to butterflies by their Russian name, *babuchka*."

Derek watched George's face contort as he spoke. His agent's brows squished together. He realized he said too much. He couldn't worry about it now, but by the end of this case, he would have to explain.

George wanted to ask a question, but kept his mouth shut. Something was amiss here. He didn't remember reading all this information in the file. He wanted to ask about it, but thought it would be best addressed later. If Derek mentioned it, he had to have the information. George just wanted to know how he knew this stuff.

Derek avoided George's stare. "I know this may seem a little like we are jumping the gun, but Dr. Chelsea has reviewed the case and agrees with our assessment that Anastasia is more than likely our killer."

"How are we going to proceed, then?" Felicia asked.

"I spoke with the director. Explained what we had, and he agreed with my plan. We are going to call the Weatherbys and go see them this morning. I believe, and Dr. Chelsea does too, that the Weatherbys are Anastasia's end game."

"How?" Kelly asked. "But more than that, why?"

George faced her. "Kelly, look at it like this. Patrick dumped Anastasia for Lucy. Even though I can't find any proof, I believe Anastasia's son is Patrick's son. The interview Patrick and Lucy gave was televised nationally. I have to believe Anastasia saw it. Her son is dead, and the wife of the man who dumped her is having a baby. That has to cut deep."

Kelly nodded. "I get it."

Derek crossed his arms over his chest. "I don't have solid proof. And this may blow up in my face. I can and will take the heat. But it could blow back on you guys. I want to set a trap for Anastasia. I think she will take the bait and come to us."

Felicia squinted at her boss. "You want to use Lucy as the bait?"

Every agent stared at Derek. "Yes."

"That could be so dangerous," Kelly said.

"Yes, I know. I believe after we speak with Patrick and Lucy, the plan will flesh out. So, sit tight while I call them." Derek walked away, heading to the kitchen.

Kelly turned towards George. "You agree with this plan?"

"I need to give him a chance to flesh it out. I don't think he has any intention of putting Lucy Weatherby in harm's way."

Kyle focused on Kelly. "Derek would never put someone in a position that would bring them harm. If he is considering this, he has a plan. We have to give him the chance to explain it to us."

Derek walked back into the room. "Patrick and Lucy have agreed to see us this morning. I would like all of us to go. For this to work, I need all of us to be on board."

Everyone gathered their things.

Kelly stood. "I will give you the chance to tell us what plan you have, but if I don't agree with it, are you going to force me to take part?"

All movement in the room stopped.

"I don't own you. You are an FBI agent. With that position comes expectations you will do your job. If you should decide you don't want to get on board with the plan I come up with, I understand. I would never force you."

Kelly opened her mouth to speak.

Derek held up his hand. "That doesn't mean I will keep you on this team. If, when the plan comes together and you don't feel it is the right plan, then you can go. I will call the director and have you transferred." Derek scanned the room. "That goes for everyone. I don't think it is my way or the highway, but if I put the plan in place, I expect you to do your job."

Kelly stared at him. "Fair enough." She respected this man. No question about that. She just didn't know if she was ready to follow him in a potential career-ending move.

CHAPTER FORTY-FOUR

George rode with Derek while the other agents followed in Kyle's car. Lola remained at the church.

George looked over at his boss. "What do you think they are talking about in the other car?"

Derek grinned. "Probably who is going to the director and have me fired."

George raised his eyebrows. "I agree."

Derek laughed. "You all have a right not to be forced to do an operation, but I can't have anyone who doesn't want to follow directions on my team. I want each of your input on the plan. And in a perfect world, we would all agree on what works best. I don't think I have ever been an authoritarian. I hope I haven't been like that. However, ultimately, the decision lies with me."

"No, you haven't. I think we are all uncertain how this will go. And it is worrisome. We have no way to predict how this will turn out."

Derek drove into the neighborhood. The estate homes in this area were large and some old wealthy residents of Phoenix lived here. "You never know how an operation will turn out. You plan and allow for variables."

He pulled into the driveway, followed by Kyle. As everyone exited the vehicle, Derek scanned the area. There was a possibility Anastasia was there now, watching. It was a risk he had to take.

Derek led the way to the front door.

Patrick Weatherby opened it before they got there. "Agent Reed?"

"Yes," he held out his hand. Shaking Patrick's hand, he motioned behind him. "This is my team."

Patrick waved them in. "Please, come in." He closed the door, then moved next to his wife, who waited in the foyer.

"First, I appreciate you taking the time to see us. And I realize you must have so many questions. Can we go into your living room?"

"Oh yes," Patrick said. "I'm sorry, please follow us."

They led the agents to a spacious area. Tall windows filled the room with bright light, but no heat. The tile floor had an inlaid pattern that drew the eye right to the back windows. A large swimming pool sat on the other side of the glass.

The agents took seats around the room.

Patrick held his wife's hand. "Can you please elaborate on how you think we are in danger?"

Derek took a deep breath. He began his explanation with the case ten years ago. As he explained the timeline of Anastasia's life, when it came time to tell him about the son he never knew, Derek considered how to phrase it.

"You're telling me that Annie started killing because I canceled our wedding?"

George leaned forward on his elbows. "I know it is hard to hear, but you caused nothing. Anastasia, Annie, has dealt with her emotions this way. It has nothing to do with you. The recent death of her son has sent her further over the edge."

Patrick gripped his wife's hand.

She placed her other hand over his. "It is not your fault. I know you want to blame yourself. Don't."

"After the death of her son. Which happened a short time ago. She started killing again. She has suffered a break from reality," Derek continued.

"Wait. She had a child?" Patrick asked. His eyes scanned the faces in front of him.

"Yes." Derek made quick eye contact with George.

"How old was her kid?" Patrick asked.

"Just under ten years old." Derek waited a beat. He saw the flicker of realization in his eyes. "There is no proof, Patrick."

Lucy glanced from her husband to Derek. "I'm sorry, no proof of what? I don't understand."

George lowered his voice. "We have no information about who the father was. We can use the records to go back and see that Anastasia's son was born roughly eight months after Patrick called off the wedding."

Her hand covered her mouth. Tears welled in her eyes. "Oh, no." She placed her arm around her husband's shoulders.

Patrick's shoulders slumped. "He could've been my son."

"We don't know that." Derek had to get the conversation off the dead child. "Patrick, Lucy, have you received any weird letters or phone calls? We believe Anastasia pretended to deliver packages. Have you found any strange packages at your door?"

Lucy shook her head. "I have had nothing like that."

Kelly sat quietly. The warmth on her cheeks from the flush that crept across her skin made her dip her chin against her chest. She now understood where Derek was going with this. She should never have questioned his plans. "May I ask something?"

Derek nodded.

"Mrs. Weathersby, I understand you and your husband gave several interviews regarding your IVF treatment. Have you received anything odd or had any odd phone calls since that aired?"

Lucy shrugged. "Well, I don't think so. We had several phone calls yesterday asking us for interviews."

"Did they ask you to go to them or come to you?" Kelly asked.

"Most want us to come to their studio." She looked at her husband.

Patrick nodded. "Except for one."

Derek straightened. "What was different?"

"A young lady called she asked if we would give an interview for the Phoenix Women's Coalition podcast. She asked to come here."

Kelly pulled up the coalition on her phone. "Did she give you a name?"

Lucy rubbed her belly. "Yes. Um," she looked at her husband. "Oh my, I—I know I wrote it down." She started to rise from the sofa and a check her note pad, then snapped her fingers. "I remember. Her name was Angelica Carter."

Kelly searched for the list of employees. She didn't find it. She excused herself from the room.

Derek watched her leave. "Can you tell me anything about the conversation?"

"Like what?" Lucy asked.

"Did she ask questions you found odd?" Derek asked.

"Yes. I mean, she apologized," Lucy said.

Patrick turned to his wife. "What did she apologize for?"

Lucy wrung her hands. "She mentioned your first engagement. Something about having to do research to get the interview okayed."

"Why would she reference that?" Patrick asked.

"She wanted to see Lucy's reaction. Did you react?" Derek asked.

"No. I thought her explanation was a valid one," Lucy said.

Kelly walked back into the room. "There is no one with that namt working at the women's coalition. And they don't have a podcast that they do interviews on."

Lucy's eyes filled with tears. "Oh, my gosh."

Patrick consoled his wife. "What do we need to do? Please. Protect my family. You can't let this woman hurt my family."

A chill ran down Derek's spine. He looked at his crew. He turned back to Lucy. "Mrs. Weatherby, could you stand up?"

Lucy shot a look at her husband. "I don't understand."

"I need to see how tall you are." Derek stood and motioned to Felicia and Kelly. "Could you two stand next to her?"

Felicia stood on the side with Kelly on the other side.

"Felicia, you are almost her build, exactly. Minus the pregnant belly," Derek said.

"What are you thinking?" Felicia asked.

Derek stepped back. "I can't in good conscious ask Lucy to go through with the meeting tomorrow. That would be too much of a risk. But I think if we could find a wig and mimic the belly, we could fool Anastasia enough to get her here and..."

"And stop her before she kills Lucy, or me," Felicia said.

"Yes." He stood in front of his agent. "If you don't want to, you don't have to. You are the most qualified. I know you have serious martial arts skills."

George stood. "Anastasia uses chloroform. How do we stop her from knocking out Felicia?"

"Do we know the amounts of chloroform Dr. Callahan found in the tissue samples from the last victim?" Kelly asked.

Lucy sat on the sofa next to her husband.

"I can stop this. I can ask them to leave," he said.

"No. Not at all." Lucy met Derek's eyes. "I will not let this woman hurt any more people. We will do whatever they need, Patrick. I just need to sit. It's a little overwhelming."

Derek nodded. He answered Kelly's question. "He found low levels."

Kelly looked at Felicia. "If you resist, not overtake her, but resist and you can feign like you are unconscious and fall. She will assume she knocked you out." Kelly faced the other agents. "The attacker has to have complete control over their victim. A struggling person will not ingest a large amount of chloroform."

Derek held up his hands. "Okay. We need to decide a few things. We can put Felicia in the place of Lucy." He turned towards Patrick. "She hasn't seen Lucy except in interviews, and she will be hyped up on adrenaline." He faced the husband. "Are you okay being in the same room?"

"Yes. But she has to know the minute I see her, I will recognize her," he said.

Derek sat back down in the chair. "We don't know what she will do. But the great thing is she doesn't know we know. I want everyone to listen. This is how I think we should approach this." He sat quietly for a moment, gathering his thoughts. He closed his eyes and envisioned the scene.

Everyone in the room glanced at each other.

"Um, Derek?" George asked.

He held up his hand. Derek's eyes popped open. "Lucy will answer the door. It will be Felicia in costume. She will make herself vulnerable by turning her back on her. Anastasia will take that moment. She knows the minute Patrick walks in, her cover is blown."

He pointed at Felicia. "The moment she grabs you, you will struggle. If she uses chloroform, you will hold your breath, struggle, and then fall to the ground. If she doesn't use chloroform, you can let her subdue you. I know you will keep her from doing anything else."

Derek motioned to Patrick. "You will come in within minutes and will be shocked when you see your wife. Make sure you look concerned. Then you will recognize her. Annie, you called her. I want you to call her that. She will take so much joy that she has the upper hand. She will use Felicia to hurt you, but she wants to draw it out."

Derek focused on the other agents. I will position the team around the home on this level, where she can't see us. I can almost guarantee she will stay within the living room area. She needs to act quickly. She wants to make you pay," Derek said, turning his attention back to Patrick. "I need you to talk to her. Ask her why she is doing this? Get her talking. Mention her son."

George snapped his fingers. "Mentioning her son will throw her. It should make her go off on a tangent."

"Yes," Derek said. "Patrick, I need you to get her to keep her talking. Felicia will be coherent, but it will look like she is unconscious." He paused. "I know this will hurt and scare you both. She wants to kill Lucy and the baby to hurt you. I don't think she will have any desire to kill you, unless you provoke her. That is why I want you to provoke her."

"I don't understand," Patrick said.

"She will drag Felicia into the room, away from the door. She has done that in every kill. When you come in, you will keep your distance. I want you to provoke her. Tell her why you left her. Say she was horrible. Say how horrible she was in the bedroom. I don't care what you say to her, but I want you to distract her for a few seconds."

Felicia stood. "That's when I will take her down."

"Yes." Derek glanced around. "We will do a run-through. Now I know I can't account for every outcome. But I think we can steer this." He stood. "We need a few things."

Patrick stood. "Whatever we need to do."

Lucy breathed out. "I need something to drink. How about we move into the kitchen? I want to ask some questions." She stood and led everyone out of the room.

The kitchen was around the corner from the living room, down a small hall. It opened up to a large bar area and small eat-in table. Through the back was a small butler's pantry.

Derek walked around and scoped out the area. He turned towards Kyle. "How fast can you get cameras rigged?"

"A couple of hours," Kyle said. "What are you thinking?"

Lucy set out some glasses and a few pitchers of different drinks. "Please help yourself. You don't need to install cameras."

All agents turned towards her.

A small smile tugged at the corners of her mouth. She pointed to every corner of the house. "Behind each corner piece is a camera. They are fiberoptic." She motioned for them to follow her as she walked into the butler's pantry. At the far end, there was a cabinet. She pushed on one area and the entire cabinet opened.

When they stepped inside, there was an audible gasp from Kyle.

"This is incredible," he said.

Patrick took his wife in his arms. "It was her idea. She wanted a safe room. The cabinets look like regular cabinets, but they are reinforced steel. Each lined with bulletproof material. These walls are the same. That panel has all the camera feeds throughout the home. There is audio as well."

Lucy laughed. "I know there is nothing funny about this. But I always told him don't cheat at the house. This is why."

Derek chuckled. "It will come in handy with teens."

She smiled. Her lips quivered. "I'm scared. I'm scared you can't control everything."

Derek stepped close to her. He thought of his visions and wanted to tell her she came to him and told him to help her. But that wouldn't go over well. He placed his hand on her upper arms. "I promise you, I won't let anything happen to your husband, you, or your son."

The other agents exchanged glances.

Lucy's brow furrowed. Before she could say anything, Derek turned away.

"This will work perfectly. We need to set up a few things." Derek turned towards Lucy. "Do you have anything we can use to make Felicia look pregnant? Or what should we buy?"

"I actually have a baby bump," Lucy said.

"I'm sorry. A what?" Felicia asked.

"It mimics a pregnant belly. We got it in our Lamaze class. I wore it so I could understand what my wife would go through when she got bigger," Patrick said as he led them back to the kitchen.

CHAPTER FORTY-FIVE

By mid-day Saturday, they had run through a few scenarios with Lucy and Patrick. Derek had called AD Fretz, who spoke with the couple. They had agreed to allow the FBI to conduct this unusual operation, and the director said he would be there in the morning to help set up.

They were getting ready to leave when Lucy spoke up. "What if she comes tonight?"

Patrick pulled his wife in close to him. "We can go to a hotel for the night."

"No. I don't want you to veer from your usual activities," Derek said.

Lucy's eyes widened. "You think she will try to come early? Do you think she might try to do something?"

"No. But I don't want her to see something that might raise suspicion. What if I had an agent stay here tonight with you?"

"Here in the house?" Patrick asked.

"He can park down the street. He doesn't have to be in the house."

"That would look suspicious. Wouldn't it?" Patrick asked.

"We can work wonders with undercover officers. You guys have security patrol, right?"

Patrick nodded.

Lucy pulled him close to her mouth. She whispered in his ear.

"Lucy wants you to stay here," Patrick pointed at Derek.

"I—I have a dog. I have agents that are much more suited to doing this. I can have one here in a few hours." Derek looked at his crew for help.

Kyle smiled. "Don't worry about Lola. She can stay with me. And I will make sure to take care of her before we come here in the morning."

George hid his grin. "I think it is a great idea."

Derek glared at the two men.

Michael wouldn't even make eye contact with him.

Derek turned back to Patrick and Lucy. "I will go home and get some items. What time do you want me to come back?"

Patrick looked at his watch. "We have family plans in about an hour. And we will be back by 7 p.m."

Derek nodded. "I don't want you to come into the house alone to-night. If you get here first, do not get out of your car. Drive around. I have a blue Jaguar; I'll be in your driveway."

Lucy took his hand. "Thank you."

"Do not open your door. I don't care... you know what? We will all wait here until you leave." He smiled at his crew then turned towards Patrick and Lucy. "You go get ready."

Patrick looked at his wife. "What do we need to do?"

She shrugged. "I will run upstairs and change. I think I can be ready in about twenty minutes." She smiled at the agents. "I can't thank you enough."

They watched her as she headed up the wide staircase.

Patrick waited until she was out of earshot. He leaned in towards the agents. "I appreciate this. The fact you all were so honest with us. Including us in the planning. It makes us both feel less, I don't know, exposed. Vulnerable."

Derek took a seat on the staircase. "Tell me about Annie."

The other agents followed suit and sat next to Derek.

Patrick leaned against the wall. "She was a sweet girl. Her family is Russian. They have a lot of money. After I canceled the wedding, I paid them back all their deposits." He sniggered. "For a few moments, I thought they would kill me. But her parents understood. Thank God they are not the Russian mafia. Annie was odd, a little OCD, but smart. She could be a little clingy. But nothing too overwhelming."

George glanced over his shoulder. "Why did you break it off? Did she do anything?"

"Nope. She would have made a wonderful wife. I met Lucy. She stirred my soul, not just my heart. I fought it for a long time. Lucy worked as a florist. I went to the shop she worked and called her to ask weird question about flowers."

Patrick sighed. "I didn't intend to hurt Annie. She was a good woman. I bet she made a wonderful mother." He pinched the bridge of his nose. "Annie was never angry or violent. She never seemed like the person who could kill someone. Let alone the way she did."

"When people have a break with reality, they will do things no one ever thought they would. The break up was more than she could take," Kelly said.

"Do you have any idea why she would kill those women?" Patrick asked.

George looked at his feet. Then at Patrick. "We think she was trying to save them somehow. From the pain she felt when you rejected her."

"Our forensic psychiatrist explained it by saying she was trying to save them from future pain that the men may inflict on them. She didn't' see it as being a bad thing," Kelly said. "She used the way she felt and wanted to spare them."

"Why start now, though? So many years later?" Patrick asked.

"When she lost her son, that was the ultimate loss. The final straw in her ability to cope with the pain. Her pain was so great, she couldn't let the women ever suffer such a significant loss. She focused on the same type of victim, just slightly different reasons." Derek glanced up and saw Lucy coming down the stairs. His throat swelled. She wore the same outfit in his vision when he saw her husband holding her dead body.

"I have to ask both of you not to say anything to your family or friends tonight. The details of the murders have never been released and no one can know what we are doing." Derek stared at that the couple.

"We will say nothing. I promise you that." Patrick took his wife's hand. We will go through our garage. How about you all follow us out?"

They all followed.

Kyle and the others left and would meet Derek and George at the unit.

Derek and George checked the garage and the car.

"I will be here at seven." Derek walked to his car. He waited for their garage door to close and for the pair to leave before he pulled out of the driveway. He scanned the area looking for anything suspicious. Things or people that shouldn't be there.

"You think we can pull this off?" George asked as they drove away.

Derek rubbed his chin. "If we don't, I will lose my career and all of you just may end up working at posts in Alaska."

CHAPTER FORTY-SIX

Before everyone headed home, the entire team went through every imaginable scenario. Although there was no way to plan for everything, they all felt they had a good idea of what to do.

The director arranged for a make-up artist to help disguise Felicia. Derek discussed at length about the chloroform the killer used to subdued her victims. They both agreed Felicia could handle herself.

Lola sat on the bed as he packed. "You're going to stay with Kyle tonight, then he will let you stay here during the day."

She tilted her head from side to side as if she understood his words.

"Then we will go somewhere. Sunday evening. Just you and me."

Lola barked and wiggled her butt.

Derek heard tapping on the glass door in the living room. He jogged in to see Kyle standing there. He unlocked the door and slid it open. "Come in. I'm packing a bag."

Lola followed and ran outside when Derek opened the door.

"I wanted to make sure I had everything she might need to sleep at my house." Kyle followed him into his bedroom.

"I have a bag of food for you. If you feed her at your place in the morning, she will be fine until we get done. And she can get in and out through the doggie door on her own."

Kyle sat in a large chair Derek had off to the side. "Are you worried?"

"I think there would be something wrong if I wasn't worried." He glanced up at his junior agent. "I think we have covered everything we can. We have contingency plans in place and hopefully, our assessment of her mental health will play in our favor." Derek zipped up his bag and set it aside. Then he sat on his bed. "What's bothering you?"

"I'm not sure what my role is."

Derek couldn't help but smile at him. "Sure, you do. I need you to stay in the comms area. You will run the show. We will all have our earpieces in and you will let us know what is going on and when to approach Annie."

Kyle wiggled in the chair. "What if I screw it up and get Felicia hurt? Or worse?"

"Kyle. You are a master wizard at this kind of stuff. I plan on scoping out the house and seeing the best place for everyone. You won't be in the room alone."

"I guess. I just know how dangerous this woman is. I know Felicia can handle herself, but still."

Derek lifted his bag and motioned for Kyle to follow him to the kitchen. "I appreciate your apprehension. It will help you pay closer attention to the finer details." Derek handed him the bag of food from the counter. "Here."

Kyle held the bag in his arms. He stared at his boss, who was more like an older brother. "I think you are handling this the right way." He looked at the microwave clock. "How about if I take Lola inside and feed her at my house? That way, she won't see you when you leave."

"I like that idea. I will lock the glass door, then leave." Derek watched as Lola ran after Kyle. He locked the door and headed to his car. Backing out of his driveway, he felt cool air brush against his arm. He turned towards the passenger seat. "I was wondering where you were."

Chrissy giggled. "This is so exciting."

"What? The case?"

"Yes."

"Chrissy."

"I won't get in the way. I would never do anything to put any of you in harm's way."

Derek drove on. The sun was setting in the west and the burst of colors looked like a giant painted canvas.

"Are you worried?"

"Why does everyone keep asking me that question? Yes. But I think we can do this."

"I bet Dr. Chelsea and Dr. Callahan are beside themselves to see this murderer caught."

Derek pulled onto the main thoroughfare. "I know they are. I also know the FBI will be glad to have this case closed as well."

There was a long silence. Derek glanced over to make sure she was still there. "What's wrong?"

"I'm not sure."

"Spill."

"I feel like something big is just around the corner." She stared at him. She thought if she had met him when she was alive, she would've fallen head over heels for him. Now, though, she loved him like one might love a brother. At least if dead people can love.

"With this case?"

"No. Something down the road."

"Another case?"

She clasped her hands in her dress. She shook her head. "I don't even know if it is good or bad. I just feel like something is coming."

Derek turned into the neighborhood. He smiled at Chrissy's reaction to the houses. She was still such a young girl. "I need you to promise me you will be on your best behavior."

"I will. I promise."

He parked in the driveway and waited. It was minutes before 7 p.m. when they drove up. The garage door opened and Derek motioned to them he wanted to pull inside, too.

Patrick pointed for him to park next to them.

Derek exited the vehicle and waited for the garage door to close. "Thank you. I don't want there to be anything that might scare her off tomorrow."

"No problem at all. Have you eaten?" Patrick asked.

"No. I don't think I even remembered to eat." Derek followed them into the home. He quickly glanced over his shoulder, but Chrissy had gone.

"We have a spare room upstairs and one downstairs. You can have your choice," Patrick said.

Lucy went to take his bag.

"Do not even think of touching that," Derek said, pulling it closer to him.

"Fine." She headed down the hall. "Come into the kitchen after you pick your room."

"I would prefer to be downstairs," Derek said.

"Follow me, then." Patrick went in the opposite direction from his wife. "I'm glad you're staying here. I was trying to not be all freaked out but, I'm just not that tough."

"You have every right to be freaked out. And you don't have to be tough." Derek put his bag on the queen-size bed, then followed Patrick out. He opened and closed doors, checking the layout.

Entering the kitchen, Lucy had a platter with sandwich fixings on it. "I hope this is okay?"

"This is perfect. You don't have to feed me." Derek took a seat at the bar.

Patrick grabbed a few sodas and bottled water from the fridge and a few bags of chips. "We are super bad at having regular dinners. Our kid is probably going to be a grazer."

Lucy laughed. "I will start having regular breakfasts, lunches, and dinners, at least for the baby."

Patrick made eye contact with his wife.

Derek noticed the interaction but ignored it. He looked around the area. "I like your house."

Patrick gave him a toothless smile. "Thanks."

Derek spun around and stared out at the lighted back porch. From the corner of his eye, he could see Patrick mouthing something to his wife. "Just say it," he said as he turned back to face them.

"Excuse me?" Lucy asked.

"You two are making that weird face, trying to communicate without me knowing." He opened a bottle of water. "You aren't very good at it. I would work on that skill before you kid becomes a teenager."

CHAPTER FORTY-SEVEN

Lucy rolled her eyes. "See, I told you."

Derek took the plate she offered.

"Build it the way you like. I have other things in the fridge, if you want something else." Lucy opened one of the diet sodas.

"This is great." Derek opened one of the sub rolls and grabbed several slices of lunchmeat. "What do you want to ask or say?" He kept making his sandwich.

Patrick rubbed his hands together. "What was Annie's son's name?"

Derek looked up from what he was doing. "Dimitri."

"Is there any possible way for me to see if her son was my son?"

Derek stopped making his sandwich. "I'm not sure how the legal procedure would work. But I bet if you mention him tomorrow, she will tell you."

"Do you think I should?"

"We ran through a lot of scenarios, and when you distract her, that could be your first question." Derek finished making his sandwich. Smiling at Lucy, he continued. "If she were to lunge at you or come after you, we will have someone right there to grab her. I promise you."

"I'm not worried. I can dodge pretty quickly, and I don't plan on being that close to her," Patrick said.

Derek looked from Patrick to Lucy. "If she doesn't tell you, I will do what I can to help you get answers. But let me ask you something. What will knowing for sure do for you? You already have a pretty good idea the boy was more than likely yours. I saw that realization on your face earlier."

Patrick sighed. "I guess knowing for sure would," he paused, looking at his lap. "It would make the sadness I feel and loss I feel—I'm not sure..."

"It would make it feel worth it," Derek said.

"Yeah. That's it."

Lucy touched his hand. "You don't need to know for sure to grieve for him."

Lifting her hand, he kissed it. "Thank you." Patrick made a sandwich. "Should I make you one?" he asked his wife.

"No. I'm pregnant, not handicapped."

Derek raised an eyebrow at her. "I do not want you anywhere near this area. You can stay in the safe room, or upstairs."

She crossed her arms over her chest. "Don't tell me what to do." She raised an eyebrow at him, pooching out her lips.

Derek glanced over at her husband, then back at Lucy.

Lucy smiled. "Did you think I was mad?"

"Kind of."

"I don't plan on being anywhere near that woman. I would like to stay in the safe room though. I want to see what is happening."

"That is fine." Derek grabbed a bag of barbeque chips and took one pickle from the charcutier tray. Taking a bite of his sandwich, he savored the flavors. "I know this is a simple meal, but I love sub sandwiches."

Patrick swallowed his mouthful. "Me too. We often have things like this for our meals."

Patrick and Derek cleaned the kitchen while Lucy sat and watched. "I could get used to this. Two men, doing all the work."

"Don't even get used to it." Patrick laughed when she stuck her tongue out.

When they finished, they went out onto the back patio. The glow from the pool lights transported Derek to another place. He thought about putting in a small pool in his backyard. There was enough room for it, he just never got around to starting the job.

After twenty minutes, Patrick stood. "I need to shower. You going to stay out for a while longer?" he asked Lucy.

"I can go to my room. You guys pretend I'm not here." Derek stood.

"Stay with me for a few more minutes." Lucy kissed her husband before he left. Facing Derek, she curled up in the lounger, bringing her legs under her. "Why did you refer to my baby as my son earlier?"

"Excuse me?" Derek asked.

"You said you would protect me and my son. How do you know what we are having? We don't even know if it is a boy or girl."

Derek shrugged. "I just assumed."

"That is not true. I think you know what I'm having. I can see it in your eyes. It wasn't an assumption."

"I guess I just said it because I'm a guy."

"No. You know. I don't know how, but you know. The moment I met you, there has been something—it feels like I've met you before."

"I've been told I have that effect on people."

"No. I think it's more than you look familiar to me. I've been having vivid dreams. Scary dreams. Everyone says it is pregnancy hormones. But I don't think so. They seem too real."

"What does Patrick say about them?"

She looked away, staring out at the pool. "I haven't told him. I keep them to myself." She laughed. "I mean, he might have me committed if I say I've been dreaming of being murdered. No, I keep them to myself."

The hair on Derek's arms stood on end. He searched the shadows beyond the pool for an intruder. Frowning, he furrowed his brow. "They say pregnant women have all kinds of heightened senses. It's their instinct to protect."

"Does everyone let you get away with not being truthful?"

"Uh, what?" Derek asked, flinching back.

"You didn't assume or make an educated guess about my child. You know my child is a boy. And I want to know how. Please, just be honest. I promise I can take it."

Derek's shoulders slumped. His chin rested against his chest.

"I will not break your confidence. No one will ever hear this conversation. You need to know you can trust me."

Derek wanted to run. He wanted to bolt. And as uncomfortable as this was, it felt—right. "I had a dream, or vision, of your husband holding you in his arms after you were murdered. It was before I knew anything about you or who the killer was." Staring at her, he waited for the laughter. For the rebuking. None came.

Lucy's lips puckered. She bit the inside of her cheek. "Was I wearing the dress I am now?"

Derek smiled. "Yes."

"I had the same dream." She laughed. "I didn't see your face, but I felt your presence. How is this even possible?"

Derek hissed out a breath. "I have no fucking clue."

They looked at each other and laughed. Laughed like old friends from years gone by.

"When did you start having the visions?"

Derek sighed. "I had a case over a year ago. I couldn't save a young girl. A serial killer had abducted her and I couldn't save her. Since that case, I see weird shit. Shit, that has no explanation. I suffered some pretty severe injuries at the hand of that killer. Maybe that has played a part." He faced her. The smile left his face. "If you tell anyone, I will tell them you're crazy."

She laughed. "They already think I'm crazy. I promise you that." Lucy tugged on the sleeves of her dress. "I knew Annie was pregnant when I met her and Patrick. I can't explain how I knew; I just did. Maybe it's a woman thing.

"I should've said something to him, but I didn't know how. I never planned to fall in love with him. And I didn't know how to approach the subject when he left her and canceled the wedding."

They both sat quietly, looking at the pool.

Derek felt incredibly comfortable in her presence, something he couldn't explain.

Lucy reached over the arm of her chair. She took his hand in hers. "I believe you were sent to us at this moment to save us. Me, my baby, and Patrick. I believe you when you say you won't let anything happen to my family. My baby."

Derek squeezed her hand. "Your son will be a healthy, strong boy. Just like his mother."

Patrick walked out, joining them. He saw his wife and Derek holding hands. "Putting the moves on my wife?" He gave Lucy a side glance.

"Yes. Yes, he is. I don't know how to tell you this, but it is his baby."

Patrick just rolled his eyes. "See what I have to put up with?"

Lucy patted the end of her lounge chair. "Sit with me." She adjusted herself so he could get closer. "I was holding onto his hand, thanking him for what he and his team are doing for us."

Patrick kissed his wife's hand. "I want to thank you. Had you not come around when you did, things may have turned out terribly bad."

"All part of my job." Derek stood. "I want to walk around the downstairs and get an idea of where I want to position people. I want my team readily available, but not where she can see them."

Both Lucy and her husband rose.

"Do whatever you need to. Help yourself if you get hungry or thirsty. There is a bathroom in your suite. Please, make yourself at home," Lucy said.

"Tomorrow morning, we have a makeup artist coming. She will help transform Felicia into you." Derek turned towards Patrick. "Once that is done," he pointed at Lucy, "you will go into the safe room. From that moment, Felicia will be your wife. I need you to pretend she is pregnant with your child. Annie needs to believe she has you where she wants you."

"I can do that. Whatever is needed."

"Also, I think she will come earlier than the planned time. She may try to give an excuse; she may even walk around the front yard trying to spy. We will have someone stationed on the street in a van, probably a cable or AC van. There is a house being remodeled just down the road. It won't look out of place for a van to be there. They will watch the street and relay to us what they see. It will be a long day."

CHAPTER FORTY-EIGHT

Derek walked through the silent house. He'd taken a shower, a very long shower, and ate another sandwich. Checking every nook and cranny, he found a few areas in the hallway where he could put two agents. They would have a perfect view of the living room.

Standing at the front door, he pretended to be Felicia and let the killer in. He closed his eyes and mimicked the movements that would force Annie to move the way he needed.

Once in the home, Felicia would need to make herself vulnerable. Letting the killer in and turning her back on her would give her the best opportunity to overtake his agent.

As he studied the entryway, he believed Anastasia would use the least encumbered path to the living room. He figured she would have to get control of her victim before the husband came in. If Derek had planned this right, Anastasia would see Felicia opening the door alone, and that would be her chance to act.

Surveying the area with a pleased expression on his face, he headed to his room. He planned the ruse as best he could. Closing the door behind him, he got undressed and slid into bed. He had plugged his phone in earlier and set it on the nightstand. Reaching over, he set the alarm for 7 a.m. He'd instructed his team to show up by 8. The other team members would be there by 9.

Derek grabbed the TV remote off the nightstand. He propped himself up and pulled the covers up. Flipping through channels, he settled on the late college football game. It didn't take long for him to doze off. Before he drifted into a deep sleep, he felt the other side of the bed go down. "I was wondering when you were going to show up."

"I've been around. Wanted to give you some space." She turned on her side. "Do you have everything planned?"

"Yes. I know I can't control everything, but I think I've done the best I can."

"Nothing bad is going to happen. I can feel it." Chrissy tried to change the channel, but she couldn't push the buttons.

Derek watched as she lifted the remote. It raised a few inches off the bed then fell back. "How can you move things? Or am I imagining this part?"

"No. Sometimes I feed off the energy around me and I can move things, or cause things to happen. It doesn't happen often. Although, it seems like the more I'm around you, the more abilities I have." A big, toothy smile filled her face. "You are putting out a lot of nervous energy. Under all that pretend calmness, you are a big tight rubber band."

"Thanks. Makes me feel like I've got this under control."

She laughed. "You do." She watched the ballgame. "I heard the conversation between you and Lucy. She's special, you know."

"How so?"

"She sees the dead. Or at least senses when they are around. She can't talk to them yet, and she doesn't understand the power she has. But she will. Her baby will have the gift, too."

Derek twisted to stare at her head on. "What? How do you know this?"

"You don't understand. One day, your veil will be gone and you will, but there are some who can see and speak to the dead. More than you. Like I said, you need to remove all of your obstructions."

"I don't have any obstructions. I have a brain that works in the real world. Not on some weird spiritual level."

"Anyway, back to the conversation. Why did you tell her?"

Derek shrugged. "I didn't want to lie. It seemed like the right thing to do."

"That's what I love about you. You always do the right thing."

CHAPTER FORTY-NINE

A loud crash woke Derek. Stepping into his jeans, he grabbed his weapon, opened his bedroom door and stepped into the hallway. Dead silence filled the entire house. Derek craned his neck, trying to hear any movement from upstairs.

He hugged the wall, easing himself towards the foyer when a scream echoed throughout the home. He ran towards the kitchen. As he rounded the corner, he saw a dark figure bent over a woman.

"Stand up. Hands in the air." Derek trained his weapon on the mysterious figure. "Do it now!"

Slowly, the dark entity stood. As it turned towards Derek, hundreds of roaches ran out from under the cloak surrounding the man's body. "Hey, boy," Josiah Craig said, standing mere feet from him. "I have a surprise for you."

Derek took a half step back. He kept his gun pointed at Josiah. One side of his head was caved in. Rotten flesh hung in chunks as maggots and worms slithered through open eye sockets. "You're not really here." Derek shook his head. "No. You are not here."

Josiah threw his head back, roaring in laughter. Black flies spewed from his mouth. "Son, I can be wherever I want to be." He stepped to the side. "I brought you something."

Derek followed the finger, pointing towards the floor. Gasping, Derek ran towards Lizzy, who lay in a bloody heap. "No."

Before he could touch her, Josiah grabbed Derek by the throat. Lifting him a few inches off the ground, he held the agent there.

Derek struggled to breathe. He clawed at the rotting flesh on Josiah's hand. The putrid smell of decaying flesh filled his nostrils.

"No, no, no. You can't save her. She will come with me. Soon. Very soon." Josiah laughed at the agent. "You can't save her."

Trying desperately to free himself, Derek only made Josiah's grip tighten. His eyelids grew heavier. His chest hardened as the last of the breath he held on to left his body. The last thing he saw before darkness engulfed him was Josiah's foot stomping on Lizzy's head.

Derek sat up in bed. He clawed at the imaginary hand. Coughing and gagging, he forced himself to inhale. His chest pounded out a rhythm that echoed in his skull. The swooshing of air between his ears sounded like a freight train barreling down the tracks.

Soaked in sweat, Derek hung his legs over the side of the bed. He reached for his cell on the nightstand. 5 a.m. His alarm would go off in two hours. Dragging his fingers through his hair, his concern focused on Lizzy. Positive, Josiah Craig couldn't physically hurt her, Derek was more concerned about what the nightmare meant.

Standing, he made his way to the shower. Turning the water to as hot as he could stand, he stripped and stepped inside. Steam circled around him. Derek couldn't focus on this, on Lizzy right now. He had to push his concern for her safety to the back of his mind.

In a matter of hours, he and his team will apprehend a serial killer. Derek had to make sure his full attention focused on the case at hand. He'd made a promise to Lucy, and he intended to keep that promise.

CHAPTER FIFTY

Derek walked into the kitchen to find Lucy at the stove. "Good morning."

"Good morning, Agent. How did you sleep?" she asked as she flipped pancakes.

"As good as one might expect. The bedroom was very comfortable." He poured a cup of coffee from the carafe on the bar. Taking a seat on one of the bar stools, he watched as she hummed and cooked breakfast.

Lucy turned around with a large platter of pancakes, eggs, and bacon.

Patrick walked in. "That smells and looks fabulous." He kissed his wife on the cheek. Facing Derek, Patrick nodded. "Good morning. Did you sleep well?"

"Yes, I did. Thank you." He motioned at the plate of food Lucy handed him. "You didn't have to do this, you know?"

"I know that. But I wanted to make sure you had a good start to the day." Lucy poured a glass of orange juice.

Derek eyed the plate of food. "This is fantastic. I was planning on just having some coffee. This," he pointed at the food, "is way better."

Helping to clean up the breakfast mess, Derek felt at ease with this couple. It wasn't an agent protecting someone kind of feel, it was more like a friendship. Which is not good for any agent to feel while on a job.

He checked his watch. Moving towards the front bay window, he searched the immediate area in front of the home. Nothing seemed out of order. Just when he was about to turn away, he saw a van pull up down the street.

Derek recognized the agent that got out dressed as a worker. He walked to the house being remodeled and entered. If Anastasia showed up, she wouldn't be suspicious of the workers walking in and out of the home. His phone pinged.

Hey, Agent Marshall here. I'm down the road from you.

I saw you pull up. Nice cover. How did you get the keys?

Director arranged for it. I will keep you posted if we see the suspect.

Thanks, and I will let you know when we are in place and ready.

Just as he was about to step away, Kyle drove past the house. Derek watched as he parked a few houses down. Michael and Felicia exited the car. Within minutes, George pulled up and parked near Kyle.

George and Kelly exited his car.

Derek moved towards the front door; he was about to open it when he saw the alarm panel on the wall. "Hey Patrick?" he called out.

Patrick stepped around the corner from the kitchen. "What's up?"

"I was about to let my crew in, but I wasn't sure if you shut off your alarm."

Patrick walked towards him. "No. It's always armed. Let me change the settings." He punched a code and reset the system.

Derek reached for the door as the bell rang. Pulling open the door, Derek stepped back. "Morning guys."

His agents walked in, heading towards the main living room. As he was about to close it, another car pulled up in front of the house across the street. Derek stepped back when he recognized Francine from the bureau. He waved her to hurry.

"Hey Derek. Sorry, had to grab something for my kit," Francine said, stepping into the home. "Where are we setting up?"

Derek pointed down the hall. "We can get Felicia ready in the kitchen.

As he and Francine entered, all heads turned towards them.

"Francine," Felicia said, walking to her. "I didn't know it would be you doing the makeup."

"Yeah, Assistant Director Fretz called me yesterday and asked for me to handle this one." Francine set her kit on the counter. She walked over to Lucy and twisted her head from side to side, looking at her facial profile. "I don't think this will be hard to mimic at all. I have a few different wigs; we can see which will work best."

Francine stared at Felicia's clothes, then turned around and addressed Lucy. "Do you have the outfit you wore for the news interview? If we think our unsub saw that, seeing Felicia in it today will help make her think she is looking at the real you."

"Yes, I do. It's a dress. Will that work?" Lucy asked.

"That will work fine. Perfect actually." Francine motioned to Felicia. "Let's get to work on you."

As Francine set up her things, Felicia changed into the dress and the fake baby bump.

Felicia walked around, trying to be as graceful as Lucy was. "I'm not sure I can pull this off. It feels very weird."

Derek took her by the hand. "Come with me."

She followed.

He stood at the door. "I want you to run through the scenario from yesterday. Let's try it a few times with the belly."

Lucy and the others watched as Felicia practiced being overpowered by her assailant.

After several tries, she felt like she knew how to fake out Anastasia enough to make her believe she had rendered her unconscious.

Sitting at the table, Francine went to work, transforming Felicia.

Kyle double checked the security system and cameras. The fact they could record and keep the footage was a bonus. He knew the team wanted to take Anastasia alive, and these recordings would go a long way towards securing a guilty verdict if it got that far.

After a few hours, Francine called for everyone. "Tell me what you think?" she directed her question at Lucy and Patrick mostly, but input from the crew would make sure Felicia was Lucy.

The men stepped into the kitchen area.

Patrick, had been in the safe room helping Kyle set up, walked in. When he saw Felicia, he did a double take. He quickly glanced towards his wife, then back at the agent. "Wow." He stepped closer. It was only when he stood close to her that he could spot the differences.

He spun around to Derek. "She looks so much like my wife." Patrick stepped closer to Lucy. He took her hand. "What do you think?"

Lucy's mouth gaped open as she studied the agent in front of her. "I feel like I'm looking in the mirror."

Everyone else stared at the two women. They all agreed Anastasia would not know the difference.

They ran through a few more scenarios. The agents were too excited and too preoccupied to eat. They nibbled on a few sandwiches Lucy had set out. They were running through a few more things when Derek's phone pinged.

He glanced at the screen. He motioned for the noise to quiet down. "It looks like a person matching Anastasia's description drove through the neighborhood."

Derek moved towards a window when his phone rang. "Derek."

"It's me," Assistant Director Fretz said on the other end. "I was about to come to the door when I saw the suspect drive by. I pretended to forget something and moved back to my car."

"What is she doing?"

"She has driven up and down the road a few times. As soon as I can, I'm going to get into the van. I'm moving my car to the driveway where the van is parked. She's early."

"I figured she would come early. Not this early, but I'm not surprised." Derek made the round-up sign to the other agents. "Let me call you back in a moment."

He turned to his crew. "That was the director. It looks like Annie," he said, focusing on Patrick, "is driving through the neighborhood. I don't' think she will wait until 4 p.m."

Everyone double-checked their weapons.

"You all know where I want you to be. Most will be in the safe room. Make sure all comms are working, and your phones are turned on silent." Derek looked at Francine. "Looks like you are stuck here. I can't afford to let you go with her driving around."

"Not a problem. I will hang out with the others in the back room." Francine removed everything from the kitchen table.

Kyle, Kelly, and Francine went into the safe room. Michael and George remained in the hallway area with Felicia. Derek planned to be in a small office just off the main living room.

They had decided this would be the perfect place for Patrick to enter from and see Annie with his wife.

Patrick moved to the side of his wife. "I love you. Please don't worry."

Lucy hugged him. "I know nothing will happen to you. I'm not worried." She kissed him.

"We are in a holding pattern. I want to close the blinds. In case she comes up to the windows." Derek closed several window blinds.

Patrick, Lucy, Michael and George, all helped.

The agents went from a laid-back moment to heightened alert. Not only was a family's safety at issue, but one of their own was going to be at the mercy of a serial killer.

CHAPTER FIFTY-ONE

Derek's phone vibrated in his pocket. "Yeah," he said, answering the director's call.

"She just parked in your driveway. She's scoping out the place. Get ready."

Derek placed his phone in his pocket. "It's time."

Everyone went to their places.

Lucy stared at Derek for a few minutes before she disappeared into the safe room.

He nodded once then turned to Felicia. "You ready?"

"I am." She took Patrick by the hand. "Hi, honey." She kissed his cheek, with her mouth next to his ear. "You got this. When you look at me, you see Lucy."

"I'm ready." He went into the office.

Derek motioned to George and Michael. They positioned themselves, and Derek went into the office. He left the door opened a crack and made eye contact with Patrick.

Patrick gave him a thumbs up.

Felicia stood in the empty living room. She knew she was being watched by all those in the safe room. She closed her eyes, taking a moment to settle her nerves. Using a mantra and breathing she used in her martial arts, she slowed her breathing and heart rate.

She focused on the movements she would need to do. She touched the fake belly, making sure it was secure. As the doorbell rang, she took a deep breath and released all the negative energy. "Show time," she mouthed to the camera directly across from her.

She crept towards the front door. Taking a moment, she shook out her arms, then opened it. Felicia smiled at the young, pretty woman in front of her. "Yes, may I help you?"

Anastasia stood at the door with a small bag draped over her shoulder. "Hi, I'm Angelica. I'm here to do the interview."

Felicia smiled. "You're a little early."

Anastasia made a pouty face. "I'm sorry. I must have got the time wrong. Is it okay if I come in?"

Felicia watched the young woman reach her hand into the pocket of her pants. She was ready. "Absolutely. Please come in. Where are my manners?" she motioned for Anastasia to enter. Felicia turned her back on her, knowing what was coming. She blew out a breath and inhaled deeply.

Anastasia pulled the cloth from her pocket. The moment Felicia turned away from her, she made her move. She reached around, using one arm to grab around Lucy's waist, just above the protruding belly. She took the cloth and covered her face. "Don't struggle, Lucy. It will be easier."

Felicia smiled inwardly as Anastasia called her by Lucy's name. She pretended to fight, then fell limp in Anastasia's arms.

Anastasia worked fast. She knew Patrick would show up, and she needed to be ready. It was luck Lucy answered the door alone. She had hoped by showing up early, she would catch them off guard.

She dragged Lucy down the hallway and looked over her shoulder. "That area should work just right. Moving with care, she positioned the pregnant woman the way she wanted.

Derek received a text from Kyle to send Patrick out to the living room. He pointed towards Patrick, who took the cue.

Patrick opened the office door just a little and pretended to be finishing a phone call. "Lucy, who was that at the door?" he called out.

Anastasia jumped. She wasn't ready. She positioned herself where Patrick couldn't get to his wife without going through her. She pulled the knife from the sheath at the small of her back. "Don't come any closer."

Patrick stepped into the living room. "What are you doing? Who are you?" He took a step towards Anastasia. He kept his focus on Felicia for a few moments, then lifted his gaze.

Anastasia's nostrils flared. "What do you mean, you don't know who I am?"

Patrick realized he had touched a nerve. "Should I know you?"

Derek could hear the conversation from where he stood. He thought Patrick was doing a good job of getting Anastasia worked up. "Patrick, slow it down." he whispered.

Anastasia clenched and unclenched her hands. She let out a guttural roar. "I'm your sweet little Annie. The one you left her for." Anastasia kicked Lucy's belly."

Felicia felt the kick, but because of the fake belly, it didn't hurt at all. She listened to the conversation. Peeking with one eye open, she could see that Anastasia had positioned herself closer to her hip area than her midsection.

Patrick made a move to stop her. "Don't you fucking hurt my wife."

"I'll do what I want." She wielded the knife, jabbing the air, pointing it at Patrick. "After all you did to me. It's time for me to make your life a living hell." Anastasia took a small step back, moving closer to Lucy.

"Stop, just hear me out. I never meant to hurt you. I tried to talk to you, but you wouldn't listen. You left me no choice but to cancel the wedding."

"That's such a lie. You didn't try to talk to me. You left me. You left me for her." Anastasia kicked Lucy's belly again. She watched Patrick's reaction as she did it. "Is this mean? Am I hurting her?" she asked as she kicked her again.

Patrick stepped closer. "I heard you had a child. What was his name?"

Anastasia's eyes widened. "How do you know I had a baby?" she pointed the knife at Patrick. "How?"

"I checked on you once in a while after we broke up."

"We never broke up. You left me."

"I saw that article about you and childhood leukemia. How is your son now? Did the treatments work?" Patrick wanted to make her come towards him so that Felicia could take her from behind. But in order to do that, she needed more room.

"You have no right to ask me about my son," Anastasia said. Her voice dropped an octave.

"Was he my kid? Did you have my son and not tell me?" Patrick asked.

"You impregnated me. You weren't his father." Spittle formed in the corners of her mouth. She jabbed the knife towards him. The muscles in her neck strained. "Everything was your fault."

Patrick held back the tears. "Why didn't you tell me? He was my son. I should've been there for him."

"You didn't deserve to have him in your life. He was a sweet boy. There was no way I would let you turn him into a bastard like you and all the other men I have known."

"I'm not a bastard. I just didn't love you anymore. Why are you wanting to hurt my wife? My unborn child? They did nothing to you. Hurt me. Not them."

"You caused this. You caused all of this."

Patrick shook his head. "I didn't cause you to do anything."

"Yes, you did," she screamed. "Don't deny it. I never would have hurt anyone had it not been for you. I had to save them. You caused all those other women to suffer. Men, you are all the same."

Patrick's brow drew together. "What are you talking about? What women?"

Derek clicked his earpiece. "If she confesses to the murders, I want her taken down. But not until I give the word."

Derek could hear Michael and George respond in his earpiece. He studied Felicia's movements from his position. She didn't verbally respond, but he saw her blink.

"I don't understand. Who did you hurt?" Patrick asked.

Anastasia squinted at him, giving him a hard smile. "I didn't hurt them. I helped them. Before you ruined their lives. I gave them the chance at peace and happiness."

"Annie, what do you mean? You're not making any sense."

Anastasia completely focused on her former lover and fiancé. The anger had boiled to the surface. She took a step towards him and pointed the knife directly at him. Her hand shook. "All those women, they had to be released. Released from the future pain they would experience when their fiancé or husbands cheated on them."

Patrick stepped back, hoping she would continue to move towards him. "I never cheated on you. I just didn't love you anymore."

Anastasia focused on the adrenaline rushing through her body. "Don't lie to me!" She had a twitchy, edgy feeling. For the first time, she let the anger and hatred consume her. It wrapped itself around her, blanketing her in a barrage of emotions.

"My son," an evil sneer spread across her face. "The son you never got to see or hold." She made a sad face. "How does it feel to know, all this time, you have been trying to have a kid and now you find out, you had one? One I kept you from ever knowing?

"I hope it makes you feel empty inside. Just like the way you made me feel when you left me for her." She glanced over her shoulder. "My son was taken from me. He became sick. I couldn't help him. No doctors could help him."

She took a step towards Patrick. Anastasia held the knife out. She tilted her head to the side.

Patrick stepped away from her. "Annie, stop."

"No. I will not stop." She took another step forward.

Felicia opened her eyes. Patrick was several feet away from her and Anastasia was facing him. She wanted to sweep out her legs, but this fake belly was making it a little hard. Quickly shifting her weight, waved her hand, making a circling motion, indicating they should move in.

Derek tapped his earpiece. "What are you seeing, Kyle?" He couldn't risk looking through the doorway. Anastasia was in his direct line of sight. If she saw him, she may react.

"Felicia is waving for you guys to move in. She is positioning herself to take Anastasia down from behind." Kyle watched the screen. "She is up on her feet."

They would have to move fast.

Derek hit the comms again. "Felicia, stand and remain quiet until I give the word."

Patrick stepped back. "Annie. I know you don't want to do this. Think of Dimitri. Would he want you to do this?" He watched as Annie's face contorted, her eyes bulged, and the hand holding the knife flailed.

"You have no right to speak of my son." Spittle flew from her mouth. "You don't deserve to say his name."

Patrick watched as her nostrils flared. The veins in her neck looked like small ropes bulging out from under the skin. He had never seen Annie like this before. He went to move to the side, and Annie blocked him, moving closer.

Felicia had to get Anastasia away from Patrick.

Kyle spoke to Derek. "Felicia is on her feet, waiting."

"Felicia, talk like you are still woozy from the drug. Get her to face you."

Felicia nodded, knowing those in the safe room could see her acknowledging the command. "Patrick, what's going on?"

Anastasia turned around. "You aren't supposed to be awake. I drugged you." Anastasia stomped towards Lucy. She looked back over her shoulder. "Now you can watch your precious wife suffer."

Felicia braced herself. She needed to draw Anastasia closer to her. "I'm really dizzy, Patrick. Everything is blurry." She looked up, focusing past Anastasia as if to make her think she was out of it and couldn't see her.

Anastasia moved quickly, lunging forward.

Derek stepped from the office and spoke into the comms. "Michael and George, take up your post."

Both agents emerged from their hiding areas and moved slowly down the hallway with their weapons drawn.

Felicia expected the move and blocked her. She grabbed the hand holding the knife and bent it at an angle, forcing Anastasia to drop the weapon.

Anastasia heard a ringing in her ears. She shook her head. "This can't happen. You're ruining everything." She broke loose and grabbed her hair. When the wig came off, her jaw dropped open as she stared at it. Her gaze drifted across the woman standing in front of her. "Who are you?"

"I'm an FBI agent and you are under arrest."

At that moment, Michael and George burst into the living room.

Derek stepped next to Patrick and pushed him behind him. "Anastasia, you need to lie on the floor and put your hands out."

Anastasia's eyes darted around the room. Her gaze fell on Patrick. "You have messed up everything. You have ruined everything." She began hitting herself in the head and screaming. "I have to finish this. I have to kill her."

She turned towards Felicia and charged her.

"Don't take a shot!" Derek called out to his agents.

Felicia crouched just as Anastasia lunged at her. She caught the woman around her midsection and flipped her over, taking her down. Felicia slammed her to the ground on her back, landing on her.

It forced the air out of Anastasia. She grunted as her head smacked the tile.

The loud crack echoed throughout the home.

Felicia checked for a pulse on the unconscious woman. "She is still alive." She rolled her over and held out a hand, motioning to Michael, who was closest to her. "Handcuffs."

Michael tossed his cuffs to her.

Lucy followed the other agents from the safe room and ran to her husband. "I'm so glad this is over."

Derek searched the satchel that Anastasia brought in. He held up a music box, just like the other left at the latest murder. He pulled his phone from his pocket. "We got her. Come on in."

Within moments, Assistant Director Fretz came in the front door with several other agents.

Derek looked at his team. "Good work, guys."

Assistant Director Fretz stared at the still unconscious Anastasia. "I can't believe she is the killer." He looked up at Derek. "Why did I expect the bogeyman?"

"It would be so much easier if they looked like the monsters they are." Derek phoned for an ambulance. "You need to assign two agents to watch her. As soon as they clear her to leave the hospital, she needs to go to headquarters."

Assistant Director Fretz put his hand on his agent's shoulder. "You did a good job. I don't know how you connected everything, but you did something the bureau couldn't do ten years ago." He walked off to speak to the two agents that were in the van.

Anastasia moaned as she slowly regained consciousness. She struggled and thrashed around. "Let me out of these. Let me out now." She growled and spat as she tried to release herself.

Felicia put her knee on her lower back, exerting enough pressure to hurt. "If you continue to struggle, I will increase this pressure until your eyes pop out of your head."

The ambulance arrived. As the paramedics checked over Anastasia, the agents from the surveillance van collected the audio and visual tapes of the entire incident.

Derek watched as Patrick held Lucy in his arms, noticing Lucy's face had paled. Blocking out everything around him, he walked towards them. "Lucy?"

She looked up. "Thank you for everything."

"Lucy, are you okay?" Derek asked.

Patrick's brow wrinkled. He pushed Lucy back so he could see her face. "Honey, you look pale."

"No, I." She doubled over. Letting out a horrible scream, she grabbed her belly. "Oh," Lucy panted. "The cramps. The baby. There should be no cramps."

Derek whistled.

The paramedics who were assisting Anastasia came over to Lucy.

"I think she is going into labor," Derek said to one of the EMTs. He motioned to the two agents from the van. "Take her into custody," he said. "They can have her looked at in holding."

The paramedic looked at Patrick, then Lucy. "How far along are you?"

"I have three weeks left." She squeezed her husband's hand when the next contraction hit. Lucy screamed out. Using the training from the Lamaze class, she panted through every contraction.

The paramedic clutched the radio on his shoulder. "This is unit 425, be advised we have a pregnant woman with three weeks left until her due date. She is experiencing full on contractions roughly five minutes apart."

Static of the radio filled the room. "Has her water broken yet?"

Lucy stood, holding on to her husband. "Maybe these are Braxton Hicks. Maybe the...." Another contraction hit. She panted through it when her water broke.

The paramedic's eyes widened. "Be advised her water just broke. We will be en route in two minutes." He grabbed his bag and a few items. "Bring the gurney over here."

The second paramedic helped position her onto the gurney and rushed her to the ambulance.

Patrick turned towards Derek, and pulled him close. "Set the alarm. The code is 2420." He shook his hand. "Thank you. I have to go. But thank you. You saved my family." His voice trailed off as he ran out after his wife.

CHAPTER FIFTY-TWO

Everyone sat at their desks at the Legacy Unit. After Lucy had been rushed to the hospital, two agents had taken Anastasia into custody. The AD had watched the security tapes before he left the scene and was impressed with how well Derek's team handled the situation.

Derek rested his head in his hands, when Felicia entered carrying some sodas. He smiled at her as she set one on his desk. "Thank you."

"My pleasure." She handed one to each agent. "These reports are horrible."

George popped the top on his drink. "I'm almost finished. Where is everyone else at?"

Michael stretched, reaching for his drink. "I just finished."

"Me too," said Kelly. "Derek?"

He sat back, relaxing in his chair. "Yes?"

She glanced at her hands. "I'm sorry for my actions earlier when I questioned your tactics."

"Kelly, you have nothing to apologize for. It could have gone left very easily, and then you could have said I told you so."

"I seriously doubt that. I guess I'm... I don't see the connections you see and sometimes I feel like I'm missing something," Kelly said.

"I'm nothing special. I just process things differently." Derek caught the stare from George.

Kyle came running up the stairs. "You got to see this." He turned one of the security screens to a local news station.

A reporter motioned behind him. "We are standing outside the FBI offices here in Phoenix, waiting for a news conference. It seems a ten-year-old murder case, along with a recent murder, have been solved." He glanced over his shoulder then turned to address the viewing audience. "It looks like the conference is ready to start."

The crew watched as the cameraman focused on a podium. AD Fretz moved towards the center of the steps just behind it. Next, the newly appointed Deputy Director Jessup came to the microphone. As the camera panned out a little, they could see Congressman Jackson and Elizabeth on the side.

Derek balled his hands into fists, digging his nails into his skin.

George and the others turned around, glancing at Derek before they focused on the screen.

Deputy Director Jessup stood behind the podium. "Today we arrested a person in connection with the murders of four women over ten years ago, and a recent murder. The FBI carried out a sting operation securing the arrest of Anastasia Parker. I cannot give any more details about the crimes committed at this time."

Several reporters clamored at the Deputy Director, barking out questions.

He raised his hands to quiet the crowd. "Assistant Director Fretz has a few things to say about these cases."

AD Fretz stepped up to the podium. "The FBI's leads had grown cold on the ten-year-old case. Had it not been for a special unit, the Legacy Unit, we may not have apprehended Anastasia Parker."

Deputy Director Jessup whispered in Fretz's ear.

Fretz took a step back.

Deputy Director Jessup waved for Congressman Jackson to come to the podium. "Before you ask questions, the Legacy Unit is a specialized unit that investigates cold cases and solves them. Congressman Jackson spearheaded the entire unit." Jessup patted the congressman on the shoulder.

"I want to take a few moments to let the victims' families know how sorry I am for their losses. It is because of the turmoil that families face when they can't get answers that led me to work with the FBI, Deputy Director Jessup, and AD Fretz to form the Legacy Unit. And I handpicked Special Agent Derek Reed to head this unit. He has been an enormous help to the families, and his team has solved some fifteen cases in the last year alone. They are the real heroes here."

The press conference lasted a few more minutes.

George spun his chair around. "Why do you think they held that news conference?"

"Election year for the Congressman. They will use this case to push his reelection campaign." Derek gulped down his soda.

"How do you think they will explain the botched handling of the first set of victims? They mishandled the entire case," Michael said.

"They will bury the first four cases. Or pin the shoddy work on the agent who handled it, and since he's dead, he can't argue with anything that might be said." Kelly glanced up and laughed. "Now, if she were dead, all of this would be much more easily buried."

Derek eyeballed her. "If Anastasia were dead, that would make it so much easier for them to spin it."

"What about Dr. Callahan and Dr. Chelsea? Could the old case hurt them?" Michael asked.

Derek paused for a moment. An uneasy feeling made his stomach flip. "No. They had minimal contact with the agent or any say in what was happening. Hell, the bureau took over everything and let the crime lab process all the forensics after the second case."

"That's good. I wouldn't want them caught up in the middle of a scandal." Michael stood. "I'm done. Does anyone need a ride?"

They shook their heads.

Kyle looked at Felicia. "Ready to swim?"

"Yes." She punched Kelly on the arm. "you ready?"

"Yeah. I want to soak in the hot tub." Kelly grabbed her things. "What are we going to do for dinner?"

"Chinese?" Kyle asked as they headed towards the door.

"Mexican," Kelly said.

Walking out, Derek heard Felicia say, "Let's get both." He leaned forward on his elbows. "What about you? What are you doing?"

"I'm going to take a long shower and sleep." George leaned back and rocked in his chair. "Are you going to tell me?"

"Tell you what?"

"How you knew so much about this case. How you knew about the baby. How did you figure things out?"

"I don't figure things out. We work as a team. And the information we all gather helps put things into perspective for me. That's all."

"That's not all." He scooted closer to Derek's desk. "I told you earlier I spoke with my grandmother. She wanted me to tell you something."

"Oh yeah. What is it?"

George smiled. "I've told her about everyone here. You know, just about the job a while ago. Yesterday, she told me she had a dream about you and I needed to give this to you."

"Me or the entire team?"

"Nope. You. She explained the dead surrounded you. And they waited for you to help them. Every time you helped one, a bright beam of light would flash. And that dead person was gone."

"Um, okay. I don't like that dream."

"Then you won't like this." George looked him in the eyes. "She wanted me to give you these." He handed him a small bag. "This is what she sent me a few weeks back. There are different ones. I know you aren't a jewelry guy, but she said you need to always have one on you. She made one for a key ring. She also sent you a necklace and a bracelet. You have to always keep one with you."

Derek opened the pouch and poured out its contents. He lifted what appeared to be an open hand with the thumb and fingers outstretched, like a flat hand. "I don't understand."

"In Africa, they refer it to this as the Hand of Fatima. In other cultures, they refer it to as the Hamsa Hand. Basically, it wards off evil spirits."

Derek stared at George. "Why is she giving me this?"

"You know why. I know why. And you don't have to worry. I won't tell anyone. But if you are going to see and speak to the dead, you need to be protected." George stared at his friend.

"I don't need to know how or why. I don't even have to understand it, but I know you see things. Whether they are coming to you in those visions or dreams you mentioned, the dead are reaching out to you."

"The dead aren't reaching out to me. I have weird shit happening because of Josiah...."

George cut him off. "If you keep denying it, you will have worse things happen. You need to acknowledge what is going on. But the dead know you can see and hear them. That makes you a target."

Derek shook his head. "A target of what, an overzealous ghost?" he chuckled when he said it.

"Laugh all you want. But it won't hurt you to wear one of those."

"Okay. What did your grandma say would happen if I don't protect myself with this?"

George gathered his things. "She said the evil that lurks among the dead will use your ability to make you go mad, insane. She said they want your soul because of what you can do."

Derek sat still. The words George said lingered in the air. "Do you believe in that stuff?"

"My grandma knows some shit will happen before it ever does. I know she is a smart and old woman. I also know there is more to what is going on with you than just visions. The Fatima Hand won't hurt you, and in the end, I would wear it." George stretched, bending his back and twisting from side to side. "You know," he said as he watched Derek grab his computer bag and his belongings to leave.

"Know what?"

"Kelly wasn't too far off with her comment. About burying the case. It won't take long for everyone to see how poorly the FBI handled this case. And that will hurt the Deputy Director's chances to be head of the FBI. After all, those four cases were from his watch."

Derek locked up as they walked to their cars. He had clipped the Fatima Hand to his car keys and now he fiddled with it. "The good thing is, it is out of our hands. We can't be blamed this time."

CHAPTER FIFTY-THREE

Derek walked into his house.

Lola charged at him, squealing and barking.

"Hey, sweetie. I'm sorry I had to leave you home alone today." He walked into the kitchen to feed her. After filling her food bowl, he scanned the fridge for his own dinner.

There was a lot of Chinese food from the other night. Loading up a plate, he popped it into the microwave. Waiting for his food, he called Dr. Chelsea. "Did you see the news?"

"No, I have not. I have been with patients all day. I am only now finishing up."

"On a Sunday?"

"This was my Sunday to do rounds at the local hospitals."

"Fun times." Derek pulled his plate from the microwave. Balancing the phone between his shoulder and ear, he grabbed two beers from the refrigerator.

"What did I miss with the news?"

"There was a news conference about the arrest of Anastasia Parker. Congressman Jackson was on hand to make sure his constituents knew he had a hand in the whole thing."

"The Deputy will milk this. He wants to be the next head of the FBI." Dr. Chelsea yawned into the phone. "Excuse me. I'm worn out."

"Go home and rest. Your music box killer is off the streets."

"I feel like the load of guilt is gone. Washed away. I know it wasn't my fault, but if I could've done more. Maybe...."

"Stop. Don't do that. Enjoy knowing it is over." Derek took a long sip of his beer.

"Thank you, Derek. Thank you for all you did."

"Just doing my job." He hung up the phone and finished his dinner. After he cleaned the kitchen, he and Lola took a stroll through the neighborhood. Walking back into the house, he unhooked Lola's leash and watched as she ran out the doggie door.

He sat down on the sofa and got comfortable. He reached into his pocket and pulled out the little black bag from George's grandmother. He looked at the bracelet and the necklace.

Something about the necklace caught his eye. Never one to wear jewelry, he put it around his neck. The thinness of the chain and the length made the necklace almost nonexistent.

He closed his eyes and let his body relax on the sofa.

Lola ran in and jumped up next to him.

He scratched her belly as she rolled over, exposing it to him. He thought about calling Patrick and asking how the baby and Lucy were doing, but he didn't feel he had the right to invade.

About to doze off, his phone rang. He glanced at the screen. Assistant Director Fretz. "Hey what's up?"

"I need you to call the secure line."

The phone went dead. Derek dialed the number and put in the code. It rang once.

"Anastasia is dead."

Derek sat up on the edge of the couch. "How? When?"

"They took her into custody and placed her in a holding cell at headquarters. One officer brought her something to eat and drink and found her dead in the cell a few hours later."

"Are they sure it was suicide?"

"That is what they are saying. And that is what the report will say."

"I don't believe it."

Fretz sighed into the phone. "I'll get the autopsy report, or at least the photos. Do you think Dr. Callahan would look at them and tell us if what they say matches up?"

"Yeah, he would. And he would keep it quiet, too. Get me the photos. I will get you an answer." Derek was about to hang up.

"Derek, I'm worried."

"I know. I am too. The deputy director will do whatever he needs to become head of the FBI. We've already seen the extent he will go to in order to make people disappear."

"We need to figure out the connection between the deputy director and the Pink Diamond case. That is our only way to stop what he is doing," Assistant Director Fretz said.

"I know. I'm working on it. I'm not sure who to trust. Someone out there has to be willing to talk." The line went dead.

Derek had a small window of time to stop the deputy director from becoming one of the most powerful people in the United States. He also knew if the deputy director found out what he knew, it would be his death everyone would be investigating. That's if they ever found his body.

Links to all my books:
[The Damien Kaine Series](#)
[The Derek Reed Series](#)
[Other Books](#)

ABOUT THE AUTHOR

Victoria M. Patton is forced to share her home with a husband, 2 dogs, and 4 cats. The strays just seem to find their house. Her kids are grown. One is in college, and the other is living on his own. She is almost an empty nester.

Her time in the Coast Guard performing Search and Rescue/Law Enforcement duties, and her BS in Forensic Chemistry help her figure out the best way to hide all the bodies and write amazing stories about the murders. If she has any free time, she drinks copious amounts of whiskey and binge watches YouTube TV, BritBox, and Tubi. She is on most social media outlets, type in her name, you'll find her.

To learn more about her and sign up for her monthly email visit her websites:

www.whiskeyandwriting.com
www.victoriampatton.com